The Celebration

Books by Mary Deasy

THE HOUR OF SPRING

CANNON HILL

ELLA GUNNING

DEVIL'S BRIDGE

THE CORIOLI AFFAIR

THE BOY WHO MADE GOOD

O'SHAUGHNESSY'S DAY

THE CELEBRATION

The

CELEBRATION

Mary Deasy

Random House New York

copy 1/

The Celebration

You are cordially invited
to attend a
Reception
honoring
The Reverend Michael J. Cournane
on
The Silver Anniversary
of his ordination
on Sunday afternoon
the twelfth day of June
nineteen hundred and thirty-eight
two until five o'clock
at the Parish House
Saint Cyprian's Church
McKinley Boulevard

June 11, 1938

AFTERNOON

Shivaun

The porter put the suitcases in the vestibule and we watched the train slow down. We went past long twisted railroad tracks, with smoke and steam all around. It was raining a little.

"You want to watch your step now, young lady and gentleman," the porter said. "Don't you be in no hurry. You stand right there till I give you the word."

"Yes, sir," Stephen said. "Is this Amorica?"

"Coming up," the porter said. He smiled at us. "You-all can't wait to get off this train, can you?" he said.

"We've been on it a long time," Stephen said.

The train stopped and the porter unfolded the steps and put the footstool down. Stephen was the first one off, after him. I heard Mother call me: "Shivaun, don't you and Stephen go wandering off now. Wait for me."

I looked around. She was coming down the steps. She gave something to the porter and he smiled and said, "Thank you kindly."

"Mother," I said.

The redcap put the suitcases on the little cart and she was busy talking to him so she didn't hear me.

"Mother," I said.

We walked along next to the train. There were a lot of people. You could hear the clangy, echo-y noises there always are when you get off of trains.

"What is it?" she said.

"Is Amorica as big as New York?" I said.

"No, stupid," Stephen said. "Don't you know anything at all? New York is the biggest city in the United States."

"Don't be rude, Stephen," Mother said.

She looked happy. We were in Amorica now. Mother was born in Amorica. I was born in Los Angeles, California, and Stephen was born in Acapulco, Mexico. Daddy was born in New York City, New York. And Granny Cournane was born in County Cork, Ireland. I was going to visit Granny Cournane. She was my step-great-grandmother. Mother explained it all to me on the train.

We walked along with the other people. Mother walked fast. Stephen stopped to look at the engine and I stopped too.

"Come on, you kids," Mother said. She smiled at us. "We have somebody waiting for us," she said.

"Who is it?" I said. "Is it Granny Cournane?"

"Granny Cournane's an old lady," Stephen said. "Isn't

she, Mother? Isn't she too old to come to the railroad station?"

"Yes," Mother said. "Your cousin Mal is going to meet us." She waved at somebody up ahead. "There he is now," she said. "At the gate."

I looked. There were a lot of people standing on the other side of the gate.

"Which one is Cousin Mal?" I asked.

"The one in front," Mother said. "The big dark one. I suppose you're too young to remember when he came to see us back home in California. But Stephen remembers—don't you, Stephen?"

"I remember," Stephen said.

"He brought you that crazy little tin sailor that you wound up and then it did a hornpipe," Mother said. "Don't you remember?"

"I remember," I said.

"You don't," Stephen said. "You're only seven."

Mother went on ahead. Cousin Mal shook hands with her with both hands. He was taller than Daddy. He didn't smile much except in his eyes, and he lifted up his eyebrows so his forehead wrinkled when he looked at Mother.

"Hello, Champ," he said. He was talking to Mother, but her name was Amy. "Long time no see."

"A very long time," Mother said. She was going to cry. Mother never cries. "Oh, Mal, it's so good to be back," she said. She didn't cry.

"Are these the kids?" Cousin Mal said. "Holy Saint Patrick, they've certainly aged since I saw them."

Mother bent down to us.

"Aren't you going to say hello to your cousin Mal?" she said.

"Hello," I said.

"Hello," Stephen said. "Why do you call my mother Champ? Her name's Amy."

"It's an old nickname," Cousin Mal said. "Don't you like it?"

"I like it all right," Stephen said. "It sounds like a boy's name, is all."

Cousin Mal looked at Mother. "Well, your mother was pretty much of a tomboy when she was your age," he said.

"Like Shivaun," Mother said. She didn't look at Cousin Mal. "I can't stop her from following Stephen and his friends around."

The redcap came up pushing the cart. Cousin Mal picked up the two big suitcases.

"Let's go," he said. "I've got my car outside."

We started to walk. It was a big railroad station but not new. Stephen walked up with Cousin Mal and I walked in back with Mother.

"Mal," she said. He looked around at her for a minute. "Mal," she said, "have you seen Father lately?"

He looked ahead again.

"No," he said.

"When was the last time?"

"Oh—two, maybe three months ago," he said. "I ran into him on the street."

Mother didn't say anything for a while. I looked at the big booths with the people buying magazines and papers and candy and orange juice. There was a man sleeping on a bench, sitting up.

"Is he still—" Mother asked.

"Still what?" Cousin Mal said.

"Still living with that—"

Cousin Mal didn't turn around.

"What the hell—he married her, didn't he?" he said. "It's all legal."

"Then he is?" Mother said.

"As far as I know," Cousin Mal said. "If you want to call what he's doing living."

The voice said over the loudspeaker: "Now arriving on Track Nine, Number seven-thirty-three—" Then we went through the big doors and the voice stopped and we were outside again. It was still raining, but not enough to get wet. The air felt soft and hot and gray.

"Sorry we haven't any better weather to welcome a set of old Californians," Cousin Mal said. "I'd apologize, but you knew what to expect."

"It feels like home," Mother said. She was looking around. "Those wonderful lazy *hot* Midwestern summers—"

"All the worst features of the North American climate," Cousin Mal said. "We guarantee to provide you with a complete set."

We walked between the cars in the parking lot.

"Cousin Mal," Stephen said.

Cousin Mal turned his head and looked down at him.

"Were you ever in Africa?" Stephen asked.

"I can't say I ever was," Cousin Mal said.

"Mother says you've been all over the world," Stephen said. He sounded as if he didn't believe Cousin Mal.

Cousin Mal looked around at Mother.

"Champ," he said, "you're going to get me in trouble if you go around making false statements about my accomplishments."

"Now, Stephen," Mother said. "I never said Africa— did I?"

"I guess I just happened to miss Africa," Cousin Mal said to Stephen. "There hasn't been much call for second-rate public relations experts on the veldt."

"Don't be funny, Mal," Mother said. "You know you wouldn't let anybody else call you second-rate."

He put the suitcases down and reached in his pocket for the key to his automobile. He had a green automobile.

"That was in the old days," he said. "Haven't you heard that well-known saying: 'Times change'?"

"A Chrysler," Stephen said. "Look, a Chrysler." He kicked the front tire. "It's not very new, is it?"

"It's an old, respectable car for an old, respectable gent," Cousin Mal said. He looked around at Mother. "Hadn't you heard I'd settled down?" he said.

Mother laughed.

"Well," she said, "Mother wrote me you'd actually been working here in town for a year."

"An old, respectable gent of thirty-two," Cousin Mal said. "With a steady job. Every moderately senile young man should have one. Good for the liver—brings up muscle tone." He opened the car door. "Hop in, kids," he said.

He went around to the back of the car to put the bags in the trunk. Stephen got in the back seat and I got in too. Then Mother got in and Cousin Mal came around the side of the automobile and closed the front door on her side.

"I'm going to go to Africa when I grow up," Stephen said. "I'm going to be a big-game hunter." He put his head out the car window to talk to Cousin Mal. "I don't suppose there's any big game around Amorica?" he said.

"Not unless you go to the zoo," Cousin Mal said. "And I understand it's not open season there just now."

He came around and got into the driver's seat and started the car. It was like being at home when Daddy was there and we went out driving on Sunday afternoon. *Daddy said, Where do you want to go? And Mother said, Don't you remember? You promised to take them to Laguna. The sun shone on Daddy and he looked old. I asked Mother once and she said Daddy was forty-eight years old and she was* twenty-eight years old. That was a long time ago—almost a year.

We drove past the corner where there is the wigwam with the hamburgers inside, and after a long time past the oil wells, and Daddy said, You know, Amy, I can't ever pass one of those things without thinking where we'd be today if I hadn't had to sell those leases.

It doesn't do any good to think about it, Mother said.

I know it doesn't, Daddy said. But there are things a man doesn't find it so easy to get out of his head. When I think of it, that you and the kids could be living in Beverly Hills with a swimming pool of your own, like the movie stars, and you could give up your job—

It's kismet, Mother said. The Gilmans weren't cut out by Providence to live like movie stars. Besides, we have the whole ocean to swim in, and I rather like my job.

She smiled at him and patted his arm. When we had passed the oil wells he was tired, and he stopped the car and got out and Mother moved over into his seat and drove. Stephen sat up in front with her and Daddy got in the back with me. He put his arm around me and I leaned against him. His arm was bony. He was thin. Mother was thin too. Mother said Stephen was the only one in our family who looked as if he got enough to eat. Juana was fat but she didn't belong to our family. She came to our house in the afternoon and cooked dinner and was there when we came home from school. She said she had six children of her own and they were all fat. But I can't put the fat on you and the Señora, she said. She called Mother the Señora.

After a while Mother stopped the car and there was the ocean down below and we went down the wooden steps to the beach. Mother and Stephen had the picnic basket.

Let me carry that, Amy, Daddy said.

Oh, we're doing fine, Mother said. You go on and take care of Shivaun.

We went down the steps. The ocean was full of sparkles and the waves came in and made a noise on the beach.

I want to go swimming, Stephen said.

Not today, Mother said. We'll go wading today—shall we?

Daddy sat down on the sand. He looked tired.

The Harringtons should have given you the key to the house, he said. What good is a private beach if you haven't any place to dress?

Oh no, Mother said. I couldn't ask them. And it's nice, anyway, to be able to have our picnic away from the crowds.

I took my shoes and socks off faster than Stephen and got in the water first. The water felt cold. I jumped up and down. Stephen came in the water too.

Don't go too far out, Mother said.

She was sitting on the sand next to Daddy. She had on a green dress. She held her arms around her knees.

Oh, she said to Daddy, it looks so lovely and cool. Doesn't it, Irv?

She took off her shoes and stockings and ran down in the water with us. She held Stephen's hand and my hand and we went out farther and the water came up to my knees. We all laughed when the waves came up. Daddy lay down on the sand and went to sleep. The water splashed up on my dress.

Oh, Mother said. That's enough now. Come on. We're going to have our lunch.

Her hair blew around. It is light-colored like mine, light brown and then lighter and then light brown again.

We came out of the water. Mother said Stephen and I could leave our shoes and stockings off, but she sat down on the sand to put hers on. Stephen saw a shell on the sand and went away. I looked for a shell too. There was a man coming down some wooden steps on the hill. He was going to go swimming. He looked at Mother sitting on the sand putting on her stockings.

Hey—Amy, he said. What are you doing in these parts? I thought it was you—I could mistake the face but never the legs.

He started to come over. He had on a white robe like a towel and slippers on his feet that flapped when he walked. He was bigger than Daddy. Daddy sat up.

Oh—hello, Mac, Mother said. She stopped putting on her stocking. I didn't know you were going to be down here this weekend, she said. The Harringtons lent us their beach for a picnic.

I stood and watched them. Mother said, Irv, I don't think you know Mac Fraser, from the paper—my husband—

How do you do? Daddy said.

The man didn't say anything for a minute and then he laughed and said, Oh. How's every little thing, Mr. Gilman?

And my children, Mother said.

Stephen was at one end of the beach and I was at the other end. We didn't come up to be introduced.

Oh, the man said again. Quite a family party, I see.

He laughed too much. He had big shoulders. Daddy said, Yes, just an old-fashioned family party, Mr. Fraser. He didn't laugh at all. Mother smiled a little, but she frowned with her eyes.

Well, the man said, I'm partial to old-fashioneds myself. He laughed again but I didn't and neither did Mother or Daddy. Nobody said anything. Well, the man said again, you've sure got a great little wife there, Mr. Gilman. We think the world of her down at the shop—couldn't run the place without her, I always say. Best little fashion writer in the business.

I'll remind you of those kind words the next time I ask for a raise, Mother said.

The man said, Ouch, and laughed again. Mother looked at him the way she does out of her eyes, so you can't tell what she's thinking. Well, the man said after a minute, four's company and five's a crowd. See you tomorrow, Amy. I'm going to have a swim.

He went on back the way he'd come. When he passed me he said, Hello, small fry, but I didn't say anything back. I went over to Mother and Daddy. They were talking low. Mother was putting her stockings on fast and Daddy was looking at the sand. They didn't notice me standing there.

Oh, he's harmless, Mother said. He talks too much, but he's perfectly harmless. Too much money and too little brains—that's all his trouble is.

Yes, Daddy said. He kept on looking at the sand. I don't think—You mustn't think I think—But he admires you, Amy; a lot of young men admire you, and who am I to blame them? You're young and you're beautiful—

And I'm Mrs. Irving Gilman, Mother said, and they all know it and so do you and so do I. She smiled at Daddy. Oh, Irv, don't let's get gloomy, she said, just because a moron like Mac Fraser makes a crack about my legs.

A football player, Daddy said. I know the type. Yes. Him I'm not worried about. But if some day a fine young man should come along, somebody that was fit and worthy for you—I used those words to you ten years ago, Amy, and I was right then and I'm right now, so right I still get the cold chills down my back when I wake up in the night and think of them.

Mother looked up and saw me standing there.

Oh—Shivaun, she said. Don't you want to help me

unpack the picnic basket? She jumped up and patted Daddy on the shoulder. No, you sit still, Irv, she said. The women of the family are going to serve this meal, aren't they, Shivaun?

She went over to the picnic basket and I went with her. We had fried chicken and hard-boiled eggs and chocolate cake, but Daddy didn't eat very much and neither did Mother. Some other people came down the steps where the man was and we heard them over behind the rocks on their beach and they talked and laughed a lot but we didn't talk and laugh very much. And after a while Mother said we'd better start for home again and so we went back up the steps to the car.

Cousin Mal drove out of the parking lot and along the street. Mother looked out the window. She looked happy. The houses weren't like the houses in California. They were taller and thinner and made of red brick and most of them looked dirty. When I asked Mother why, she said it was because Amorica was a very big city and this was the old part, and most big cities were dirty and smoky in the old parts.

"Your mother and Aunt Una have been moving heaven and earth trying to get Gran out of the West Side," Cousin Mal said. "But you know Gran: she'll stick to Number Thirty-three till they carry her out feet first."

"How is she?" Mother said.

"Flourishing," Cousin Mal said. He didn't say anything for a minute. Then he said, "She'll live to be a hundred."

Mother looked at him.

"Poor Mal," she said. "You never can forgive her, can you?"

"I haven't anything to forgive her for," Cousin Mal said. "She made life one happy living hell for me when I was a kid, and I've chalked it up to experience, and that is that. It was all a long, long time ago."

"She's always been so wonderful to the rest of us," Mother said. "It seems so queer—you're the only real grand-child she has; the rest of us are sort of courtesy relations. Of course, she's always sparring with Aunt Dolly and Aunt Una, but that doesn't mean anything; the whole Cournane family was born with boxing gloves on."

"She can't forget I'm half wop," Cousin Mal said. "My mother committed the unforgivable sin in Gran's book when she married a Cesti instead of a Sullivan or an O'Brien."

Mother glanced around at us just for a second.

"Then what about *my* kids?" she said. "Mal," she said, "for goodness' sake, you don't think—"

"You said it yourself," Cousin Mal said. "You're only courtesy relations; you haven't the sacred blood of Tom Dineen circulating in your veins. Gran may have married Grandpa Cournane after the sainted Thomas died, but that doesn't mean she expects any of the Cournane breed to live up to the standards of the Dineens. You could have married an Eskimo and all she'd say about it would be, 'What more could you expect of a Cournane?' "

They talked so low then I couldn't hear the words.

"Mother," I said.

She turned her head around.

"Mother, is Daddy part Eskimo?" I said.

Mother laughed and I could see Cousin Mal's eyes in the little mirror in front and he was laughing too.

"Oh, Shivaun," Mother said, "for heaven's sake, don't try to listen to things you don't understand. Of course he's not part Eskimo."

She turned around in the seat again and talked to Cousin Mal. *Your daddy is a Jew, Eloise said. She put out her tongue at me. Yes, he is, she said. And you're a Jew too*

—even if you do go to the Catholic church. It doesn't make any difference. You're still a Jew.

I didn't answer her because I didn't know. I put out my tongue back at her and went home and asked Mother, Am I a Jew? It was evening but the lights weren't on yet. It was after dinner in summer. Mother was sitting in the living room writing something at the desk. She looked around at me.

Come here, she said.

I went and sat on her lap. She smelled good.

Did somebody say that to you, Shivaun? she said.

Yes, I said. It was Eloise.

Eloise?

The new girl next door, I said.

Oh, she said. Well, it may be a good idea if you don't see too much of Eloise. She doesn't sound like a little girl I'd like to know.

Then she explained to me about people. People who live in America are Americans, but everybody's fathers and mothers, or their fathers' fathers and mothers, came from somewhere else before they lived in America. That is why they are Irish or English or German or Italian or Spanish. Daddy's father and mother came from Ireland, but a long time before that their fathers and mothers came from Palestine and that is why he is a Jew. And Jesus was a Jew and the Blessed Virgin was a Jew when they were living on earth, but there are people who don't like Jews. And that is all there is to it. Some people do not like cats either. But I like cats. Mother is Irish and Daddy is Jewish, so Stephen is half Irish and half Jewish and so am I. But we are all Americans too.

"Is Cousin Mal part Eskimo?" I said.

"No," Mother said. She and Cousin Mal were still laughing. "Shivaun, I'm not going to be able to live through

this visit if you want to know the pedigrees of all your relations," she said. "You'll just have to take them at face value;
there are dozens of them, and I can give you my personal
assurance that none of them is part Eskimo."

She and Cousin Mal talked to each other in the front
seat. They talked about New York. *Mother went to New
York for the paper and she saw Cousin Mal there. Juana
stayed with us and Daddy was home all day and he drew
pictures of horses and trains for us after we came home from
school. When Mother came back we showed them to her
and she said, You should have been an artist, Irv. And
Daddy said, Yes, I should have been an artist. Or anything
but any of the things I've ever tried to be. I couldn't have
done worse, that's one thing sure. That was the night
Mother cried. I woke up at night and the light was on in
Mother and Daddy's room and I could hear her crying. She
said, Oh, Irv, don't talk about it, don't talk about it. It's not
your fault; it's just the way things are. And Daddy said, It is
my fault, and they talked low and then I went to sleep.*

Cousin Mal stopped the automobile in front of a house.
It didn't have any front yard except a little one made out of
red bricks with an iron fence around it. The house was made
out of red bricks too.

"Are you coming in?" Mother said to Cousin Mal.

"No," he said. "I'll just bring your bags in and then I've
got to get back to the salt mines."

He started to open the door of the car.

"Mal," Mother said.

He stopped opening the door and looked at her.

"Mal," she said, "I want to see Father."

"Do you?" he said. He didn't say anything for a minute. After a while he said, "I thought you were a smart girl,
Champ. And that isn't smart."

"I can't help it if it isn't," Mother said. "I still want to
see him. Do you know where he's living?"

"No," Cousin Mal said.

"Could you find out?"

"Maybe I could, maybe I couldn't." He said, "How do you know he wants to see you?"

They talked low. Mother said, "I want to see him, Mal. I want you to help me find him. He is in the city, isn't he?"

"Oh yes," Cousin Mal said. His voice sounded different. "You could have been sure of seeing him a couple of months ago if you'd been willing to lay out fifty cents," he said. "She had him lecturing at a local movie house one night on corruption on high levels in local politics. I have it on good authority that his act was a scream." He stopped talking. They both stopped talking. "I just don't want you to get hurt any more than you have to, Champ," Cousin Mal said.

"I won't get hurt," Mother said. She smiled at Cousin Mal. "I'm not the pushover I used to be," she said. "I've developed some fast footwork and I've learned how to roll with the punches. Watch me and see."

"Yes," Cousin Mal said. "I'll just do that."

"And you'll help me find Father?" she said. "Today? Tomorrow? You know all the places, Mal."

"Oh, sure," Cousin Mal said. "I know all the places." He opened the car door. "All right," he said. "I'll pick you up around noon tomorrow. That'll give us time before you'll be due out at Father Michael's for the reception."

"He wouldn't possibly go to Father Michael's himself?" Mother said.

"To the reception?" Cousin Mal said. "That would be a fine case of the skeleton walking out of the closet and sitting down at the wedding feast. They'll probably have the Bishop and hell's own number of reverend Fathers there, you know—maybe even the Cardinal."

"Yes," Mother said. "I didn't think. I just thought—he and Father Michael were always so close."

"You haven't been around for a long time, Champ," Cousin Mal said. He got out of the car. "Jack's not close to anybody now," he said, "unless it's the little man in the white apron who sells him the bottle." He came around the car and opened the door for Mother. "You still want me to find him for you?" he said.

"Yes," Mother said. She got out of the car and looked around at us. "Shivaun, Stephen," she said. "Here we are."

We got out of the car. Cousin Mal went around to the back to get the suitcases. Mother opened the gate and went up the steps of the house. The door opened before she rang the bell and there was a lady. She was older than Mother but she made her mouth redder than Mother made hers, and her hair was red like a movie star's, not like a person's.

"Amy," she said. "Well now, for heaven's sake, it *is* Amy, isn't it? And you don't look a *day* older, what a *lovely* suit, did you have a nice trip, and these are your babies, of course . . ."

She talked so fast it made me dizzy trying to keep up. She was beautiful but old. Mother called her Aunt Dolly. She kissed Mother.

"Come here and say hello to your aunt Dolly," Mother said.

"Their *great*-aunt Dolly," the lady said. "Uh-h-h!" She shivered all over. "Doesn't that sound old! Sounds like an old woman, and I'm not ready for that *yet*; you ask any of my clients in Atlanta if I'm ready for that yet."

She kissed Stephen and me, but she didn't stop talking.

"Why, only the other day," she said, "I had one of my clients say to me, 'Mrs. Clohessey,' he said, 'I want you to tell me something, and I want you to tell me the honest truth: how long have you been in this business? In this bill-collecting business, that is—*how long*?' Well, I told him the truth, of course; I said, 'Fifteen years.' And do you know he didn't believe me? Said he'd been around for a long time and you couldn't fool *him*—"

"Fifteen years," Mother said. "Has it really been that long, Aunt Dolly? I can remember when you and Uncle Gus—"

"Oh, *Gus!*" Aunt Dolly said. "If Gus could see me now, he'd turn right over in his grave. Out in *all* kinds of weather, bumping up against *all* kinds of people—and you know how particular Gus always was about me—" She stopped talking and looked at us. "But what on earth am I thinking about," she said, "keeping you all standing out here? Mal, bring those suitcases right in, and you'd better stay a minute and say hello to Mrs. Cournane; she said she just knew you wouldn't come in."

"Sorry, Aunt Dolly," Cousin Mal said. "I'm late now." He said to Mother, "I'll see you tomorrow then, Champ."

"Mal, you're a regular *devil*," Aunt Dolly said. She took hold of the lapels of his coat and shook him. "Here I've been standing up for you all afternoon to Mrs. Cournane, said of course you'd come in, and now you let me down. She's just going to sit there and *crow* over me. Said you wouldn't come to Michael's reception tomorrow either, and I said, 'Why, of *course* he will, Mal's a wonderful person—' "

"Flattery will get you nowhere," Cousin Mal said. He smiled at us. I was sorry he was going. "See you, kids," he said to Stephen and me. "So long, Champ."

He went out the gate and got into the automobile. Mother watched him. He waved at her when he drove away.

"Well, *you* come in anyway, Amy," Aunt Dolly said. "Your mother isn't here yet—phoned over to say she had to work late, on a Saturday afternoon, mind you, as if the Mayor's office and the whole City Hall would just collapse if she walked out to see her only daughter come all the way from California—*and* her own grandchildren that she's never even laid eyes on. But Mrs. Cournane and Josie and I've just been waiting for you with bated breath—"

We went into the house. It was dark in the hall and smelled quiet and old. We went into a room with Aunt Dolly and there were two ladies and they were old too. One was older than the other one and that was Granny Cournane. She had on a black skirt and a black-and-white waist and she was sitting in a chair next to a little marble table with a fern on it. The other lady was her niece. Her name was Josie and she was not related to us.

"Well, here they are at last, Mrs. Cournane," Aunt Dolly said. "Amy and her babies—all the way from California."

"I'm not a baby," Stephen said.

Everybody looked at him.

"He doesn't look like you, Amy," Granny Cournane said. Everybody kissed Mother and then she brought me over and Granny Cournane kissed me too. Granny Cournane had wrinkles in her face and there was a mole on her chin with black hairs coming out of it. She put her arms around me and her chest was fat and soft. I liked it. "But this is a Cournane," she said. "She couldn't deny it, God help her, if she wanted to."

Mother smiled at her.

"Why should she want to deny it?" she said. Granny Cournane had a queer way of talking and then Mother talked like her too. "Aren't the Cournanes a fine Irish family," she said, "and who should know that better than yourself?"

"A fine set of Irish bedlamites," Granny Cournane said. "There isn't a one of them but Father Michael that I'd give the time of day to."

"Present company excepted, I *hope*," Aunt Dolly said.

They all talked and I looked around. There were shutters on the inside of the windows and some of them were closed. It was dark after the outside. The furniture was all covered with slippery black where you sat down.

"Where's Mal?" Granny Cournane said. She looked around. "Ah, don't tell me," she said. "He wouldn't come in. There's a blackguard of a grandson for you. I haven't laid eyes on him since Christmas."

"He had to get back to work, Gran," Mother said.

"He has time enough for everybody else in the family," Granny Cournane said. "From all I hear, if they pay him a salary for the time he puts in on that job, they're charitable people, and that's a fact." She turned to Mother. "Arrah, listen, Amy, do you know what he sent me for Mother's Day?" she said. "A pot of geraniums. *Geraniums*, no less. And hasn't been inside this door since Christmas."

Aunt Dolly said, "Well, you're too *old*, Mrs. Cournane. You know Mal always has some girl on the string—can't be bothered with old women like us." She talked to Mother. "Amy, I get to thinking sometimes—remember years and years ago, when you were still in high school, and Mal and that young man you were going with had that awful fight right on the front lawn of your house? Nobody even *knew* he was jealous, but he turned up there just as you were coming home; Rosemary was ready to call the police—"

Mother looked at Stephen and me.

"Mal left our suitcases in the hall," she said. "Suppose I bring them upstairs now."

She got up, and Aunt Dolly laughed and got up too.

"My goodness, Amy," she said, "this *is* the twentieth century, you know; *little pitchers* are terribly old-fashioned now. And when I think of the way *you* were brought up. Rosemary would talk about anything in front of you—Jack's drinking, the Marlow girl, all of it—"

"That's fine," Mother said. "But I still think my kids had better stick to *Peter Rabbit* for the time being."

She went out to the hall and Aunt Dolly went with her and the lady named Josie went running out too. I looked at Granny Cournane and she looked at me.

"Shivaun," she said. "Is that what they call you?"

"Yes, ma'am," I said.

"Well, it's a fine Irish name, thanks be to God," she said. "And how old might you be, Shivaun?"

"I'm seven," I said.

She looked at Stephen.

"And how old is this young gentleman?"

"I'm nine," Stephen said.

Nobody said anything for a while. I could hear Mother and Aunt Dolly and the lady named Josie going upstairs. Granny Cournane reached over to the little marble table next to her and picked up a rosary. It was a big black one made of wood. I looked at Stephen. If we were going to say the rosary we had to kneel down. But Granny Cournane closed her eyes and began to pray by herself. I looked at Stephen again and he made a face at me. It was a big dark quiet room, and I was glad I could hear the people on the street outside.

After a few minutes Granny Cournane stopped praying her rosary and opened her eyes again and looked at me.

"You don't go to church. Do you?" she said.

I looked at Stephen.

"We go to St. Hilary's Church," Stephen said.

"Oh," Granny Cournane said. "Is it a Catholic church?"

"Yes, ma'am," Stephen said.

"That's good," Granny Cournane said. "Because I'd tell her to her face if you didn't."

"Tell who what?" I said.

"Your mother," Granny Cournane said. "That she wasn't bringing you up right. Sure she's a fine girl, but she wasn't brought up right herself, God help her."

She closed her eyes and started to pray again.

"Granny Cournane," I said.

She opened her eyes.

"Can we go upstairs?" I said.

"You've got legs and there's a staircase," she said. She reached over to the table next to her and took two peppermints out of a little glass dish. "Here," she said. "Here's a peppermint for each one of you."

We took the peppermints.

"Thank you," I said.

"Thank you," Stephen said.

We went out to the hall. When we were there, Stephen said, "Come on. I'll race you up the stairs."

He won. Mother came out of a room upstairs when we got to the top.

"Where's the fire?" she said.

"Granny Cournane gave us some peppermints," I said. "She's praying her rosary."

"Well, come on in here," Mother said. She went back in the room. It had white lace curtains and a big bed. "This is where you and I are going to sleep tonight, Shivaun," she said.

Aunt Dolly and Josie were hanging Mother's dresses up in a big wooden cupboard. They were talking.

"Your aunt Una's staying out in Silver Woods with Tommyo and his family," Aunt Dolly said to Mother. "Of course *she* wouldn't miss it for the world."

"Father Cournane's such a fine man," Josie said. She talked very fast and almost in a whisper. "Isn't it nice that he can have so many of his family around him for this wonderful occasion? Coming from far and near."

"The Cardinal's never appreciated Michael," Aunt Dolly said. "In *my* opinion, Michael would have been a bishop himself by this time if he hadn't made enemies in the wrong places."

Mother laughed.

"Oh, Aunt Dolly, that hasn't anything to do with it," she said. "Father Michael's just not ambitious; that's all. He's satisfied at St. Cyprian's."

"Maybe he *was* satisfied at St. Cyprian's," Aunt Dolly said. "Though for a man as brilliant as Michael always was, and studying over in Rome and all, it's *not* very likely. But that new church has been just a millstone around his neck. And the people! Ugh!" She put both hands out as if she was pushing something away from her. "Troublemakers. That's what they are. Nothing but trouble, trouble, trouble, from Sunday morning to Saturday night."

Mother laughed again and sat down on the bed.

"Oh, Aunt Dolly," she said, "how do you know? You're down in Atlanta, and Father Michael never writes."

"Well, Una does," Aunt Dolly said. "She's up here in Amorica every few months, and of course she always goes to see Michael. His housekeeper can't *bear* her."

"Can't bear Aunt Una?" Mother said. "Why, what does she do to her, for heaven's sake?"

Aunt Dolly waved her hands.

"Oh, you know Una," she said. "She's so used to being the chairman of every committee and the patroness of everything that goes on for the benefit of the church in Columbiana that she even orders the Bishop around down there. I suppose he's used to it, poor man, but Michael's housekeeper *isn't*. She told Una once to stay out of her kitchen, and they had words—something about some chops, I think. Una says the woman's a devil on wheels, but you know that's a pretty good description of Una too."

Josie kept on putting things away. Her eyes looked big. Aunt Dolly went to the window and pulled the lace curtain aside.

"Your mother said she'd be here by five, *sure*," she said. "We're all having dinner out at Michael's, you know—a sort of private family celebration before the big doings tomorrow. I told her she might as well come straight on here from work so we could all go together."

"How is she?" Mother said.

"Rosemary? Oh, she's fine. She still plays tennis twice a week—says it helps her keep her girlish figure. Well, she always was a string bean, you know. Like you, Amy."

She pulled the curtain a little farther aside.

"Here she comes now," she said. "You'd better go down, Amy." Mother got up. "And *don't* talk to her about your father," Aunt Dolly said. "It'll just set her off."

Mother looked at Stephen and me.

"Shivaun, Stephen," she said. "Do you want to go downstairs and meet your grandmother?"

"We've already met her," Stephen said.

Mother smiled.

"That's your *great*-granny Cournane," she said. "This is your real grandmother—my own mother."

"What do I call her?" Stephen said.

"Well, I don't know," Mother said. "We'll ask her—shall we?"

We went down the stairs. Aunt Dolly went with us, but Josie stayed in the room. Mother opened the front door. There was a tall thin lady with a red hat and dark hair and a dark-blue suit. She looked at Mother.

"Amy," she said. "Well, my word—Amy."

She kissed Mother. I didn't want to be kissed any more so I hid behind Stephen.

"Hello, Mother," Mother said.

"If you don't look simply scrumptious," the lady said. "Hollywood all over you, you lucky girl." Her eyes went so fast she saw me hiding behind Stephen. "And the children —" she said. "What gigantic creatures—Amy, these *aren't* yours!"

Mother smiled.

"They're worried about what to call you," she said. "You see, they already have one Granny Cournane."

"Why don't they call me Aunt Rosemary?" the lady said. "*Grandmother* sounds so terribly old—and we working girls can't afford to be old, can we, Amy?"

She wasn't going to kiss us. Aunt Dolly came down the steps and she talked to her, and we all went into the room where Granny Cournane was. Aunt Rosemary said I looked like Mother and she looked at Stephen and asked did he look like his father.

"Isn't it terrible?" she said. "I can hardly remember what Irving looks like any more. His hair is sandy, isn't it? Like Stephen's?"

"What there is left of it," Mother said. She smiled. "It's getting a little thin."

"Well, yes—I suppose so," Aunt Rosemary said. She sat down and got a cigarette out of her purse. "He's only seven or eight years younger than Jack, isn't he?" she said. She stopped before she lit the cigarette and looked at Mother. "You know about Jack, of course?" she said. "That he's married that girl? I must have written you."

"Yes," Mother said.

"It's only an infatuation, of course," Aunt Rosemary said. "Like the Marlow girl, only apparently this one wouldn't settle without the wedding ring—little as she knew it could mean to Jack. He may have gone through the cere- mony, but naturally he knew it could never change anything in the eyes of the Church."

"Well—" Mother said. She looked at Aunt Dolly. "Let's not talk about it, Mother," she said.

"Oh, I don't mind talking about it; why should I?" Aunt Rosemary said. "I faced all these things years ago— that your father was absolutely incorrigible when it came to drink and women. I might be a little happier, I'll admit, if his taste ran to something of a higher class than this Rae Jacowski—Mrs. Cournane, of course she calls herself now. I've never seen her, but from the description—"

"They say she's *good*-looking, Rosemary," Aunt Dolly said. "Dark, you know—exotic. And of course she's so *young*—younger even than Amy."

Aunt Rosemary didn't pay any attention to Aunt Dolly.

"Naturally, it was the mother who engineered it," she said. "Apparently she thought she'd got hold of something in Jack—thought since he'd once been mayor there must be *some* profit to be squeezed out of him. They're both very ambitious, I hear, mother and daughter. Came out of some little back alley somewhere and got hold of him the usual way. Well, at least they'll never starve as long as they have him. Paul Willis says Jack could still walk along Lake Street any day between twelve and two and borrow enough money to keep a respectable household of four going for a month."

"How do you like working for Mr. Willis?" Mother said. "It sounds awfully strenuous—secretary to the Mayor."

"Well, darling, it's not half so strenuous as being the Mayor's wife; I can tell you *that*," Aunt Rosemary said. She crossed her knees and swung one foot up and down. "Oh, Paul's all right," she said. "Of course, I suppose he thought he was giving me the job for old times' sake, but he's found out by this time that I'm a darned good secretary too."

"Rosemary," Granny Cournane said.

Aunt Rosemary turned her head and looked at her.

"Rosemary, what do you suppose that blackguard of a

grandson of mine sent me for Mother's Day?" Granny Cournane said. "A pot of *geraniums*, no less. And hasn't been inside this house since Christmas."

"Oh, I've given Mal up long ago," Aunt Rosemary said. "Nothing he could do would ever surprise *me*."

"Bringing him up like he was my own child since he was six years old," Granny Cournane said, "and now he won't so much as cross the doorsill to pass the time of day with me."

"By the way, he was the one who introduced that girl —that Rae Jacowski—to Jack; did you know that?" Aunt Rosemary said to Mother. "Isn't it typical of him to know a creature like that?"

Nobody said anything for a minute. The lady named Josie came downstairs and said hello to Aunt Rosemary. She asked Aunt Rosemary and Mother if they would like a cup of tea, and they said they would, and then she asked us if we would like to go out to the kitchen with her while she made some lemonade for us.

"Is it all right, Amy?" she said to Mother. And Mother said, "Josie, you're an angel."

We went back to the kitchen with Josie. It was bigger than any kitchen I ever saw before, and it had a little black stove in it and a big round table and a big cabinet with blue-and-white windows in it. Josie put a teakettle on the stove and got a pitcher and some glasses out of the cabinet with the blue-and-white windows. They were talking in the other room.

"Do you want to squeeze the lemons?" Josie said.

"Yes," I said.

"Let me," Stephen said.

"You can put the sugar in," Josie said to me. "And then you can stir it up."

She got the lemons out of the icebox. I watched her. I didn't know what to call her.

"What shall I call you?" I said to her. "You're not any relation to Stephen and me, are you?"

She smiled at me.

"Oh, you just call me Josie," she said.

"All right," I said. Stephen squeezed the lemons. "We've got a lot of relations, haven't we?" I said to Josie.

"The Cournanes are a large family," Josie said. She was busy all the time, getting cups and saucers and things out of the cabinet. "You'll meet some more of them this evening," she said. "Father Cournane, and your mother's aunt Una, and her son Dr. McGrath and *his* wife and children."

"In California we haven't any relations at all," I said. "Have we, Stephen?"

Stephen finished squeezing the lemons and I put the water and the sugar in and stirred it up.

"You ought to come to Amorica oftener," Josie said. "It's too bad you live so far away."

Stephen watched her pour the lemonade in the glasses.

"I've been to Texas and Lake Arrowhead and San Francisco," he said. "And I was born in Acapulco, Mexico. But I've never been to Amorica before."

"Well, you must come soon again," Josie said.

"Why don't you come to California?" Stephen said. "You get to sleep three nights on a train."

Josie said she'd like to sleep three nights on a train, but she said she thought it would cost too much for her to go to California.

"I suppose the oranges really grow on trees out there, don't they?" she said.

"What do they grow on here?" Stephen said.

"Oh—here," Josie said. "Why, they don't grow here at all, you know. It's too cold for them."

"It isn't cold today," Stephen said.

Josie made the tea and put everything on a big tray and

carried it out to the other room. We could hear them talking in there. They were talking about Mother's job on the paper. Aunt Rosemary talked the most.

"Weren't you the lucky one to fall into a job like that?" she said. "Trips to New York and all—and I'm stuck in that little office fifty mortal weeks a year."

Mother said something; we couldn't hear.

"But you always were a lucky girl, Amy," Aunt Rosemary said. "I remember when you were at Ste. Marie's; you always managed to get the top boys. Baxley Gerolt and Monty Ferris—everybody used to tell me you were sure to marry into the top drawer of Amorica's Four Hundred."

Mother said something again; we couldn't hear.

"I want some more," Stephen said.

He reached for the pitcher.

"No," I said. "It's not polite. You've got to wait for Josie."

"*Do* I?" he said.

"Mother said we had to be polite," I said.

He got up and went over to look out the screen door.

"Oh, that's all very well for you to say, Amy," Aunt Rosemary said, "but we can put two and two together, you know, even if you do live two thousand miles away. Why didn't Irv come with you on this trip, for instance? Now *don't* look at me as if I'd just dropped the collection plate in church. Of course it was either money, or he simply didn't want to—"

"I suppose it's never occurred to you," Mother said, "that Irv might be tied up with his business in California."

We heard the cups and saucers tinkle. Stephen put his hands in his pockets and looked out the back door.

"Oh, Irv's business," Aunt Rosemary said. "Really, Amy, you don't live in China, you know; we do hear *something* about what's going on. Irv hasn't had enough *business*

of any kind to tie him up anywhere since that Texas hotel
deal blew up in his face."

I sat at the table and looked at the lemons floating
around in the pitcher. *Mother came in and took off her hat
and said, All right, kids, we'll eat down in the dining room
tonight. I'm sorry I'm so late. Are you awfully hungry? I
said, Yes, but Hattie made us some lemonade.*

*That was in Texas. It was almost before I could remem-
ber. We lived in a hotel and when you looked out the
window everything was down below and you could see the
stores and the street with the automobiles going by and
the tops of people's heads going along on the sidewalks. It
was Daddy's hotel, Mother said. He and Mr. Knight owned
it.*

*Mother was hot. She went in the bathroom and washed
her face and then she went in her room and closed the
door. When she came out she had a white dress on.*

All right, she said. We can go down now.

Is Daddy going to eat with us? I said.

Daddy has some important business today, Mother said.

*She opened the door and we went down the hall to the
elevator. You had to be quiet in the hall. Sometimes the
doors would be open and you could see the colored ladies
making the beds, and sometimes through the transoms you
could hear people talking. One night there was a lot of noise
and Daddy went out to see what it was and the next morning Hattie said there were twelve broken glasses in the room
and it looked worse than when her cousin Billie got married in Houston. Hattie's feet hurt her most of the time.
We asked her every morning if her feet hurt her, and she
always said they did.*

*When the elevator came we all got in. Joe was running
the elevator and we said hello to him.*

You-all been mighty quiet today, he said to Stephen and me. I ain't seen hide nor hair of you all day.

Mother said we had to stay upstairs, Stephen said. But we're going to eat our dinner in the dining room tonight.

Fried chicken, Joe said. He opened the elevator door to let us out. That's what you-all'll be eating tonight, he said. How about that now?

We liked Joe. He said he would let Stephen run the elevator when he got a little bigger. Stephen measured himself every night on the wall.

There were people in the lobby, but it was late so there weren't many people in the dining room. We sat down at a table in the corner and Arthur Lee came up and Mother told him what we wanted to eat. She didn't talk to us except when we talked to her. Most of the time she was looking at the door to the lobby. Arthur Lee brought some tomato juice and put it down in front of her.

I want some tomato juice too, Stephen said.

All right, Mother said. Here, you can have this.

She put it on the paper mat in front of him. The mat had a picture of the hotel on it, with a flag flying on top of it. I didn't think the picture looked much like the real hotel, but Mother said that was because they made it when the hotel was new.

Arthur Lee brought us some fried chicken and biscuits, and Stephen and I ate ours but Mother wasn't hungry. She was still looking at the door. After a while I looked up and there was Daddy coming in. He looked hot and he was wiping his forehead with his handkerchief. He saw us and he came over and sat down.

Well, Irv? Mother said.

Arthur Lee came up and asked Daddy what he would like to have.

Nothing, thanks, Arthur Lee, Daddy said. You might just bring me a glass of ice water.

Arthur Lee went away and Daddy looked at Mother. His face looked funny.

Well, Amy, it's over, he said. The bottom's dropped out.

Mother didn't say anything. She just nodded her head and sat there with her hands on the table. Arthur Lee came back with the water.

Nice fried chicken tonight, Mr. Gilman, Arthur Lee said.

No, Daddy said. It's too hot to eat, Arthur Lee.

Arthur Lee went away again. Mother said to Daddy, There really isn't a chance then, Irv? Knight won't—?

Knight is a crook, Daddy said. His voice sounded funny too. I could dress it up in fancier words, Amy, he said, but I couldn't say it any better than that. And I am a fool—

No, Irv, no, you're not, Mother said. You couldn't have known how it was going to turn out.

I ought to have known, though, Daddy said. It was my business to have known. A man with a family has no business taking a risk like that.

Mother smiled but she didn't look like smiling.

Oh, Irv, it's not as bad as that, she said. We'll go back to California and start all over.

At my age? Daddy said. You're young still, Amy, so starting over looks easy to you, but at my age—

Stephen said, Are we going to go back to California? Hot dog, are we going to go back to California?

Mother looked around at him as if she'd forgotten he was there.

Have you finished your chicken, Stephen? she said. How would you and Shivaun like to go back upstairs now?

I want some dessert, Stephen said.

All the while Daddy sat there looking straight ahead of him with that funny expression on his face.

It may be the best thing, after all, Mother said. A hotel is no place to bring up children. We'll all be better off back in California.

Daddy just sat there. He put his elbow on the table and leaned his face on his hand.

What a terrible thing, Amy, he said. What a terrible thing. I tell you, I don't know where to turn. I never thought this could happen to me.

Stephen said, "There's a dog here that wants to come in the house."

He was standing at the screen door. I got up and went over and looked out. There was a little yard with a wooden fence around it. The dog was standing on the other side of the screen door looking up at Stephen and making a noise in its throat. It was a black-and-white curly dog. It looked slow and fat and one eye looked queer.

"I suppose it's old," I said. "Do you think it's old, Stephen?"

"Old as the hills," Stephen said. He squatted down and patted the dog's nose through the screen. "He wants to come in," he said.

"Maybe he lives here," I said. "Shall we ask?"

I wanted to go back in the other room where Mother was. I could hear them talking there. Aunt Rosemary was still talking the most.

"Of course Michael could have done something," she said. "He's the only one who ever had any influence on Jack. And naturally it affected him, too—a marriage like that, that's no marriage at all, in his own immediate family. What on earth do you imagine the Cardinal said about it? But Michael gets worse every year; he simply sits back and lets people walk over him. They say that assistant of his, Father Kaspar, is practically running St. Cyprian's now."

"You go and ask," Stephen said to me.

He was still squatting down looking at the dog. I went into the other room and everybody stopped talking.

"There's a black-and-white dog outside," I said. "He wants to come in."

"Well, let him in then," Granny Cournane said.

Mother looked at Granny Cournane.

"A black-and-white dog?" she said. "Gran, it isn't the Captain?"

"Isn't it, though?" Granny Cournane said. "He's fifteen years old and blind in one eye, but at that he can get around better than I can."

Mother jumped up and ran out to the kitchen. She opened the door and the dog came in and she knelt down and put her arms around him.

"Don't you know me, Captain?" she said. "Don't you remember me?"

"Do you know him?" Stephen said.

"Yes," Mother said. "He was my dog when I—before your father and I were married. Gran took him when I went away."

The dog whined.

"He knows you," Stephen said.

"No," Mother said. "I don't think he does." She stood up. Her eyes looked shiny. "He's so old," she said. "It was a long time ago."

"He knows you, all right," Stephen said.

Mother reached down and stroked the dog's head.

"It's so long ago," she said.

The dog looked up at Mother and whined again.

June 10, 1927

Amy

While I was putting the dress on I heard Mother telephoning downstairs, and without having to understand the words, only by the tone of her voice, I knew it had begun again. Once, when I was fourteen, Father said to me: "Champ, it's necessary for you to grow up to be a woman, but in the name of God, when you do, remember that the tongue is an instrument of communication, not of war." It was easy to remember, with Mother leading the words out with banners and bugles in the quiet house. I tried not to listen, hooking the dress in front of the mirror. Behind me, in the mirror, the Captain jumped up on the bed and sat there looking at me, his tongue out, panting a little in the warm summer air.

The long box of roses, American Beauties, was lying on the bed, fresh from the florist's, the red caught like blood in a nest of thin green paper. Sister Madeleine Sophie wanted lilies, symbol of purity ,but Sister St. Bernard said Ste. Marie graduates always carried roses. Mother ordered mine, speaking with authority over the telephone from the hall littered with the half-packed boxes of her best Haviland. To explain the way the house looked, she told people she and I were going on a trip right after graduation day. But of course everyone knew. They might have printed it in headlines in the newspaper and nobody would have been surprised: MAYOR AND WIFE ARRANGE QUIET DIVORCE; DAUGHTER OF FORMER GOVERNOR BREAKING UP HOME, INJURED WIFE ALLEGES.

I heard her voice, talking on the phone, then the click of the receiver, then the quick tap of her heels as she walked to the stairs. She came up; in the mirror I saw her framed beside the roses and the bed. The Captain jumped down guiltily to the floor.

"Amy, for the love of Mike," she said, "can't you keep that beast off the bed?"

She was wearing blue linen with a white sailor collar; she looked as breezy as if she'd just stepped off a yacht, except for the slight permanent frown between her brows.

"I'm sorry," I said.

"Yes, I can see that." She gave the spread a jerk to set it straight, then came over behind me. "Here, let me do that." She fastened the hooks of my dress; I felt her eyes going over me critically. "Skirt could be a little shorter," she said. "I told that simple-minded fitter at Vogue's. When a girl has slick legs, she may as well show them."

"It doesn't matter," I said.

She looked at me intently, stepping back from the mirror.

"Of course it matters," she said. "There's nothing else that does matter more to a girl your age than how she looks."

"Why?" I said.

Her eyes came up hard, hitting against mine.

"Why? Amy, you're a little fool," she said. "Are you still thinking about that—?"

"Stop it," I said.

"Because of that ridiculous business the other night with Mal and that young man—?"

"Mother," I said. "If you don't stop it—"

"Of course, darling; I know exactly how you feel," Mother said. "Good heavens, I've had crushes on the wrong sort of young men myself; I know what it's like. But you're such a popular girl, Amy; every third boy you know is perfectly wild about you."

She went on talking. I sat down in front of the mirror and picked up a comb. The Captain sat beside me on the floor, watching Mother, his tongue lolling out. In the mirror the breeze blew the curtains out a little and then sucked them gently back against the screens again. It was a lovely room.

"Let me do that," Mother said.

She ran the comb through the waves, pushing them into place. She did everything well; once Father said to her that if she were marooned alone on a desert island she'd have the monkeys organized, trained, and equipped within six months to satisfy all the needs of man. So I couldn't help wondering if she'd been as efficient in grooming herself, planning the campaign for a husband, as she was now in grooming me and planning mine. Grandfather Champion, a druggist and not a very successful one, could hardly have been much help to her, so when she met John Cournane, who was already an assistant in the District Attorney's office, was it because he was the handsomest young man she had ever seen or because she could look ahead to the highly successful law office on Lake Street and the mayoralty at forty-three, and perhaps some day the governorship except for a girl named Ermina Marlow, whom she could not of course possibly have foreseen?

"You're so *young*, Amy," Mother said. "Oh, I know you think you've been around, but at your age you can't even begin to understand. Of course it was absolutely none of Mal's business, but even he could see—" *You're no damn rotten good, he said to me. And I never knew till then how it was, love, really, something turning over inside you when you look, touch; you can't even try to fight it any more than you can fight breathing or your heart beating—*

I looked at Mother in the mirror and she shrugged.

"All right," she said. "We won't talk about it. I don't want to upset you; Sister St. Bernard will never forgive me if I don't deliver her valedictorian to her as fresh and calm as a daisy." She went on, "I told your father we'd all come back here to the house after the exercises. There'll only be the family, of course. Then you and I will have plenty of time to change and catch the eleven-forty for New York. I have everything packed."

"Yes," I said.

"We'll have a wonderful time in New York," Mother said. She laid the comb down on the dresser. "There are all sorts of people I want to look up—the Lords, and the McEvoys—"

"Yes," I said. "I'd rather not hear about it."

Her voice changed.

"If you think this is easy for me," she said. "Going on

as if nothing had happened, keeping up a front. It's only for your sake—"

"I know. I'm sorry."

"We can't let it ruin both our lives because your father has made up his mind to ruin his," she said. "And, for all we know, it may not happen even now. I've talked to Father Michael again; he's promised to get Jack off somewhere alone tonight."

I turned around but I didn't say it: "Don't you know, can't you understand, he can't even bear to be in the same room with you any more?" I thought of his eyes, his polite manner, polite and defiant and trapped like an animal, a child—

"Mother, don't," I said. "Please. Don't you know it won't do any good?"

"Oh, Amy, don't be an *egg*. What do you know about it? Father Michael has a lot of influence with Jack."

I could see her looking at herself in the mirror, planning it out. Nobody watching her would have known; she looked gay and confident, Irish-blue eyes and shining black hair, a figure like a girl's in the blue linen dress.

"Jack thinks there's nobody in the world like Father Michael," she said. "I'm surprised he hasn't listened to him before this." *Just because Michael's the pastor at St. Cyprian's, does it mean we have to live on Johnson Avenue too? Mother said. The house was brown but she had it painted white to make it look larger. I was nine years old then; we moved in the day after my birthday. After dinner Father Michael and Father wanted to talk but she said, We'll have a game of mah-jongg, Michael; there's no reason for you to be behind the times because you wear your collar backwards. I saw his kind bitter observing eyes.*

She went over to the bed and lifted the roses from the

box. The Captain watched her warily, his tail thumping slowly on the rug.

"When did these come?" she said. "I didn't hear the bell." She shook them out, looking at them critically. "Well, I suppose they'll have to do."

"They're lovely."

"I had your father's office on the phone five minutes ago," she said. "I told them, if he wasn't here by half past three we positively wouldn't wait. You'd imagine that creature of his would at least let him be on time for his own daughter's graduation."

"He has things to do, you know," I said. "You'd think, to hear you tell it, he never went near his office to do a stroke of work."

"Father Michael warned him," Mother said. "As long ago as when we were living in that horrible little house on Johnson Avenue, he warned him what would happen if he went on the way he was going. I know because I put him up to it." *Talk to him, Michael; tell him I won't stand for his drinking—*

If you wouldn't have it in the house, Rosemary, encourage him—

But what has that got to do with it? People come here; I can't, for the sake of his career, when they expect— And he's a grown man, not a child.

She would sit there, drumming with one foot on the floor, smiling impatiently when the old people from St. Anne's or Father Michael's parishioners came to the house, saying, I'm awfully sorry; I have a headache; would you excuse me? And Father trying to cover it over, laughing, telling them stories to make them laugh, so that in five minutes nobody cared and that only made it worse. Playing the clown for those people, she would say; after all, who are they? Butchers, bakers, and candlestick-makers. I suppose you're thinking it's so many votes, but do we have to live with them too? You can't even imagine anybody from Johnson Avenue joining a country club; instead, do you realize a Mrs. Dennehy was here today—her husband has a little bakery, I believe—and wanted me to join her kaffee-klatsch club, every other Thursday? When I said, No, thank you, she looked as if I'd shot the Pope. And Father, Well, there goes the Dennehy vote. And she, You don't actually think I could, should— And he, Rosemary, after the rarefied atmosphere of high society in which both you and I grew up it's hardly likely I'd expect you to associate with anybody beneath the rank of a D.A.R.

She looked at her watch and said to me, "Are you ready? We may as well leave; of course he isn't coming."

"We can wait a few more minutes," I said.

"I don't want you to be late," she said. "Rushing in at the last minute with your face on fire, getting up on that platform for all those people to see you. Meg Gerolt told me Bax and Monty Ferris were going to be there; they won't miss seeing you graduate even if they miss their own college graduation—"

I wanted to tell her I didn't give a damn about Bax Gerolt or Monty Ferris, but I knew it wouldn't do any good. If she could only look twenty years into the future, see which of them was going to make more money and live in the bigger house, she wouldn't even have to lie awake nights wondering which one I ought to marry. Only there had to be some reason why it was so important to her. She sat there in the first row, the place of honor between Father Michael and Father. The little school hall smelled thinly of coal smoke and camphor, everybody nodding and smiling at her a little nervously: Merry Christmas, Mrs. Cournane, Merry Christmas. Mr. Pflaum, the milkman, came out on the stage in a red suit and whiskers, singing

"*Jingle Bells*" *while Miss Laura Dennehy determinedly ac-companied him on the piano. Then the children in white cheesecloth, all with tinsel wreaths, the ones who lived down the street from us too but whom I didn't play with because they went to the St. Cyprian parish school and I went to a private academy. All the while Mother sat there smiling oversweetly, rigid, her furs too expensive, just pat-ting her gloved hands together, bored, protesting, No, really, Michael, I actually thought it was sweet, so nice of you to ask us—*

Till we were home and from my room I heard them in the hall, she saying, And there I sat watching my milk-man, my own milkman— And Father, It hasn't done you any visible damage. And she, Do you hear me? We're leaving, we're leaving; I don't care if he is your brother. There's a house on Winchester Avenue, in the kind of neighborhood where we belong; you can call the agent to-morrow.

We went downstairs; the Captain's feet padded softly behind us on the steps. Sadie was in the hall. She started to ask Mother about dinner but then she stopped, smiling at me.

"Oh, Miss Amy," she said, "that's a pretty dress. You know what you look like? You look like a bride."

"I haven't time now, Sadie," Mother said. "I told you this morning, I've left a list of everything in the kitchen. There'll only be the family; a few friends of Amy's may drop in a little later, but she can entertain them on the porch; it'll be nicer out there."

"I didn't ask anybody," I said.

Mother looked at me, fitting on her gloves.

"Oh—I must have forgotten to tell you," she said. "Meg Gerolt said Bax wanted to come over to say good-by. And of course if he comes, you know probably Monty—"

"I don't want—"

Father came in the door before I could finish it.

"Well, Rosemary," he said. He was always too polite to her, as if he were some kind of foreigner who had never heard of Western manners and was practicing them now, overdoing the experiment a little. "I see you're all ready," he said.

He smiled at me; it might have been a wink. Mother shrugged.

"I suppose you realize you're late—as usual," she said.

Sadie discreetly disappeared.

"Far be it from us," Mother said, "to disturb your more pressing social engagements—"

"Yes," Father said. "As a matter of fact, I was laying a cornerstone. If I manage to stay in this job long enough, I expect to become expert enough with the spade and trowel to apply for a union card."

"I wouldn't count on that if I were you," Mother said. Her voice always rose three tones when she spoke to him, her hardest, gayest voice, as if she were at a party and wanted to make sure everybody knew she was having a good time. "What is it Paul Willis always says about politics?" she said. " 'In this business, a man has to choose between having a good time and having a good job—' "

Father didn't answer; he looked at me.

"It looks beautiful today, doesn't it?" he said to Mother. "You know, Rosemary, in spite of our sins, we've managed somehow to produce between us a very handsome and intelligent young woman."

"Whose graduation you had to be prodded not to forget to attend," Mother said. "But, of course, that's not surprising; it seems there are other young women in the world—" *I met her at the front door just as I was coming in from school. She had on a wide hat, velvet, and a coat*

*with a cape and a little white fur collar, like a child's coat in
the eighteen-nineties.*

Mother said, This is Miss Marlow, Amy. Now I want
you two to be good friends.

Oh, she was pleased enough to have her in the house
before she knew, running after her, Governor Marlow's
daughter, the name, prestige, still there even though the
money was all gone now: a widow and two daughters trying
to make ends meet in a small apartment, the older doing
society notes for the Herald and the younger, Ermina,
helpless, soft, inefficient, in an office down at City Hall
and then Father—

Bringing her into this house, Michael, Mother said.
The two of them together, here under my nose—

But if you invited her yourself, Rosemary—

Yes, invited her before I suspected—I was sorry for her
sitting around in corners in some dowdy made-over dress
from before the war, and that mother of hers talking from
morning to night about her late husband the Governor and
the Boyds of Virginia. As for her being so beautiful, I never
could see it, but I suppose blond curls and blue eyes and
that helpless look will always take the men in. But how
could I ever have imagined anything like this? You know
Jack; he's never been the type to go in for sentimentality—

No, he hasn't. Has it ever occurred to you he may
only be sorry for her too?

Of course, that's it; stand up for him, but you won't
convince anybody but yourself. The whole world knows
about it by this time; Una heard it all the way down there
in Columbiana. She came up here and began commiserat-
ing with me on losing my husband, when everybody knows
if Tom McGrath hadn't died when he did, he and Una
wouldn't have been able to live together in the same house
another year. Acting as if her own married life had been one

long sweet dream of bliss; well, I don't have to tell you about that; you patched up their troubles often enough.

They had their difficulties; most married couples do, but if there's real affection, understanding—

I suppose you're hinting now that it's my fault. I know all the Cournanes have always thought Jack could do no wrong; you've always been willing to look the other way when he did anything you didn't approve of, like all the other people in this town, electing him mayor on the strength of his good looks and his wit, as if none of the rest of it mattered as long as he could make a good after-dinner speech and look handsome in white tie and tails. Well, I think he'll find out he's gone a little too far this time. A divorce will make very interesting reading in the newspapers, and if he marries that girl there isn't a Catholic in town will vote for him.

Then he has actually told you he wants a divorce?

We've talked it over. What else is there to do? He won't ask the Church for a separation because he wants to marry that girl. Of course, she's seen to that. Where would she be if he and I were simply separated and he stayed in the Church? No, he wants a complete break; he's like a boy of seventeen—calf-love—can you imagine that?

All right, I'll talk to him again, but, Rosemary, you'll have to help.

I've done all I can; nobody can accuse me of not being a good wife to him. I've come downstairs in the middle of the night to make coffee for him when Irving Gilman or one of his other City Hall cronies brought him home, sobering him up so he could appear before his admiring public the next morning. One night he sat up there on the bookcase and recited Shakespeare, Hamlet, to us for an hour before we could get him to come down. He said he ought to have been an actor instead of a politician, all that about

*O what a rogue and peasant slave am I and the rest of it.
Well, it couldn't have been any worse for me if he had been.
What kind of life have I had of it with him? You know
yourself what he could have been if he'd had the ambition
that some men have—the governorship, Washington, the
Senate—but instead he's satisfied with anything they hand
him. He wouldn't even be mayor now if Paul Willis and
Irving Gilman hadn't done most of the work for him.*

"Since we all seem to be ready," Father said, "I sug-
gest we go." He opened the front door; you could smell the
June afternoon in the air, the freshly cut lawn. The car was
standing in the drive, the long black limousine with Eddie,
the chauffeur who went with the other perquisites of
Father's position, at the wheel. "Irv said he'd meet us at the
school," Father said. "He's leaving on his vacation today,
but he said he wouldn't miss Amy's big moment."

We went down the steps.

"Why he shouldn't miss it I'm sure I don't know,"
Mother said. "Just because he's a member of your official
family is no reason for him to act as if we'd adopted him
into ours. He sent Amy a perfect monstrosity of a lavaliere
for her graduation—very expensive and in very bad taste.
You'd think he thought he was her fiancé."

Eddie got out and opened the car door. He had something on his mind; he looked abstracted.

"Evening, Mis' Cournane—Miss Amy," he said.

Or maybe it was just bad humor; he didn't like to
drive Mother because she always wanted to go fast. Eddie
liked making elaborate swings around corners before an
admiring populace, and he adored parades.

"He ought to get married and have a family of his
own," Mother said. She was still talking about Irving Gilman. "Heaven knows he's old enough; he must be thirty-
seven or thirty-eight if he's a day."

She got into the car. Father said, "Irv? He's a con-firmed old bachelor; you'd be wasting your time trying to make up a match for him."

"Well, I don't like him mooning around here after Amy," Mother said sharply. "It was different when she was small— though I must say I never cared for it even then." *He brought me a box of candy for my birthday; it was a Sunday afternoon and I was having a party. Mother insisted on asking the Duncan boys but only one of them came, a stuck-up prig with glasses; he spent all his time pulling Connie Yates's braids and mooing like a cow. Mother said, Isn't that amusing? Oh, Amy, listen to that; isn't it amusing? But it didn't do any good; he kept right on after Connie Yates as if I weren't alive, so after they'd gone she began the course of instruction. Little boys like to be noticed, Amy; Teddy was your guest and he comes from such a nice family, the kind of little boy you ought to culti-vate, et cetera, et cetera, till I felt like the world's most un-successful ten-year-old. I wished I never had to have another birthday as long as I lived. Then Irving Gilman came, brought me a box of chocolates as if I were grown up and popular and beautiful. He sat there watching me open them. You know what I said to the girl at the counter, Amy? he asked. I said, I want a box of chocolates for the finest young lady I know.*

The car started off down the drive. Mother kept on talking about Irving Gilman but I didn't listen; I was think-ing that it was the last time the three of us would ever go anywhere together and that after tomorrow all that would be left would be Mother and I. And Bax Gerolt and Monty Ferris, of course; I mustn't forget them. I could toss a coin and decide which of them to concentrate on, and then it would all be settled and if I didn't get tired of smiling too soon I could start down the road toward a divorce of my own, beginning with a big wedding with six bridesmaids written up in all the newspapers and a honeymoon in Nassau. I had the roses lying in my lap on the white dress: supposing I were on my way to the church to meet Monty Ferris or Bax Gerolt, all I really needed was the veil.

The car went along the streets with the fine new houses and the broad June midafternoon lawns and somebody's bridge club with Packards parked in the drive. Mother said, "I hope Josie's been able to persuade Mrs. Cournane not to come; I told her she'd only be bored and uncomfortable. I don't know what the Yateses and the Shiels and the Lowheimers would make of her, and for Amy's sake I don't care to find out."

"Well, I wouldn't worry about it," Father said. "The Yateses and the Shiels and the Lowheimers all had grandparents too, you know."

"I've met old Mrs. Lowheimer. She's a perfect dowager —white hair, black velvet, a silver-headed cane—"

"Her husband made his money in pork-butchering," Father said. "Their coat of arms is a hog rampant on a field of slops."

He looked tired; you could see the fatigue gathered in the strong single line between his brows. If he would only stop joking I could find out before it was too late what he was really feeling. We never talked about it; Mother was the only one who talked about it.

"Oh, Jack, don't be vulgar," she said.

He felt me looking at him and he glanced over at me, but answering Mother.

"Yes," he said. "All life is vulgar; that is an invaluable lesson that it would pay you to learn, Rosemary. It will save you so much trouble in the future."

Mother shrugged.

"I can be as down-to-earth as the next one when I see

the reason for it," she said. "But I believe in having *some* standards."

The back of Eddie's neck was rigid, listening. He would tell it all over town, down at City Hall, over back fences on Lincoln Street: "The Mayor he says to her and she says to him—" Add it to the legend of Jack Cournane. I never knew how much of it was true when I saw it in the papers or heard people talking about it to each other; as Mother said, his family were the last people in the world to know how he really spent his time. Evenings when I was small after Mother had gone downstairs he used to come into my room sometimes in the dark and tell me long fantastic stories, dramatizing them for me under his breath, the witch squeaking like a bat, the barrel-tones of the giant, till Mother came to the foot of the stairs and called, "Jack, Jack, are you going to keep that child up all night?" And, I remembered, once or twice coming in late from school and finding him sitting in the living room with three or four friends over whisky and soda, being taken on his lap, amidst masculine laughter and attention, feeling like a princess, all of them listening, looking at him, at us. *Miss Smithson said it would be all right for me to wait in Father's office. Well, Amy, she said, I hear you'll be graduating from high school this month. The letter was lying open, half-finished, on the desk: "Ermina, my darling, Yes, it's settled now and the worst is over. I know this is one of the many times in my life when I've managed things badly. May God forgive me for what I've done, but there's no meaning in life for me any longer without you. I know I couldn't go on without your love—" I didn't read any more; I wanted not to have read that much. It was like seeing him—always so humorously cynical and sure of himself—now naked and defenseless, ugly with truth. I went out and said to Miss Smithson, I'm sorry, I can't wait. Will you tell Father I've gone on?*

They were talking; I heard their voices.

"All I'm asking you to do," Mother said, lower now, looking at the back of Eddie's neck, "is to give Amy this one day. She can have that to remember, anyway."

"Mother, don't," I said. "Please. It's all right."

I looked out the window; you couldn't have asked for a finer day. Sister Madeleine Sophie said whenever she prayed to St. Jude they had a fine day for graduation, but why St. Jude she didn't know. The patron of lost causes: even in Amorica the weather isn't that bad. Up the street the crenellated Victorian walls of Ste. Marie's rose familiarly against the blue summer sky. A car drew up ahead of us and I saw Rose Antonio's head in the back seat between her father's and her mother's. When the car stopped, a dark neat young man got out first: her fiancé. He had inherited, at twenty-two, a chain of restaurants, and he and Rose would be married in July. But it was a love match; the rest of us watched Rose, sedate and happy, walking with him, dancing with him, ready to preside over his home and bear his children. If it could just be simple and easy like that, knowing the minute it happened to you, not too late—

Eddie stopped the car and came around and opened the door. Through the gate you could see the folding chairs on the lawn under the trees, the sunlight dappling the garden-party hats and the white flannels and the black habits of the nuns. I always thought that being a nun at Ste. Marie's would be like staying a little girl all your life, lost in the magical dream of innocence, irresponsibility, except for being teacher instead of learner in the daily monotony of the class. Sister St. Bernard had to struggle with bills, plumbers, contractors, provisioners, like the manager of any other business, but when the rest of them laid their heads on their pillows at night they were as free as prisoners or schoolchildren. We sat in class feeling guiltily our own dark knowledge, for some of them had entered the convent as well-bred girls of sixteen from good homes before the time when well-bred girls of sixteen kissed, sat in parked road-sters, wore lipstick, tasted whisky from silver flasks. *Mal said to me, That jerk you're going around with, sneaking out to roadhouses alone—what in hell does your mother have to say about that? And I, Are you going to tell her? Are you? Are you?*

I had to go into the building to join the other girls, so I told Mother where I'd meet her and Father afterward. I went right on in; I didn't look around as they walked across the lawn toward the folding chairs because I already knew what their progress would be like. Mother said once you might just as well take a brass band along when you went anywhere with Father; everybody knew him and everybody wanted to talk to him. So he would be smiling now, the Irish wit, good humor, there exactly as they expected them to be, so that none of them would be able to read sleepless-ness, worry, or whisky, in his good-humoredly smiling eyes; and afterward he would come home and sit in the study with one light on, not reading or working, just sitting with the devil to keep him company, he said once, joking about it, but you could feel the horror. He hated to be alone; maybe that was how he punished himself, sitting there thinking about it afterward.

I went up the steps and into the cool wide hall. There was a statue of the Blessed Virgin in one corner and on the wall a dark oil painting of the founder of the order, a placid face you could never remember. The faint clean virtuous shut-up scent of a building maintained and inhabited by nuns surrounded you at once, so that even without seeing one of them you moderated your walk and lowered your voice a little. There was the sound of voices from one of the classrooms, so I went back. The others were all there, in white, with the roses. I walked past a group of them gathered around Sister Madeleine Sophie to where Carolyn Lesseur stood beside a window, talking to Connie Yates.

"Well, I see you made it," Carolyn said.

She mocked me out of a witchlike tangle of dark hair; she was my best friend, if I had one. Mother said popular girls never had other girls as friends, only as sort of comrades-in-arms. She never cared for me to bring girls home, looking at them jealously to see if they were prettier than I was, or if their clothes were more becoming. I was a terrible disappointment to her till I was about fourteen and all at once it was the style to be thin and not look like the girls on the boxes of chocolates and the boys started flocking around the house.

"Did your father come?" Carolyn asked me.

"Yes," I said.

"Then St. B. will be in her glory; she's got the Bishop and the Mayor too. She was angling for the Cardinal, but even she didn't expect that this side of heaven."

Connie stood a little sulkily, feeling herself excluded; after a moment she drifted over to join the group around Sister Madeleine Sophie.

"Lord, what a creep," Carolyn said. "Telling everybody in sight she's going to Manhattanville in the fall. Helen Tuohy's going to Trinity; they can get together on holydays of obligation and compare catechisms."

"What about you?" I said.

"I'll probably marry Roger. He says his father will send him out to the West Coast office if he wants; we could have a slick time there." She looked at me. "When are you going to take Bax up?" she said.

I pretended to think about it.

"I don't know—probably never."

"Don't be a dope. He's crazy about you." She dropped the subject. "I like your dress."

"Thanks. It was Mother's idea."

"Mine would have me wearing Mother Hubbards if she had anything to say about it. Honestly, Champ, you're lucky."

I didn't say I wasn't. She drooped out the open window, her arms crossed on the sill, looking indifferently across the broad green shadow-pooled lawn. Behind me I could hear Hortense Shiel whispering and giggling in a corner with someone.

"I did. No—c-c-cross my heart, I did."

"Then what happened?"

Mady Lowheimer's voice—slow indolent drawl of incipient not evil simply amorality, the placid refusal or mere inability to see any problem otherwise than as one of self-gratification. Carolyn glanced around over her shoulder at them.

"Horty had a big evening last night," she said. "Get her to tell you about it."

"What?"

"She was out with that fellow from State—you know the one she's been talking about. They had a big time."

When I looked around I saw Horty's cropped red head and eager freckled shanty-Irish face—incongruous above the organdy froth of her graduation dress—bent in secret enjoyment beside Mady's blond indolent listening silence.

"Champ, come on over."

Carolyn went over with me; we made a tight hot knot of secrecy in a corner of the clean barren varnished room.

"Tell her," Mady said, to Hortense.

"What—again?"

The red head flirted from one to the other of us, gratified. If a lucky grandfather hadn't made a fortune in plumbing supplies she would have been the leader of some South Boston gang, red-haired, reckless, ignorant, happy; as it was, the nuns at Ste. Marie's had to cope, not successfully, with her cheerful inability to concentrate or comprehend, an evil compounded by the fact of her having the largest allowance and the most indulgent parents in the class.

"It isn't anything," she said to us, grinning. "You k-k-kids'll all be doing the same thing one of these days. I just b-b-beat you to the gun."

"Not without a ring on my finger, I won't," Carolyn said emphatically. She looked, not at Hortense, but across the room to the others who were gathered—lightly chattering, gay, innocent, dull—around Sister Madeleine Sophie. "I've learned all my lessons like a good girl," she said. "I know when to stop."

"Pshaw!" Hortense gestured eagerly with both hands, boasting. "It doesn't make any d-d-difference to me. If I get in t-t-trouble, my folks'll send me to Europe, or C-c-"

"California," Carolyn said. "Wouldn't you love that. Is that what's behind all this?"

"I have to see Sister Pierre," I said.

I walked off. Around Sister Madeleine Sophie they were talking about summer vacations: "Sister, I'm going to Michigan— Oh, Sister, Mummy's taking us to Colorado Springs—"

"Amy," Sister Madeleine Sophie said.

I stopped.

"Yes, Sister?"

"Amy, I just want—for a minute—before it's time to go outside—"

She stepped away from the group with a gentle agitated clash of the rosary hanging at her waist and brought me out into the hall.

"Amy, dear," she said, "I just wanted to tell you—
we're all so sorry—"

Her round trustful face looked up at me with timid
sympathy; I suppose she would have spoken to me in
exactly the same way if my parents had just been killed in
an accident or an explosion, only with fewer inhibitions, as
she was more used to dealing with death than with divorce.
I tried to think of something to say. She patted my arm
gently.

"You've been praying hard for them, of course?" she
said.

"Yes, Sister—that is, I—"

"And I'm sure Father Cournane's been praying too,"
she said. "After all, God is sure to hear such prayers."

She sounded as if it were so easy. And maybe it was,
if all you ever said was, "Thy will be done." But what about
it when you prayed, "God, please take me out of all this
bewilderment, humiliation, pain, that You, the world,
somebody anyway has planned for me, so I can be safe,
arrogant, and happy. Let other people suffer, learn, be re-
vealed unto, but let me be safe."

"And it isn't as if it reflects on you in the least, Amy,"
Sister Madeleine Sophie said encouragingly. "You're our
brightest student; we're all so proud of you. And before
long you'll marry one of those nice boys"—*who take you
around to roadhouses, Mal said, big sports with their hip-
flasks and cigarettes, and you—what do you think you're
trying to prove? Convent-school girls—if you'd take one
good look at yourselves—*

I smiled and said I wasn't thinking about that right
now; I was thinking about my valedictory address and I had
to see Sister Pierre. I could hear my voice sounding just
as convincing as if I really meant it, and the smile must have
been all right too because she didn't seem to notice any-

thing. She just patted my arm again and said, "All right, dear," and I walked off down the hall.

I thought I might find Sister Pierre in the office and I was right; she was in there talking over last-minute arrangements for the exercises with Sister St. Bernard. I could hear them talking as I came up to the door; it seemed that the members of the string quartet, professional musicians from the Amorica Symphony Orchestra, who were to play for the commencement, hadn't arrived yet, and Sister St. Bernard was talking to somebody about it at intervals over the phone. She had her full lower lip pinched between the thumb and forefinger of her left hand as she sat at the desk, listening over the phone.

"I see no excuse for that," she said firmly. "No excuse whatever."

Sister Pierre looked up and saw me standing there.

"Oh—Amy," she said.

She came over quickly, with her rapid graceful step. She was the best-looking nun at Ste. Marie's; Helen Tuohy said she came from a wealthy French-Canadian family in Montreal and that she had gone into the convent after the man she was engaged to marry had died the week before their wedding day. I didn't believe the story; it sounded too pat and romantic. Especially since I knew one nun in the Charities who really had had that kind of history, and she was small and near-sighted and sallow, and had a disposition like a shark.

Sister Pierre brought me across the hall, where she could talk to me without disturbing Sister St. Bernard.

"How do you feel?" she asked, smiling at me. She was talking about my speech.

"All I can remember is 'Your Eminence, reverend Fathers, ladies and gentlemen—' "

"Your Excellency," she said; "Bishop McClarney is

here, not the Cardinal." She put her hands on my shoulders and gave me a little shake. "Amy Cournane," she said, "you know every word of that speech backwards; there's no use in your trying to tell me you don't."

"Yes," I said. "All right. I suppose I do. When I get up there, anyway."

"You're going to do perfectly splendidly," she said. Then she looked at me and stopped. "Amy," she said. "Don't—you mustn't—"

"I'm not going to," I said. "I didn't even know it was showing."

"It won't help at all for you to cry about it," she said.

She put her arm around me. It made me remember my first day at school, when Mother had gone away and left me there and I had cried all down the front of Sister Ambrose's starched bib. There is something awfully comfortable about nuns when you are in trouble; they never seem to have any of their own. Like angels removed and happy in the sight of God. Of course it only seems that way, because they have their bad moments like everybody else, Sister Semphorian worrying herself sick, for example, when the roof leaked all over the chapel, all the vestments, everything, the night before the Bishop's visit, and then the afternoon she and Sister Paul quarreled about whose class went to lunch first, Sister Paul's blazing face and voice shouting from the stairs, and afterwards when Sister Semphorian died they said Sister Paul did penance for a year.

"Amy," Sister Pierre said. "Now stop this. I simply won't let you—"

"Yes," I said. "I'll be all right in a minute."

I couldn't take out my vanity and powder my nose even in front of Sister Pierre; in spite of all the evidence to the contrary it was still an accepted belief at Ste. Marie's that make-up was something young ladies wore only on the stage.

"You're a fine girl, Amy," Sister Pierre said. She sounded kind and severe. "And you're going to have a fine life; nobody in the world can stop you from that."

"Can't they?" I said.

I wished I could talk to her about it, but what could she say to me except that I'd done what I wanted to do and I'd have to make the best of it, and that Father was doing what he wanted to do and I'd have to make the best of that too? The only people who seem to understand what you're talking about when you're in trouble are people who are in the same kind of trouble themselves, and if they knew anything constructive to do about it they wouldn't be in that particular trouble.

"And here I thought you didn't know how to cry," Sister Pierre said. "You're the only girl in school who hasn't dissolved into tears in *my* class, at any rate."

"You're too tough," I said. "They're all afraid of you."

"And you aren't?"

She smiled at me. She was the kind of nun girls get a crush on: she could play hockey or discuss Marxism with you or just sit there at her desk at the front of the class looking like Joan of Arc with her pale handsome face and flashing dark eyes. But they were all afraid to talk to her and when you talked to her she was just like anyone else. I suppose if you could talk to an eagle you'd find it was saying the same things as the robins; it would be some unlikely-looking crow or starling that would have the really original things to say.

Sister St. Bernard came out of the office, clapping her hands together sharply.

"All right," she said. "All right, girls. Freshmen, form in line. Sister Cyril—Sister Margaret Louise—"

She never raised her voice; she just stood there now talking to that empty hall as if she expected the entire student body and all the teachers to materialize there before her when she clapped her hands, like something out of the *Arabian Nights*. It almost worked that way, too; when you go to a convent school and you hear a clap of the hands you automatically move, like a private in an army when a drill sergeant shouts. In two minutes the freshmen were lined up in pairs along the hall, the sophomores were forming on the stairs, and Sister St. Bernard was confronting a guilty-looking string quartet who came rushing up the steps from a taxi, carrying their instruments.

"There is no excuse for this, gentlemen," she said to them solemnly. "The Bishop has been kept waiting—and the Mayor. There is no excuse."

One of them was trying apologies when I went back to join the others in the graduating class, but I could have told him it wouldn't work. *I don't want to hear any excuses, Granny Cournane said. The young blackguard, eighteen years old and you'd think he was the King of Ireland, independent as an old mule since he's got that job and making money of his own.*

She brought in the plum pudding flaming with brandy. Grandpa Cournane sat there watching her at the head of the table, heavy and silent, thinking his own stubborn thoughts in the midst of all the gaiety and Christmas cheer.

Oh now, Mrs. Cournane, Father said, youth will have its fling, you know. Mal may have better places to spend his Christmas than with a parcel of relatives who're either a bit too old or too young for his taste.

He hasn't been near here, Granny Cournane said triumphantly, since he walked out two months ago, bag and baggage. That's the gratitude I get for raising him—that Italian all over again—

Aunt Dolly said, Well, Mrs. Cournane, I suppose he got tired of the rough end of the broom.

We formed in line behind the juniors. From the lawn outside we could hear the string quartet begin the processional and after a while the line began to move. I walked last, with Betty Schomaker, carrying the roses. *Mal walked in loaded with presents and began distributing them stubbornly, paying no attention to Granny Cournane. He had on a new suit. Spent every penny you had in the world, I'll wager, Granny Cournane said.*

Well, what if I have? I haven't asked you for anything, have I?

She wouldn't open the package for a long time. Grandpa Cournane got a muffler. He had something for everybody, a locket on a chain for me with a little blue stone in it. Mother said it was cheap afterwards, going home; she wouldn't let me wear it, so I kept it in a box till we moved away from Winchester Avenue and it was lost.

The air felt fresh and warm, the sunlight striking down on us when we emerged slowly from the doorway and went on down the steps. Carolyn turned her head and winked at us but Betty looked straight ahead, seriously. The chairs on the lawn were a blur of color. I couldn't see Father; then I saw him on the platform beside the Bishop, with Mother on the Bishop's other side. I started to laugh and checked it just in time when Betty looked at me in astonishment. The string quartet was playing "Pomp and Circumstance," sawing away busily in their dark coats to make up for lost time. *The band was playing "Three O'clock in the"—no— "Dream House," all of us sitting at the table when Horty came in with him out of the May night beyond the dim lights, the moan of the jazz.*

Look what I f-f-found, she said.

She was giggling, having a fine time. Lord knows where she picks them up. She has a genius for it because I never could, but I knew right away as soon as he looked at me—

His name is M-m-mitch, she said. He's from K-k-kansas City—or is it St. Louis?

He didn't say anything, just looked at us tolerantly but a little warily too. Bunch of fresh kids, I suppose he thought. Still he didn't want to get into anything he couldn't handle.

Isn't he wonderful? Horty said. Look, you k-k-kids, I found him; just remember that, you hear? Remember that.

She was a little drunk. He kept looking at me and I knew even then—

Father saw me and waved as we took our places on the platform. Then the music stopped and Father Cleary stood up to give the invocation. He was a mild old Irish priest who talked to God in a soothing singsong voice about "the gooda of the sowlsa of these young womena." Father Michael was sitting in the front row with Granny Cournane and Josie, Granny Cournane looking hot and important in a black dress and a black hat with the long veil she still insisted on wearing as mourning for Grandpa Cournane. Mother said she looked like a cross between a banshee and a Red Cross nurse who had fallen into a coal bin, but nobody could get her to give up that veil. People used to turn and look at her on the street.

The music began again; the program said: "Choral Number—'The Heavens Are Telling the Glory of God' from *The Creation*—Haydn."

"For the *last* time," Horty said under her breath, as the quartet began the familiar opening phrases.

Sister St. Bernard, across the platform behind the Bishop, saw the movement of her lips and frowned.

We sang; the audience waved fans politely and listened. When the music ended I gave my roses to Betty and stepped to the front of the platform to make the valedictory address. It was like a phonograph record; once it was started

I didn't even have to think. I said we were going out into the world with fondest memories of our days at Ste. Marie's, and that in the years that stretched before us we would never forget *He said, What's your name?*

Amy. Amy Cournane.

The Mayor's daughter?

Yes. What of it?

Nothing, he said.

I looked at him. I thought, If you're scared, damn it, if you're scared— Because I meant to do it even then; I meant to. He was big—fine muscles, heavy-lidded eyes that looked at you arrogantly but he wasn't really. He was scared of me, scared of my name. He knew what I wanted, though. Why did I have to? Oh, why? Father—

"Leaving the quiet halls of Ste. Marie's," I said, "will be for all of us an experience akin to that of leaving a safe harbor for a voyage to a destination still unknown, across seas that may well be turbulent as often as they are calm. But, storm-tossed mariners though we may be, we shall all have a never-failing compass to guide us." *When he kissed me I thought, He's never kissed a girl like me before. Horty came out yelling, Where are you? C-c-come on; I see you. She was slamming car doors all up and down the line.*

He said, When'll I see you again?

Do you want to?

Sure, I want to. Listen, kid, you've really got the goods; you're not like the rest of these—

Have you got a car?

I can get one.

I wanted to say, Look, what do you do for a living? But I didn't bother because what difference did it make? He was going to be the one anyway, somebody I'd never have to see again, not like Bax or Monty. By this time next month he'd be in New Orleans or Paducah or Walla Walla, Washington—

". . . with gratitude toward our parents, our teachers, and our Alma Mater," I said.

They applauded politely, so I supposed it had been all right. I could see Sister Pierre looking proud and satisfied over at the end of one of the rows. Mother was smiling and saying something to the Bishop; then the string quartet began to play and I went back and took my roses from Betty.

"Oh, Champ," Carolyn whispered, "what wonderful mush. Did you make it up all by yourself, my dear?"

"What would you have said, *my dear?*" I whispered back.

We didn't look at each other, talking without moving our lips for Sister St. Bernard's benefit.

"I'd have said, 'Thank God, today I get my parole,' " Carolyn whispered.

The Bishop had to speak next; he was frowning a little, patiently, as he listened to Mother whispering to him under cover of the music. Trying to collect his thoughts, probably, while Mother was dinning it into his ears about Father, telling him how he might be able to do something even if Father Michael couldn't. The Bishop turned a slight patient purple as he listened to her. One of the local newspapers had christened him "The Fighting Bishop" because when he took up a cause, a new orphanage or hospital or no coeducation in church schools or whatever, he never stopped short of total victory, and I could see the signs on his face now of the kind of choleric energy that had justified his title. He was a magnificent man, tall, well-built, iron-gray-haired, but I didn't think even his magnificence would be able to make much of an impression on Father.

I got in the car. We drove out and had a couple of drinks at the Fiddle Club. We didn't talk much. He kept feeling for my knee under the table. I was cold; I kept shivering, but after all it was May, spring, and in the spring a young man's—

Come on, he said. Let's get out of here.

He had a bottle in his pocket. I knew I was a little drunk and I was glad. I kept saying to myself, It's got to be tonight or I can't— I couldn't even tell him where to go and he didn't know the town; he picked the first park he saw. I thought, If Mother could see me now— I wanted her to see me, too, I wanted her—

I could go for you in a big way, kid, he said. Just like a movie, a cheap movie—the park, the trees, the mist. I started to laugh.

What's so funny? he said.

You, I said. Me.

The Bishop stood at the front of the platform, teetering back and forth occasionally from heel to toe, speaking easily, in a firm, grating voice. He said we were very fortunate young women, and that we owed a debt of gratitude to our parents, our school, our church, and our country. Everybody looked a little more solemn, listening to him, as if they had suddenly found themselves in church. I watched Father, wondering what he was thinking about, me or Ermina Marlow *Is this what Father does? Is it?*

What the hell are you talking about?

Is this what Father does?

Come on, kid, you're doing fine.

Is this what Father does?

The Bishop talked for quite a while. It was getting toward late afternoon; you could see the tree-shadows getting longer and the lazy feel, the cool shadow of the building, all the light dresses and white flannels, like a garden

party. It was so peaceful I wanted to cry. I saw Irving Gilman sitting alone in one of the back rows, his head bent
forward a little, listening to the Bishop: non-Catholics always seem to imagine priests are going to say something
different, holier, more important than anybody else that
they had better not miss. He had sandy-red hair, blue eyes,
and a sharp rufous face that I liked. Father said he was a
theoretical genius and a practical nuisance when it came to
business—his hereditary talents spoiled somewhere along
the line by too close an association with Irish dreams. He
was in love with me; I knew that. You know things like
that but you never think about them because if you do you
will have to wonder how, why, feel sorry, worry about maybe
something you did, didn't do, spoiling it, and there aren't
enough people anyway you ever like as much as that.

"I am *dy-eeng*," Hortense muttered. "Mammy—mammy—I want to g-g-go home."

Betty looked scandalized. Carolyn whispered to me,
"There's Monty Ferris glaring at the back of Bax's neck.
Why don't you put him out of his misery, Champ?"

Sister St. Bernard clicked her tongue once, sharply,
and Hortense stared innocently into space; then the Bishop
stopped talking and started to give out the diplomas. I was
the third one to be called up. When the Bishop said, "Amy
Champion Cournane, *magna cum laude*," I saw Father
clapping on the platform and down below Bax pounding
his hands together and Irving Gilman in the back row
louder than anyone, his face flushing up. I kissed the
Bishop's ring and took the diploma tied with the Ste.
Marie colors. It all seemed unimportant or irrelevant, im-
material, and incompetent, however it was they said it in
the law courts A197350, *Rosemary C. Cournane vs. John
B. Cournane for divorce, custody of child, and alimony.
Aunt Una said, Of course you realize, Rosemary, it will be*

in all the newspapers. And Mother, What am I supposed to do about that? That's Jack's business. If he hasn't enough influence—And Aunt Una, He is a prominent man, Rosemary. It will be in all the newspapers. She shook her head reprovingly. I don't know how I can ever go back to Columbiana and explain it to the Bishop, she said.

The Bishop gave out the last diploma; the string quartet played the school song and everybody sang. Mother was the first one to reach me; she kissed me briskly and said, "Come over and talk to the Bishop; he was terribly impressed by your speech." For a minute I thought I couldn't because it was such a damned shambles, Father over there chatting with the Bishop as if neither of them had ever heard of mortal sin, and everybody kissing, Granny Cournane hot and whiskery, black-smelling, Josie soft, timid, Father Michael a little shy, nuns, girls, even Mrs. Gerolt, prospective mother-in-law: Bax luckily wouldn't dare before everybody.

Irving Gilman came up.

"Amy, may I have the privilege, too?" he said.

He kissed me carefully on the cheek, smiling at me afterward.

"You should run for Congress," he said. "Oratory—!" He lifted both hands in mock amazement.

"Irving, don't you *dare* put an idea like that in her head," Mother turned on him. She was talking to the Bishop and Mrs. Gerolt. "Amy's not even thinking of a career," she said; "she was simply cut out to be a wife and mother."

She smiled at Mrs. Gerolt, who smiled back. *Listen, Champ, Bax said, you know my folks are all for it. How about it now? What's the use in our fooling around like this any more? My dad'll stake us to a house out in the Silver Woods Country Club section; hell, he'll be able to*

*afford it—son-in-law of the Mayor, that oughtn't to do the
business any harm—*

Bax said over his mother's shoulder, "That's what I've
been trying to tell her, Mrs. Cournane."

I couldn't say anything because the Bishop was there,
hovering like God the Father over the main altar in church,
but Father said firmly, "Amy's too young to be thinking
about marriage; she'll have to have at least two more years
before she even knows a hawk from a handsaw." He turned
politely to the Bishop. "I understand that the most plau-
sible interpretation of that passage," he said to him, "is that
the word *handsaw* is a corruption of *heronshaw*, a dialect
form meaning *heron*."

Mother, of course, could have killed him. She tried to
drag the conversation back to Bax and me, but Father
Michael was handing me something, a little box.

"For your journey through life, Amy," he said to me.
"I'm afraid I'm a bit late—"

It was a gold St. Christopher medal.

"She can take it with her on the trip to New York."
Mother waved it away. "That was sweet of you, Michael.
Only, of course"—she looked at the Bishop—"there just *is*
the possibility that we won't be going to New York after
all. Jack, Sister St. Bernard has been kind enough to say that
if you and the Bishop—since you two busy men *are* together here now—would like to chat a few minutes in
private, she'll be delighted to put any room in the building
at your disposal—"

She must have talked about it beforehand to the
Bishop, because he looked uncomfortable but determined,
but Father flushed: I didn't remember ever having seen
him look so furious. People sort of melted away, the way
they do when they'd love to stay and listen but if you have
any manners at all you know you can't. Father said some-

thing to Mother, low, just ". . . Rosemary . . . ever . . .";
that was all you could hear, and the Bishop like God the
Father hovering—

"Irv," I said. "Wait a minute. I want to go home. Will
you take me home?"

He was going, too, but he stopped and looked around
at me.

"Why, Amy," he said, "don't you want to go with—?"
Then he looked at Mother standing there talking to Father
and the Bishop, low too but too fast; people were watching
out of the corners of their eyes. "Sure, Amy," he said.
"Sure thing. You come along with me."

We walked across the grass; people spoke to me but I
couldn't say anything back. Everything was all green shadows, tree trunks, calm blue sky, with people jerking across
it like puppets on strings.

"Now it's all right, Amy," Irv said. "It's all right;
we're almost there now. There's my car."

He had a nice plain comfortable old Dodge that nobody would ever look at twice, no chauffeur or limousine;
you could drive along any street in the United States and
nobody would stare. He opened the door.

"Are you all right, Amy?" he said.

"I'm fine. I'm the belle of the ball, the star of the
piece, the top freak in the circus—or no, that's Mother.
Irv, would she care, would she *care* if she had to do it all
on the stage with people paying to see it?"

I pounded with both fists on the car door. It was a
silly thing to do; I was still carrying the roses and some of
the petals fell off, and I dropped the box with the St.
Christopher medal. Irv picked it up. He put his arm around
me.

"Amy," he said, "if there was anything at all I could
do—"

"Nobody can do anything. Not Father Michael, not the Bishop, not the twelve Apostles. Wouldn't you think she could realize that?"

"Your father's in love with that young lady, Amy," Irv said slowly. "And love does funny things to people. He doesn't want to hurt you or your mother; it's like something driving him—"

The way he said it I knew what he was thinking and that was when I started thinking too: All right, all right, if he wants that it's better than Bax or Mother, New York, pouncing on every unattached young man in sight with the proper amount of money, family connections—and I, the way Mal said, "You're no damn rotten good—"

I got in the car. Irv came around. He sat there next to me and looked at me for a minute, but he didn't say anything. It felt safe, sitting there with him, and I didn't care what in hell they were doing back on the lawn, whether Mother was playing Lady Macbeth in front of the entire faculty, student-body, and assembled audience, or the Bishop and Father had squared off, Marquis of Queensberry rules, charging admission, the way I'd said.

Irv started the car.

"Amy," he said.

"I'm all right," I said. "Just don't let's go right home; can you drive around a few minutes till I'm all over it?"

"It's a terrible graduation day for you," he said. His voice sounded sterner than I'd ever heard it before. "I've never criticized Jack," he said. "God knows I'm the last man in the world to feel I have the right to do that—but he should have waited—"

"What difference would that have made?" I said. "If this is the way things are going to be, they may as well start today as any other day." We drove along the tree-shaded road, past the bright prosperous houses. "Only I feel—" I said.

He shook his head.

"If there was something I could do," he said. "I'm so fond of you, Amy; you know I'd do anything in the world to help you."

"Yes," I said.

I wanted to say, "There is something," but I didn't; I didn't know how you went about asking somebody to marry you. Because that would be the end of it all, really the end, and I wouldn't even be Amy Cournane any more then, I'd be Mrs. Irving Gilman, and we could go away someplace where nobody would ever call me Champ and there were no young men to be nice to, or mothers, bishops, Mal saying, "You're no damn rotten good—" We just drove around for a while and Irv talked about the traffic and a new building going up and what a fine day it was till all at once I remembered and said, "Oh, Lord, Irv, why didn't you tell me? Father said you were starting on your vacation today—driving to Washington; you ought to be on the road now, oughtn't you?"

"It's all right," he said. "I can start tomorrow."

"Yes," I said. All I had to say was, "Take me with you," but I didn't say it. There was too much time between us and seeing me grow up, but that was the reason really why it was all right now, because he was so much older, peaceful, and it wouldn't be like Bax or Monty instead of Mal and every time they started something it didn't come off, till Horty told me one time Monty complained, "That girl is just naturally cold," but it didn't stop him from coming around *The night Father was elected somebody brought in some champagne and we all drank to the new Mayor, everybody but Irv; he doesn't drink, never has. Paul Willis kidded him about being Father's nursemaid, staying sober to see he got home all right, and Irv said, Well, it's a funny thing, but I've never gotten any pleasure out of it, Paul. When I was a young man I tried it plenty of times but I found it never gave me any pleasure, so I gave it up and I've never been sorry. He looked at me drinking the champagne that night and said, Amy, I know it's a special occasion, but maybe your mother wouldn't like it. He was always the best of the lot, Father said—telling about the time the big Pole came down to City Hall looking for Father, something about a permit, so excited he couldn't speak the little English he knew, said the Mayor, the City, was ruining him. Before they could call a policeman he was in Father's office and he and Irv there behind the desk. Father said it was a glorious sight to see Irv, five feet nine and a hundred and forty pounds, like David and Goliath: the Pole was six feet four. We each got one of his arms, Father said, and around we went like a merry-go-round, with him trying to shake us off. It took three policemen to get him out.*

"A vacation isn't a very important thing to me, Amy, when your happiness is concerned," Irv said. "If there was anything I could do for you here, I'd call it off altogether."

"Would you?" I said.

Every time I thought about going back to the house, to Mother and the relatives and everything packed, Bax hopefully on the porch in the June dark, I thought all over again that there had to be some way, somebody who cared what happened to Amy Cournane, not just the Amy they could see, touch, use, exhibit, but the one inside, the one who was really me.

"Irv—" I said.

"Yes, Amy?"

We were just driving around; it was a beautiful day. I thought if you could just sit there moving but you wouldn't have to move too, everything just frozen the way it was, except new things to look at, with somebody else driving on a fine June day and never have to go back—

"Irv," I said, "would you marry me?"

He looked at me; the car almost jumped the curb. He had to wrench the wheel to straighten it out; then he pulled up carefully to the curb and stopped the car there. He sat there with his hands on the wheel.

"Amy," he said. He just looked straight ahead for a minute; then he looked at me. "Amy," he said, "you know you oughtn't to say a thing like that."

"Yes," I said. "I suppose not." And then, "All right. If you don't want to."

"If I don't want to—" He looked at me again; his face was flushed and I only looked for a second, but I saw tears come up in his eyes. "Amy," he said, "there's nothing in the world I'd want more, but you're—just upset, you don't mean that—"

"Yes," I said again. It was like something happening to somebody else; all I had to do was sit there and the words said themselves. "Would it be so bad?" I said. "I mean, if we did."

He sat there too.

"You're not in love with me, Amy," he said after a while. He sounded as if he were trying to be calm about it but his voice was shaking. "If you were in love with me that would be a different matter altogether," he said. "But you're a young girl, and I'm twenty years older than you are. I'm thirty-eight years old, Amy; did you know that?"

"Yes," I said. "And Father is forty-five, and Ermina Marlow is—what is it—twenty-two or twenty-three? And they are going to live happily ever afterward."

He didn't say anything. I sat there and looked at the line of brick houses running up the hill. It was somewhere around the University, in an old part of town; I'd never been there before. At the corner there was a little grocery with a sign in the window that said SALADA TEA.

"And there's something else," Irv said after a while.

"You know when my father was born they spelled his name a little different than Gilman. As a matter of fact, it was Goldmann; my grandfather changed it when my father was a boy. Maybe you knew that, Amy, but you may not have thought—"

He looked at me and I said, "It doesn't matter. I suppose none of it matters if you don't want to."

He didn't say anything again. After another while he put his head down on the steering wheel and I thought he was crying, trying not to, and I knew then it was going to be like losing something or finding—maybe some kind of responsibility, because I'd done this myself; it was like an end or the beginning of something new—

"Irv," I said. "Irv—don't. Please."

There wasn't anybody around. He raised his head, averted, and got his handkerchief; he kept his head turned away.

"If I was ten years younger, Amy—" he said. "I'd give everything I ever owned if I thought I could make you love me."

"We get along," I said. "Don't we? We'd always get along. I haven't got anybody else. If I go to New York with Mother I'll marry somebody just to have it over with, Bax Gerolt or somebody else she picks up for me."

Irv shook his head.

"That's not right, Amy," he said. "You know it's not right. You've got your whole life before you, and you don't want to do something now, right at the start, that will make all the years to come bitter for you."

"That's easy to say, isn't it?" I said. "My whole life. Only I've got to live now, too."

"Yes," Irv said. He looked at me. "If I thought I could make you happy, Amy," he said. "But how could I flatter myself? It's only because you're upset—"

When he came up we heard the car slew around on the gravel. We both thought it was a policeman; we had just half a minute to try to look respectable. Then I saw him—no coat or hat; he looked so funny I thought, He's sick. He opened the car door and jerked me by the arm.

Get out of there, he said.

Hey, what the hell, Mitch said. Do you know this guy?

Yes, I know him. Mal, go away.

The hell I will. You're coming with me.

He pulled my arm so hard I almost yelled. He could tell, of course, the way we looked. I hit him.

Go away, I said. Go away.

I was crying. Mitch pulled me back in the car.

What the devil's this all about? he said. You married or something?

No, he's nothing, nobody—

Your boy friend? Well, all right, bud. Look, I know it's tough but these things happen—

He's not my boy friend. Why did you follow us? You've been following us, haven't you? Sneaking around—

Mal said, You get on out of that car. I'll kill you, I'll kill you both—

Now, take it easy, sonny. She's all right. It happens to a lot of girls. Just go on home and keep your mouth shut.

I'm going to shut your mouth, mister.

You want to try?

He started to get out of the car but another automobile went by. We all just froze. The headlights picked Mal out standing there in the mist.

Look, this isn't going to do anybody any good, Mitch said.

He was scared and I knew it—not of Mal; he was bigger than Mal, knew ways to fight Mal had never heard of,

probably, but I was the Mayor's daughter and if there was
going to be trouble he didn't want any part of it.

You're not walking out of it like this, Mal said.

He walked around the car and put his hand on the
door. I could see Mitch trying to start the car fast. Just as
the door came open he did. The door wrenched out of Mal's
hand and knocked him flat as we went by.

What are you trying to do—kill him? Stop, do you hear
me?

He's all right—just knocked him down.

I looked back and saw him getting up, receding into
the distance, a white running blur.

Damn it, where did he come from? Mitch said. If you
knew he was following us, why the hell didn't you say so?

I didn't know, I didn't.

Well, he's in love with you, anyway. I can't say I
blame him; you're a hot little number, sister.

Shut up. Let me out of this car.

What—right here? Listen, get hold of yourself. So this
guy knows something—you can handle him, can't you?
Give him a piece of what I got and he'll keep his mouth
shut.

I sat there. It was like dying; you couldn't feel that way
and not die. Trees, the streets, went rushing by.

I'll take you home. Say you went to a movie, felt sick—
You'll be all right.

The streets rushed by.

This is some ritzy neighborhood you live in, kid. I drove
by your house the other day and asked somebody where the
Mayor lived; I figured I might as well see where the package
was wrapped.

I sat there. The mist was thickening; it began to rain.
When the car pulled up at the curb I jerked the door open
and he grabbed my arm.

Look, kid, wait a minute; I want to talk—

Let me go.

Sure, in a minute. Listen, about that kid—if he makes trouble, don't you make any for me.

Let me go. Do you hear me—?

You went right along with me, didn't you? You knew what you were doing.

The car door was open. I pulled away, jumped out, almost fell out. He got out too.

Listen, if you've got any ideas—

A car's brakes squealed behind us. Mal got out and came up running. Mitch said, *Look, sonny, haven't you made enough trouble for one night?*

You come near her again and I'll kill you. You hear me?

Take it easy, bud.

Don't call me bud. Mal looked at me. *You go on in the house.*

Why? What are you going to do?

None of your damn business. Go on in.

No.

He looked at me.

Do you know what he is? Do you know what kind of dirt you've been messing around in, or don't you care? You go on in the house and let me talk to him.

You don't have to talk. Mal, please go away. Just go away.

There were lights on in the house, cars passing by, the spring lawn damp and cool, the trees.

Look, sister, I'm getting out of this, Mitch said. *You settle things with your boy friend.*

Not till I've settled with you, Mal said.

He looked as if he was crying. I couldn't stand it. I started to cry too.

He looked at me.

You're no damn rotten good, he said. You know that, don't you?

Mitch started to walk away. Mal stopped looking at me and turned around.

God damn you, you think you can walk out like that—

He grabbed Mitch by the arm and hit him. It was raining harder. Mitch hit him and he fell into the shrubbery along the front walk. Mitch ran for the car and Mal got up and made a dive after him. They both went down. There was somebody walking a dog across the street and all I could think was, *They'll call the police.*

They kept on fighting. I could see Mal, his white shirt torn in the darkness and his hair plastered down wet; he looked terrible. Mitch was just trying to get away but Mal wouldn't let him. Then I saw the blood coming out of the corner of his mouth.

Stop it, I said. Stop it. Stop it.

I pulled Mal back and his elbow hit my chin when he jerked away. He didn't even know I was there. Mitch hit him and he fell down in the bushes again but Mitch couldn't get away; Mal wouldn't let him alone.

Then I heard the window go up and Mother's voice calling Eddie, and the next minute Eddie came running around the side of the house with a wrench in his hand and the Captain behind him barking like mad.

Don't, I said. Don't. It's all right. Don't.

Miss Amy, Eddie said, fo' Gawd's sake, whut's goin' on heah?

He looked blanched in the pale light. Mal and Mitch stopped fighting and stood there, panting. The porch light went on and Mother came out.

What is it, Eddie? What on earth—Amy—

She saw me and came running down the steps.

Amy, are you all right? What's happened?

I'm getting out of here, Mitch said.

He ran for the car and jumped in. Eddie said, Shall I go after him, Miss Amy? He hurt you any?

Mal Cesti, Mother said, what is this all about? Have you and that young man been fighting? Who is he? What have the two of you been doing?

Mal stood there without saying a word. Mother looked at me.

Amy Cournane, she said, come up here out of that rain and give me an explanation of this disgraceful—

I looked at Mal.

Did he hurt you? I said. He hurt you, didn't he?

What the hell do you care?

Come on in the house. Your lip's cut.

He just looked at me. You can't die just because you think you have to. I thought, I never even knew it was like this, I never knew, oh, why didn't I know—?

I'm going on home, he said, but if I ever see you with him again—

Mother said, Amy, do you hear me? Mal—you too— come in here. Mal Cesti, what would your grandmother say if she could see you?

He didn't say a word to her, just turned around and walked to the car and drove away.

Well, how do you like that? Mother said. Amy Cournane, you come right here. I want to know what's been going on tonight.

It isn't anything. I was out with somebody and Mal followed us. I guess he was jealous. Mother, please, I'm tired. I'm going right to bed.

Mal jealous? That's ridiculous; what on earth right has he to be jealous of you? Who was that young man? Anyone I know?

She kept on talking and I said I had a headache and

went to bed. I knew she'd find out from someone, and two days later she came home and said she'd heard I'd been out with a very unsuitable young man, nobody seemed to know anything about him, and she wanted me to promise I wouldn't see him again. We all have these crazy crushes, she said. You'll get over it. Now just promise me you won't see him again. Locked the barn door after the horse was stolen. I said, Yes, yes. All I could think of was Mal, because I never even knew it was like that, I never knew, oh, why didn't I know, and he said, You're no damn rotten good—

"Here we are," Irv said. The car stopped in front of a little two-story white house, flush on the brick sidewalk, with a sign in the window. "Amy—?" he said. "Are you all right? Are you sure—?"

"Yes, I'm sure," I said.

It was getting dark; there were trees along the street and you could still see the gold in the calm sky at the end, but under the trees it was half dark already. The air was so quiet and soft you could smell the roses lying in my lap like perfume.

"I even have the white dress and the flowers," I said. "I won't be missing a thing. Are we going to go in?"

I didn't feel anything except how peaceful it was and safe with Irv sitting there beside me. He put his arm around me and I leaned my head on his shoulder, just breathing the peaceful perfume and waiting.

"You ought to be married in church, Amy," he said. "I don't want to take you away from your religion; you know that."

"Yes, I know."

"I don't know anything about that sort of thing, but your uncle could fix it up, I suppose, so we could be married later in a church. I wouldn't want you to do anything you'd regret, Amy."

"I know you wouldn't," I said. "It'll be all right."

"You're sure, Amy?"

"Yes. I'm sure."

We got out of the car. It felt old and settled and quiet and peaceful, with the brick sidewalks and the houses people had been living in for so long that you didn't have to worry any more about all the troubles they'd had in them. When I was nine Father explained Time to me by showing me his watch with the second hand going round and round in its own little circle while the minute hand hardly seemed to move; everything that happened to you in a single day, he said, was, in comparison with the span of an average man's life, like a fraction of one of those hurrying seconds to the interminable slow sweep of the minute hand around a complete revolution of the dial. I used to think of that afterward whenever anything bad happened to me, because nothing could be so bad you couldn't stand it when it was going to be over in one or two or a half dozen of those little flicks of the second hand that were past so quick you could hardly say you had even seen them go by.

So I stood there on the sidewalk after Irv had rung the bell and thought about all the days of my life flicking by, fast, like the little round of seconds on the watch, going round and round till after a while what had happened three or five or a dozen of those little circles ago wouldn't matter any more, and it wouldn't make any difference what Mal knew about me or what he thought because he would be lost somewhere in that maze of fast-ticking little circles that would never stop long enough for you to remember.

"Is Mr. Hilary in?" Irv asked, saying the name on the sign in the window, and the woman smiled and said, "Yes." She looked at us, a little puzzled. "Do you want—?" she said.

"Yes," Irv said. "We'd like to be married."

We went inside. It was a cozy little house, like stepping inside a warm apple dumpling because they were just finishing dinner, and Mr. Hilary came in hemming cordially in his throat, white-haired and rosy-cheeked, like an indulgent English vicar except for the accent straight from Virginia.

"Yes, of course," he said. "Yes, of course. Yes, of course. Now if I can have your name, sir, and your address, and the name and address of this lovely young lady—"

It was getting dusk and there weren't even electric lights to spoil it—instead, the milder gaslight that made me remember going into the living room of the house on Johnson Avenue after dinner when I was small, the darkness over the shadowy shapes of furniture, walls, doors, frightening, unfamiliar, till Father came in from the dining room, reached and lighted the gas chandelier, the incandescent mantle shedding the soft reassuring light like a bounty, making everything peaceful, well-known again.

We didn't have a ring but Irv had one he wore on his watch chain, a heavy twisted gold one that had belonged to his mother. It was a little too small for me but it would do.

"What was she like?" I said.

"Who?"

Mrs. Hilary went to get her daughter to be the second witness.

"Your mother."

Irv shook his head.

"She was a very beautiful small dark woman—not like you, Amy, except that she was beautiful. My father always said he was such a lucky man. And now I'm a lucky man, too, luckier than I've ever deserved to be."

"Don't say that. Please don't say that, Irv."

"Why not? It's the truth."

We waited. There were chimes somewhere ringing the hour and I thought about being married, really married, not even your own name any more, Amy Cournane peacefully dead one mild June evening in cozy gaslight, dead and buried in Irving Gilman's beautiful mother's Jewess's ring, and Mal saying, "You're no damn rotten good."

"Here we are," Mrs. Hilary said, bustling cheerfully in. "Now I think we're all ready to begin."

We stood up. I felt Irv reach out and take my hand and he smiled at me, everybody smiling, waiting, then serious, because it was time to begin, and I remembered Father Michael saying, "Every man sins his own sins," Father and Ermina Marlow, who would meet him coming out of his office, Mother said, by accident or design, who knows, maybe because it was just planned that way, each of them set as a snare for the other, a sort of obstacle course before you won salvation, like the temptation of St. Anthony or St. Paul's thorn in the flesh, only neither of them would get a passing grade now. And if Governor Marlow hadn't had the bad luck to die broke, and if somebody hadn't felt sorry enough for his daughter to give her a job at City Hall, which God knows she was no more qualified for than one of Renoir's children in a park, blue velvet, white fur collar and all, and if the people of Amorica hadn't elected Father mayor, and if Horty hadn't said, "Look what I found," this would never have happened.

They were all looking at me and I said, "I do." It was so easy I almost didn't believe it except the ring on my finger and Irv kissing me and Mrs. Hilary saying, "I hope you'll be very very happy, my dear, and I wish you both the best of luck." "Mal hasn't any luck," I remembered Father saying once. "Some people are born without it, and if they're like Mal they make up for it by being twice as hard, twice

as enduring, twice as willing to put up with the meaning-
less insults life prepares for us all." Father could say that
because he was lucky himself, got everything he wanted;
people seemed to fall all over one another trying to be the
first to give it to him. So when I asked him about Mal he
said, graver than usual, Hamlet-like, "Mal hasn't any luck;
it's always the wrong place, the wrong time—Mal's an indi-
vidualist, you see; he does everything his own way, accepts
nothing except on his own authority, and had the mis-
fortune to be brought up in the most rigidly traditionalist
atmosphere that could be devised in twentieth-century
America, by a pious, strong-willed, simple Irishwoman who
would not change a single one of her few but powerful
basic concepts of life for God Almighty Himself, Who, by
the way, would not even succeed in convincing her He was
the actual True God unless He agreed with her on the
principles of fish on Friday, Mass on Sunday, and skirts
decently covering the knees."

It took such a short time that when we went outside
to the car again it was still not dark except under the trees.

"I can't believe it," Irv said. When he looked at me I
felt the new way again, like losing or finding, I couldn't
tell which, and the responsibility like an end, beginning.
"I can't believe it," he said. He got in the car, sat there
beside me. "I'll try very hard to make you happy, Amy."

"I'll try, too," I said. "Or not happy. Peaceful. Because it's all settled now, isn't it?"

There was still a little gold over the horizon, and when
he started the car and drove out from under the trees the
light came again, very soft and clear, fading little by little
as the seconds went round and round in their circle making
it all the past, even the moment before the past, and now
this moment the past, and before long all the other moments too, and I thought, We'll have to be married by a

priest before it's really settled, the door locked, the key thrown away, so as soon as we get back we'll go to Father Michael. This is one time he can help, not like the last, when he said, "Amy, the saddest thing of all is that we can never lead other people's lives for them, not even the people we love best. It's as if we were each solitary on a ship setting our own course; sometimes you can't even signal across." And I, "Yes, but you and Father—he listens to you; you're the only one—" And he, "He listened." And I, "You mean you won't?" And he, "Can't." And I, "You're a priest; you tell people what to do every day." And he, "Very few of them listen, I'm afraid. I've had the feeling lately that I'm a sort of signpost for them written in a language they no longer understand. Did it ever occur to you, Amy, that though I am a priest there are also priests who are not very successful at their jobs?"

The car ran steadily east, away from the glow, and even out from under the trees it was beginning to be dark now. Irv asked me if I wanted to stop soon and have something to eat, but I said to wait because when we stopped I wanted it to be for the night so it would be all over then and not even Mother, who would be the most disappointed of them all, would care to try to have it annulled. Of course I hadn't any luggage, but Irv's bags, all packed for his trip, were in the back of the car, and I could buy something the next morning when we sent the wire to Mother: IRVING AND I MARRIED YESTERDAY WILL WRITE SOON LOVE TO ALL AMY. There would be an extra charge for ALL, but I wanted to include everybody, Father, Mother, Gran, Bax, Father Michael, Sister Madeleine Sophie, Sister Pierre, even Mal. They were all the past now and only Irv and I were the present, and so it would be all right to send LOVE TO ALL.

The car ran on; it was full dark by now.

June 11, 1938

EVENING

Thressa Dawes

When he told me who was coming I counted them up and sure enough it came out that there'd be thirteen sitting down at the table. It wasn't bad enough having that whole family of his to cook for the night before the celebration, when he might know I'd be up to my ears in work already, but it had to come out thirteen too. And of course, with him being a priest, I couldn't just say that's bad luck, can't you ask one more, or better still ask half the others to stay home. Because I knew it wouldn't make any difference if

I did have the whole Married Ladies' Sodality swarming over the house all week, acting like they were doing me a favor waxing up the floors that were waxed already better than any of theirs would ever be, and hanging curtains, and turning the place upside down getting things ready for the reception; I still knew who was going to be doing all the work. Thressa Dawes, if you wanted it in good plain English; that's who was going to be doing the work.

So when Father Kaspar came in about quarter to six I was so sick of it, that houseful of women underfoot all day pretending to be working when all they really wanted to do was stick their noses in every room, cupboard, and closet in the house, and me trying to roast two seven-pound chickens in an oven that wasn't even big enough for one, that I told him straight out I had half a mind to just up and quit.

"Oh, don't say that, Mrs. Dawes," he says. If they were all like Father Kaspar it'd be a different sort of world, but that kind comes few and far between, Roman collar or no Roman collar, as you find out when you've been keeping house for them as long as I have. "Don't say that, Mrs. Dawes," he says, "just when I'm getting fat and comfortable on your cooking."

Well, there wasn't any need for him to talk about getting fat, because if you wanted to see a fine figure of a man you wouldn't have to look any farther than where he is. Laura Dennehy says when she sees him getting up in the pulpit at High Mass she always thinks of St. Michael the Archangel, and the looks isn't all of it; he has the disposition to go with it too. If the Cardinal had the sense God gave little green apples it'd be Father Kaspar who'd be pastor of St. Cyprian's Church today, and Father Cournane would be off in a monastery, or a Chinese mission, or someplace else where it doesn't make a bit of difference whether you know how to get along with people or not. They say he was picked out, when he was in the seminary, to be sent to Rome to study there, so they must have thought he had something in him, but the only thing I can say is that it's a pity they didn't keep him over there when they had him. He might have been some use to His Holiness the Pope, but as a parish priest, I say, you can give him back to the Indians with my compliments.

Anyway, I was mad enough by that time to say something along that line to Father Kaspar, but of course he wouldn't hear of it. You've got to say that for him, he never has a word to say against Father Cournane, as much as those Kittredges and Heffernans and old Miss Lizzie Clemens like to talk about him putting himself forward in the parish.

"Oh, you mustn't say that, Mrs. Dawes," he says. "You know Father Cournane's made St. Cyprian's what it is today."

"Yes," I says, "and if he keeps at it much longer he's going to be right back where he started with it, saying Mass in an empty loft over a grocery store. The collection was off a good three hundred dollars again last Sunday."

"How do you know that?" he says, smiling a little.

"I got it out of Father McBride," I says; "you don't think His Nibs or Walter Kittredge would tell me a thing like that, do you? But, as I started to say, I haven't heard yet that the banks have gone out of the business of collecting interest on the mortgage of a church, whether it's Catholic or Protestant or Holy Roller."

He smiled again.

"Well, I think we'll have to let Father Cournane worry about that, don't you?" he says.

He came over and opened the oven door a little so he could look in. There are a lot of men I wouldn't have fooling around in my kitchen, but Father Kaspar is different; he appreciates good cooking and he's never slow to tell you so. Father Cournane, now, would sit there at the table and look just as happy if you served him up a pair of old shoes boiled in glue. No wonder he's as thin as he is. It's no compliment to my cooking, I always tell him, to have you walking around the parish looking like they could set you up in somebody's field to scare the crows away. Clothes and all too, I could say, though I never have. Holes in his socks the size of silver dollars, and I suppose he'd never think to get a new pair no matter if there was more hole than sock, if his relations didn't buy him some once in a way at Christmas. It's gotten to the point where I'm going to come straight out and tell him one of these days I'm through trying to darn them; he can get himself some new ones or go barefoot. Like I tell those people that go around saying he's a saint, you ought to have to try to darn his socks. There isn't a priest alive, anyway, that hasn't got some fool of a woman saying he's a saint, but I've been living with them for twenty years and I've yet to see the one I'd get down on my knees and pray to, alive or dead.

"Chicken," Father Kaspar says. He took a good look inside before he closed the door again. "And two of them," he says. "We *are* going to have a feast tonight, aren't we?"

"I don't know about that," I says. "With thirteen of you at the table tonight, you'll be lucky personally to get what went over the fence last."

"Thirteen?" he says. He looked surprised. "I thought only Father Cournane's niece from California and her children—"

"Did you ever know the day when any of that crowd passed up a free meal?" I says. "There'll be Mrs. Clohessey and Mrs. John Cournane and Mrs. McGrath, *and* all the rest of the McGraths. Well, it's not my business, I'm only hired to work here, but I will just say this: if that Mrs. McGrath comes nosing around my kitchen tonight, I won't be responsible for what happens. She may tell the Bishop what to do down there in Columbiana, but she's not going to order me around in my own kitchen."

I meant it, too. She may play the fine lady, she and Mrs. John Cournane, with the rest of them around here, but she won't get away with it with me. I know all about the Cournanes, and where they come from; my aunt Julia used to live right next door to the old man over on the West Side, in St. Anne's parish, and she said he was plain as an old shoe, went to work every morning carrying his dinner pail like anybody else, and snored in church on Sunday during the sermon. Believe me, whenever I see a piece in the society page about one of those McGraths, I remember that. Because I don't care how high a bird may fly; just show me its nest and I'll tell you what it is.

But, of course, Father Kaspar wouldn't hear anything either against Mrs. McGrath, and just turned the subject off to something else. As a matter of fact, what it was that he asked me was whether I was going to the Married Ladies' meeting after High Mass the next day. I knew what he was getting at, but I didn't let on; all I says was, "Did you ever know me to miss a meeting, let alone an election?"

"No," he says, "I never did. But I thought, with the distinguished visitors that may be coming tomorrow, and a house full of people—"

"I wouldn't care if it was His Holiness the Pope that was coming tomorrow," I says. "I wouldn't miss that election even for him. If there's only one woman in this parish who's got enough sense to vote against Mrs. Walter Kittredge going on running that sodality for another year, at least there's one, and her name is Thressa Dawes."

"Well," he says, "it's going to be pretty close, I hear."

Not letting on that he cared one way or another how it came out, but of course he didn't have to say anything to *me*. Everybody in the parish knew that when Jimmy Heffernan's wife died six years ago and he got that widow over on Orange Street in trouble—at his age, seventy if he was a day—and her parading around the streets as big as you please with her belly, brazen was the only word for both of them, and Father Cournane was in the hospital then with his appendix, Father Kaspar said he couldn't stop people from having Jimmy Heffernan for their undertaker if that was what they wanted, but he could stop him from coming inside St. Cyprian's Church with the coffins. He might have known, with Walter Kittredge hand in glove with Father Cournane all these years, and Mrs. Walter Kittredge being Jimmy Heffernan's sister, what would happen. And sure enough, as soon as Father Cournane was out of the hospital he patched it all up, married the two of them one evening at the parish house with her six months gone if she was a day, and inside of the week there was Jimmy Heffernan marching up the middle aisle of the church again in his striped pants and cutaway coat, looking like widows and babies had never crossed his mind.

Naturally Father Kaspar was put out about it. Like I say, if we had him for pastor here at St. Cyprian's there wouldn't be half the parish parading into church when the Mass is half over and sneaking out again the minute the Communion is done, or little sluts of girls coming up to be married with their belongings all on show, their dresses cut halfway down to their waists in front. They say when he was over at St. Ignatius' he sent one of them out of the church one day till she'd pinned a handkerchief in the neck of her dress, with the wedding party right there in church and all. Now Father Cournane would no more think of doing that than he'd think of flying to the moon.

They'd have to come into church like September Morn before he'd notice anything was wrong.

So I knew, anyway, which side Father Kaspar was on when he said that about the Married Ladies' election.

"Yes," I says to him, "it may be close, but if there's half the married women in the parish with the sense of goslings, there'll be some changes made around here Sunday, and one of them will be Mrs. Walter Kittredge sitting down with the rest of us and watching somebody else run that sodality."

"Well," he says, "Mrs. Milligan is certainly a very able woman. A very able woman, and very energetic."

That's the way he is, always a good word for everybody. Now I never heard Father Cournane so much as say he thought Mrs. Milligan could start the *two times* table and come out with the right answer all along. He still holds it against her, is what I think, about that picket fence she wanted to put up last year around the lawn in front of the new church to keep the children from running over it. Because they weren't even the children from St. Cyprian's School, that the nuns could have any control over; they were from the public school, running across the grass because it was a little shorter maybe that way, or maybe just out of pure devilment, and who likes to see a nice new sodded lawn, that cost I don't know how much out of the parish's pocket, being trampled over like that? A nice white picket fence would have put an end to that in a hurry, and not have cost too much either, but no, to hear Father Cournane telling it, it was as bad as if she wanted to paint the steeple bright blue. "A picket fence around a Gothic church," he says; "oh, I hardly think that would be suitable." Talking in that quiet way he has, you know, as if he was afraid somebody might hear what he had to say. Well, I don't know about *suitable*, but I do know about those

children, and if there's any other way to stop them but a
fence, they must have invented it when I wasn't looking.

So then Father Kaspar got behind it, and between him
and Mrs. Milligan, and Francis Jaeger being president of
the Holy Name, they kept after him till he changed his
mind. But like I say, he's never had a good word for Mrs.
Milligan since. Not even though she's practically taken
over the Altar Society and is in the church morning, noon,
and night. She's a hard worker, that woman. Two children,
and a husband that drinks when he isn't working, and she
still has time to do more for the church than any three
other women in this parish.

Anyway, speak of the devil—while we were talking
about the Married Ladies' election and Father Cournane,
who should walk in but His Nibs himself. He'd been hearing confessions and was still in his cassock, and he had
that discouraged look on him he always has on a Saturday
afternoon. It's no wonder, with the kind of customers he
has. All the hard cases in the parish go to him, when they
go to confession at all; you'll see them sometimes lined up
three deep waiting to get in, when Father Kaspar's box
is empty and they'd have nothing to do but step into it and
tell their tale to him. They'll even steer clear of Father
McBride, who isn't dry behind the ears yet and comes out
of the box every Saturday looking as surprised as a nine-
year-old who's just learned about smoking behind the barn.
I said to Laura Dennehy only the other day, "If they'd
committed murder," I says, "Father Cournane'd probably
tell them to say three Our Fathers and three Hail Marys
and that would be the end of it. I'd give a good week's
wages," I says to her, "to hear what he says to them in that
box."

And she says, "Well, Thressa, why don't you find out?
You could go to him yourself some day, you know."

"Yes," I says, "and that would be a fine idea, wouldn't it? Telling him every time I got mad enough at the way things are run in this parish to let out a *hell* or a *damn* in my kitchen. No, thank you," I says, "I go to the Passionist Fathers for my little sessions, and it'll be a long cold freezing day in the middle of July before I kneel down in Father Cournane's box."

Well, like I said, there he comes pussyfooting into my kitchen, with Father Kaspar and me still there talking about the election.

"Oh, Mrs. Dawes," he says, hardly looking at me when he talked to me, the way he does, like he had too much going on inside to bother about *you*, "I wanted to speak to you," he says, "about the dinner tonight—"

"You leave the dinner tonight to me," I says. "If it don't suit you, you can tell me about it afterward, but you can see I've got my hands full now."

I was washing greens for the salad, and if there's one thing I hate it's a man breathing down my neck when I'm trying to work. What I felt like telling him was that if they didn't like what I was cooking for dinner they knew what they could do, which was go someplace else where there was a woman to cook it who wasn't up to her ears in work and fuss the way I was, but I kept that back. I have some respect for the calling if I haven't for the man. And Father Kaspar put in then, like the real gentleman he is, and said he was sure Father Cournane could leave all that to Mrs. Dawes, she knew how to put a fine dinner on the table as well as any woman in the parish, and so he got him out of the room. I suppose he thinks my cooking's not good enough for high society muckamucks like that precious set of McGraths with their airs, and that Mrs. John Cournane that couldn't even hold onto a husband when she had him —not that he was worth having, nothing but an old drunken bum if you want to put a name to it, won't even come around here any more, Father Cournane meeting him on street corners and handing him out a dollar here and a dollar there; of course he thinks nobody in the parish knows about it but my second cousin Tillie Wrampelmann lives on Adams Street herself, knows where he lives, knows all about him.

Well, and what else could you expect with the way he carried on in this town when he was mayor, having a grand time for himself on the people's money, I suppose, running around with that girl, what was her name, the Governor's daughter, Marlow, that was it. Mrs. Jaeger pointed her out to me one day on the street in town coming out of Casson's, said, "That's her, the Marlow girl, the Mayor's sweetie." A beautiful little thing she was, too, blue eyes and all those blond curls, like Mary Pickford. She was with her mother, at least I guess her mother, fat old dragon all in black. They say she was the one broke it up after it all came out about what was going on in the Mayor's office. That's what I call shutting the door after the horse is stolen, but at least she married her off, what did I hear about that, two three years later, some rich broker from out in Boston. Some men aren't particular about damaged goods as long as they're nice and soft and pretty to look at.

But they say the Mayor carried on terrible, don't I know it myself, that afternoon he came here looking for Father Cournane when he was out on a sick-call and I says, "Won't you sit down and wait?" I says, like I didn't know anything about what was going on. "He'll be back in a few minutes." I didn't go away, just stood there kind of waiting in that big old reception hall, we were still in the old parish house over on Johnson Avenue then, what was it, 1927, 1928, because it was all in the papers then about the scandal at City Hall, big headlines every day, and all about the investigation. So I thought he just might say something to me, let it fall by accident, and I could have something to say then to Mrs. Walter Kittredge, thought she knew it all with her cousin down in the waterworks that was always telling her things before anybody else in the parish had heard them.

But he just sat down, didn't hardly seem to know I was there. I could have kept on standing in front of him all day, I suppose, like I was a post or a table or chair, if I hadn't said something about the weather. He looked up then and said, "Oh yes, a fine day," or words to that effect. I don't think I ever in my life saw a man look so sunk. Well, it was his own fault, if I do have to say it. What did he expect, getting a divorce from his wife so he could marry that chit of a girl who wouldn't even have him after all, and all that scandal about the Mayor's office, two three of those men getting sent to jail on the head of it, and I suppose that's where he should have ended up too if truth were told, only for his being the Mayor, though they did say he hadn't done anything wrong himself, just been careless, trusted the wrong people.

I had a chance to get a real good look at him sitting there that afternoon. Well, yes, a handsome man, you can't get around that; you'd never think him and Father Cournane were brothers. Not too tall, but that lovely profile, regular matinee idol; they say he wanted to be an actor once and I shouldn't wonder. And dressed in one of those nice light-gray suits, as neat as a pin, dashing I suppose some would call it, even if he did look like he hadn't had any sleep in a week. I wanted like anything to fall into conversation with him just by accident so he wouldn't suspect I was trying to find anything out, ask him something about the health of his family, his sisters, Mrs. Clohessey, Mrs. McGrath, or that daughter of his, Amy, that ran away

and married a Jew, moved to California. That made quite
a stir too, old enough to be her father; I wonder what kind
of Catholics those Cournanes are with their Jews and their
divorces. She used to come around to the parish house
sometimes when she was still in school, Ste. Marie's, but
that didn't stop her from smoking, running around with
her skirts as short as the law allows. They say she had the
fellows all raving for her but I never saw anything in her,
skinny as a rail and that streaky blond hair, cool way of
looking at you, as if she saw right through you. Well, she
was gone now, married and off in California, probably preg-
nant by this time if I had the nerve to ask, but he just sat
there staring at the floor; you might as well have tried talking to a post.

So after a minute I went on back to the kitchen. It was
kind of spooky, him so quiet out there, the clock ticking,
knowing he was there but not a sound out of him, and then
Father Cournane came in. I heard them talking to each
other out there in the reception hall.

"Oh, hello, Jack," Father Cournane says. "I didn't
know you were coming around today. Have you been here
long?"

And then the Mayor says, "No," and something else,
low, that I couldn't understand, and they went in the study
and closed the door.

Well, I'm not making any claims to be higher-minded
than the next one; naturally I was curious about what was
going on. So I just happened to remember I hadn't dusted
in the reception hall that day, and I picked up a dust rag
and went on out. The study door was closed, and for a few
minutes all I could hear was Father Cournane's voice and
of course I couldn't understand any of that. When he's
preaching on Sunday you have to listen with all your ears
to be sure whether he's talking Greek or English. Now

when Father Kaspar preaches it's a pleasure to hear it; he'll jolt you up right out of your seat sometimes telling you about hell, the Last Judgment, his voice rolling around like thunder in that big new church.

Anyway, I was almost ready to give it up as a bad job when the Mayor started to talk too. Not that I could understand that, either; he was crying, I think, so all I could catch was something about that girl, Mina, he called her, her name was Ermina, Ermina Marlow, that was it. And I could hear Father Cournane talking to him, trying to quiet him down, I suppose. It gives me a funny feeling to hear a man cry, especially a man like that, wouldn't do it if you cut his arm off but all for love, the power we have over them. Makes a woman think, like Fred in my own time when I said I was going to leave, all packed up because I'd had enough of him. Well, I could have been foolish too in my day, that washing-machine salesman, but Fred was a good provider, I thought, after all. Much good I ever got out of him but at least I'm not like some women, I can always say I was a faithful wife for sixteen long years.

I edged over a little closer to the study door, not exactly listening, but just keeping my ears open; you never know what you're going to find out in this world just by keeping your ears open for what falls in. People you'd think to look at them butter wouldn't melt in their mouths in there telling things you'd only expect to hear down in a police court.

So I heard the Mayor say then, "Mike, you can't understand—" And Father Cournane says yes, he did, and the Mayor says, "Not this, I can't go on living without her, Mike, it's that bad, you don't know." And Father Cournane says maybe he was right, and nobody really understands another man's grief but God, but how we had to go on living all the same, alone or not. And then there was a noise like somebody hitting a fist on the desk and the Mayor says, damn it, it was only that old harridan keeping her away from him, and if he could see her, the girl he meant, he could straighten it all out and everything would be fine. And he wanted Father Cournane to go to see her himself, fix it so he could talk to her, but Father Cournane says, "Jack, can't you understand, in the eyes of the Church you're still married to Rosemary; divorce or no divorce, how can I help you?"

Which was as it should be, time somebody was telling him that, but the Mayor kept right on like he hadn't heard it. They say those Cournanes are a stubborn set and I wouldn't doubt it after that. He was in there arguing with Father Cournane for a half hour that I heard myself, till Father Redlinger, that was the assistant then, came in and I had to go back to the kitchen. What happened after that I wouldn't know. But I did manage to get another peek at him when he left, about half an hour after that, and I'd say by the look of him he hadn't got what he wanted. Father Cournane looked awfully down, and the Mayor looked like if somebody would just hand him the gun he'd go out and shoot himself. But just as they got to the door Father Cournane put his hand on his arm and the Mayor looked around, I suppose he was trying to smile, and says, "Oh, all right, Mike, I guess I'll live."

And Father Cournane says, "You'll work it out, Jack," and then says, "Come and see me again soon."

Well, I was hoping he would myself; naturally a person likes to know what's going on, with the whole thing in the papers and all. It must have been six months before it got off the front page, and I noticed that that Mrs. McGrath never once stuck her nose inside the front door while it was going on, laying low down there in Columbiana for a change, and Mrs. John Cournane banging out of the house without a word for anybody when she'd come, which wasn't often, thank God, since she and Father Cournane had it together about him not being able to make it up between her and the Mayor. Well, like I always say, if a woman needs a priest to help her hold a man, she hasn't got the necessary essentials herself. You could hardly blame the Mayor when you looked at *her*; the only reason I could ever think of that he married her in the first place was because they needed somebody in the family who could stand up toe-to-toe with that Mrs. McGrath.

But she ought to be glad enough things turned out the way they did when she looks at him now, a total disgrace to put a mild word to it. You'd think a man that was going to act that way would stay in New York, or wherever it was he went after he resigned, but no, he has to come back here and disgrace his whole family, a fine thing for a Catholic priest to have a brother in the gutter. I used to see him sometimes in town six seven years ago, when he was still selling what was it, vacuum cleaners, then it was insurance, living down at that Brown Hotel where all the old bums go when they've got a dollar or two in their pockets, dirty old men, spending it first on drink, then on a burlesque show or in one of those houses, if there's any left then for a meal and a decent night's lodging. I will say that for him, he always managed to keep himself neat, frayed cuffs if you got up close enough to notice, but they'd seen the washtub, and if you didn't look at his eyes, bloodshot, and a bit of weight he'd put on, you'd say he still looked the same.

That was before he took up with that Jacowski girl, of course; now I never saw *her*, but I'd dearly love to. Young enough to be his daughter, Tillie says, and going around in an old jacket and a tam-o'-shanter like one of them anarchists, but the bracelets and earrings on her like the Queen of Sheba. Raiding the dime store for all that junk. And calls herself Polish, or Russian, or one of those nationalities, Tillie says, when she's as dark as Benjamin and the mother too.

I remember when His Nibs first heard about that, the wedding, that is; it was all over before anybody knew a thing about it. I'll never understand how I missed it, because if there's one thing I read in the paper every night it's the death notices, marriage licenses, real estate transfers, before I even get to the serial story or the women's page. But with one paper and three men throwing it around the house, it's a wonder I ever get to see anything at all.

So the first I knew about it was when Lizzie Clemens comes marching in here one day, a rainy Friday morning it was, with that black toque of hers on that she's had since the Civil War, high-laced shoes and skirts to the top of them. If that's what it's like to be in your eighties, I hope the good Lord takes me before that time comes. But at least I won't have to go parading up to Communion on the first Sunday of every month with the Young Ladies' Sodality the way she does. They ought to have an age limit, single or not, because she's been prefect of that sodality since the parish started, and naturally those young girls won't go to meetings when they're run by an old woman with one foot in the grave. And who doesn't look like she's ready to put the other one in, either, for a good long time to come. Why, she can remember seeing Indians over at Ames's Corner in their feathers and blankets. There ought to be some way a person could get her out of there.

Anyway, in she marches, with that old black pocket-book of hers hanging on her arm, and opens it up and hands me a piece cut out of some newspaper.

"What's this?" I says, and she says, "Read it and see."

So I started to read it. Well, it was the marriage licenses, I could see that, but it took me down to about the fifth or sixth name till I knew what she was driving at. That was when I came to it, as big as life—"John B. Cournane, 55, salesman, Brown Hotel, and Rae Jacowski, 22, advertising copywriter, 2982 Adams Street." You could have knocked me down with a feather. I knew he was running around with all sorts of women; you show me the man with a little money in his pocket—and I don't care how little it is, either—and no family ties who isn't. But I never expected anything like this. It was nearly ten years since that Marlow business was put a stop to, and I'd never even heard this new girl's name.

"Do you think it's him?" Lizzie says to me.

"Why," I says, "of course it's him—'John B. Cournane, 55, salesman, Brown Hotel'—who else in the world could it be? But who is this girl? That's what I want to know."

"I never heard of her before," she says.

"Well, she's young enough," I says. "Unless they printed her age wrong. That can happen too, you know."

As I knew myself to my sorrow, that time I had my purse snatched coming home from a bingo game in 1934, and they had me in all the papers, "Mrs. Thressa Dawes, 58." Fifty-*eight*, after I told that policeman fifty-four as plain as anybody could say it, and not many women wouldn't have shaved off more than two years anyway, with all that publicity, and looking as young as I do for my age. If I had that policeman here I know what I'd do to him. Because there are people in this parish who think to this day I'm two years older than I am; they read it in the paper and that's good enough for them.

I looked again at the piece of paper Lizzie'd given me.

"Is this last night's paper?" I says to her. "I don't know how I missed it; I thought I went over that paper with a fine-tooth comb."

"No," she says, "it's Wednesday's. I was scrubbing my kitchen floor, and I laid the paper down when I finished, to keep from tracking it, like I always do, and there it was. Do you think they're married already?" she says.

"If they aren't, it won't be this paper's fault," I says. "They're always behind like an old cow's tail; my niece's baby wasn't in the birth notices last month till it was two weeks old." Then I thought of something else. "I wonder if Father Cournane knows about this," I says.

"That's what I was wondering," Lizzie says. "The poor man, he has his share of the world's troubles with that family of his."

Oh, of course, he can do no wrong for her, sitting there with her head on one side, like a monkey if I ever saw one with that toque of hers; all she needed was a tin cup and an organ grinder alongside of her. Says it was his prayers brought her through the pneumonia three years ago; like I say, there isn't a priest in the world without some fool of a woman going around claiming he's a saint. The way I look at it, it'll take more than pneumonia to do in anybody as old and tough as she is, whether there's any praying done or not.

"Well," I says, "anyway you've got it right about his family. But this is worse than anything yet. At least when that niece of his ran away and got married by a justice of the peace, he could fix it up and marry her in the Church. But Mr. John B. Cournane's already got a perfectly good wife, no matter if they did get themselves divorced by the court."

"Maybe they aren't married yet," Lizzie says. She took the paper back from me. "I came right over," she says. "I thought maybe Father Cournane might want to do something to stop it."

"Yes," I says, "and he might want to do something to

stop that rain outside too. He's got about as much chance with the one as he has with the other."

It ended with her leaving the piece of paper with me to show to Father Cournane when he came home. That was around noontime. Father Kaspar came in at the same time as he did, was right there in the room, but I couldn't see the sense of trying to keep it a secret from him when it was all there in the paper for anybody to read, so I just started right in on it. I just took the piece of paper out of my pocket and handed it to Father Cournane.

"Here," I says. "Lizzie Clemens brought this over this morning. It was in the paper Wednesday night."

Well, he took it from me and started to read it. I couldn't tell when he got to the name, because he kept his head down, reading, and for a minute I thought maybe he knew all about it after all. But he just kept standing there, and it got to be too long, and finally Father Kaspar started to say something. That was when he looked up and said, "Will you excuse me?" or something like that, and bolted off into his study and closed the door.

Father Kaspar looked at me.

"What was that all about?" he says.

"About Mr. John B. Cournane," I says. "His marriage license was in the paper Wednesday night, that's all."

"His marriage license?" he says, his eyebrows going up.

"Don't look at me," I says. "I don't know any more about it than you do. It says he's marrying a girl named Rae Jacowski, twenty-two. Anyway, he managed to get a young one."

Which is a mystery to me, why a young girl should want to marry a man fifty-five years old, and one who drinks too much even to keep a decent job, but there's no accounting for tastes. And I'll have to admit he's still a good-looking man, and has the manners to get around any woman.

The day after we found out about that marrying business, for instance—Father Cournane'd been trying to get hold of him all that Friday evening, and all the next morning, but he never seemed to be able to find him. He'd left messages that he wanted to see him, though, and sure enough, on Saturday afternoon, when Father Cournane was over in the church hearing confessions, there was a ring at the doorbell and when I answered it it was Mr. John B. Cournane himself.

"Good afternoon," he says, taking off his hat to me like I was a duchess. "I hope I'm not intruding," he says, "but I've received—from a rather unreliable source, it's true—a report that my brother would like to see me."

Well, he'd been drinking; I could see that. Not that he couldn't walk in that hall as straight as a soldier on parade; they always did say, back in the old days, he could drink all the rest of those politicians down at City Hall under the table and still make a speech afterward that would bring the tears to your eyes.

"I hope I'm not disturbing you," he says to me. "Not deranging you in any of your countless busy little household arrangements?"

"No," I says. "As a matter of fact, I'm all finished with my housework. I was just on my way upstairs to get cleaned up."

Because I looked like a sight, my dust cap still on, and an old dress I ought to've given to the Vincent de Paul six months ago, but he didn't seem to notice that at all. I will say it for him, he's got lovely manners.

"Then, by all means, don't let me detain you," he says. "The thought of you adorning yourself in your boudoir above will sustain me while I wait."

And down he sits in the hall. I hadn't even told him where Father Cournane was or when he was expected back, but that didn't seem to bother him; he looked like he was satisfied to sit there till the cows came home.

"Father Cournane's hearing confessions," I says, after a minute.

"Is he, indeed?" he says. "Wiping away the tears of the penitent—a very laudable occupation. Apparently he felt the need for one more—"

"I beg your pardon?" I says.

"Penitent," he says. "Me. I'm wearing the sackcloth, but I seem to have forgotten the ashes."

Now you try to make sense out of that. Just the same, I wasn't going to go away yet; if he felt like talking, it wasn't up to me to stop him.

"I hear we have to congratulate you," I says, thinking if I didn't take the bull by the horns I'd never find out anything at all.

He looked over at me with his eyebrows going up.

"Do you?" he says. "On what grounds, may I inquire?"

"Well," I says, "most men think when they get married it's the proper thing for people to congratulate them. But maybe you're not married yet—"

"Oh yes," he says, nodding his head up and down as solemn as a judge, "I'm married. I am definitely married. And so you'd like to congratulate me, Mrs.—?"

"Dawes," I says.

"Dawes," he says, after me. "What a lovely name."

"I don't know about that," I says. "But I married it, and I've got it, and I'm likely to keep it."

"I wouldn't be too sure of that," he says. "Mature femininity such as yours is prone to underestimate the power of its charms."

If he wasn't serious about it, he didn't show it. Of course I knew what it was, Irish blarney, all those politicians can turn it on and off like any faucet in your kitchen, but it doesn't do any harm, I suppose, to make a woman feel good with a few civil words. Father Cournane, now, if I was to put on a new dress every day in the week, would never think of giving me a compliment on it. Lizzie Clemens says a priest oughtn't to notice how a woman dresses, but I say he's got eyes, hasn't he, like the rest of us, and it wouldn't hurt him to put himself out once in a while to tell a person she looks nice when she does.

So I says to Mr. John Cournane, "Well, I don't know about mature, but I hear you got yourself a young one, anyway; twenty-two years old, it said in the paper."

"Did it?" he says. He looked at me in that peculiar way he has, like he could look right through you, drunk or not, and see everything that was going on inside you. "The newspapers have a remarkable reputation for accuracy," he says, "so I suppose we may take it that that fact is correct."

"And is she good-looking?" I says, thinking it was a pretty queer business that he didn't know himself how old the girl he married was.

"To tell you the truth," he says, "I hadn't noticed."

Now, how do you like that? Marries the girl and can't even tell you how she looks. I shouldn't have said it, I suppose, but it just slipped out: "You hadn't noticed?" I says. "Then why in the name of goodness did you ever marry her?"

Well, it never even fazed him. He just looked at me with his eyebrows up, like what he was telling me was the most natural thing in the world, and says, "She expressed the desire to be married—so I married her. Any gentleman, Mrs.—Dawes, would have done as much. Besides, I believe she *is* a fetching piece."

That was when I realized how drunk he was. I know what people say about him, but even he wouldn't have sat there in a priest's reception hall and talked like that if he'd known what he was saying. Well, it was plain as day what had happened; the girl had roped him in when he was in no condition to know what he was doing, and I doubt very much if he'd been sober since. A little harpy like that, thought because he'd been somebody once she could get something out of being Mrs. John Cournane. Advertising copywriter, my foot—they had another word for that kind when I was a girl.

So I was standing there, not knowing what in the world to say to him, when luckily the front door opened and Father Cournane came in.

"Oh—Jack," he says, not smiling, looking from me to him. "Did you get my message?"

Mr. John Cournane stood up, steady enough, once he'd got to his feet.

"Through circuitous routes," he says. "By back alleys and secret messengers." He looked around at me. "In the meantime," he says, "I've been having a most interesting chat with your charming housekeeper. Do you know she is a fascinating conversationalist? We've been discussing love —and marriage—and such tender subjects—"

Father Cournane didn't say anything, just took him by the arm and tried to steer him over to the study door.

"In a moment—in a moment," Mr. Cournane says. "Is there really any need for this unseemly haste?" He looked around at me again. "I haven't bidden this sweet lady adieu."

"Come along now, Jack," Father Cournane says. He looked around at me too; I guess he knew there wasn't any use in trying to put a good face on it before me. "I wonder if I could trouble you to make some coffee, Mrs. Dawes," he says to me.

"Ah—coffee," Mr. Cournane says. "Mike, you have a mundane soul. I am drunk on the liquor of tender glances

—which is unaffected, I believe, by coffee, black or otherwise."

Well, I left him still arguing with Father Cournane
about going into the study, and went back to the kitchen
and made some good strong coffee. It makes you sick to see
a man like that, could be anything he really wanted to,
making such a fool of himself over women. Because that's
what's at the bottom of it all, if you want my opinion—first
that wife of his, then that wishy-washy Marlow girl, and to
finish it off, a little Jewish chippy. That ought to be enough
to do for any man. What kills me is that, with all the decent women there are in the world, they have to pick up
with trash like that.

Anyway, I made the coffee and brought it out and
knocked at the study door. Father Cournane opened it for
me.

"Oh, Mrs. Dawes—thank you very much," he says,
and before I could so much as open my mouth was going
to take the tray from me so that would have been the end
of it, as far as my finding out any more went, only Mr.
John Cournane put in then, from where he was sitting
over at the other side of the room, "My brother seems determined to interrupt our little chat, Mrs. Dawes. Won't
you come in and sit down? We were talking about love,
I believe?"

His Nibs never even turned around.

"That'll be all, Mrs. Dawes," he says, taking the tray
away from me.

Well, I won't say he closed the door in my face, but it
was near enough to it. So I just stood there and listened; if
he hasn't got common ordinary good manners, I says to myself, why should I have any better?

I could hear Mr. John Cournane saying, "What is
this sudden aversion of yours, Mike, to Mrs. Dawes's sweet

company?" and Father Cournane muttering something, and then Mr. John Cournane again, says, "Privacy is a luxury in which I no longer indulge," and Father Cournane says, "Jack, Jack." I couldn't understand it all; after a few minutes Mr. John Cournane quieted down, and like I say, Father Cournane always talks so low you can't tell what he's saying unless you're right in the room. But I could make out that Father Cournane was asking him about the girl, found out quick enough how the land lay there, I suppose, but there was nothing he could do about it: Mr. John Cournane just kept saying she was a fetching piece and after all he was bound in honor. If I'd been Father Cournane I wouldn't have wasted my time on him; I'd have had that little bitch in my study and told her exactly what I thought of her. Could have bought her off, too, I'll bet my wages, if he'd reached down in his pocket for five hundred dollars. But no, he'd never think of that. All he did was talk to Mr. John Cournane about how he wasn't really married to that girl, and what he owed to Rosemary, et cetera, et cetera. "Rosemary," Mr. John Cournane says. "All I owe Rosemary is a bill for services." Just like that; I'd love to have seen her face if she'd been there and heard him.

After a while he sobered up a little, more like himself, but he was still stubborn as ever about that girl.

"No, Mike," he says, "it's my life, and I don't think I have to point out to you that so far I've required the minimum of assistance in making a mess of it. And I've already taken on one little helper now, so I don't think I could use another one."

And Father Cournane says something about God knows he's never been much help to him, and Mr. John Cournane says, "I'll tell you something, Mike, if I hadn't always known there was such a man as you alive in this world, there'd have been times when I'd have given up on

the whole human race, including myself." And Father Cournane says, "Just so you haven't given up on God," and the
other one says, "I'm afraid it's the other way around; not
even God can enjoy contemplating forever such a ridiculous
comedy of errors as I've been producing and starring in for
the past ten years."

Now if it'd been Father Kaspar in there, he'd have laid
down the law to him good and proper; well, of course he'd
have done that long ago, long before this Rae Jacowski ever
got in the picture. I heard him one night talking to that
Lutz boy, got that girl over in Brownville in trouble and
wasn't going to marry her; he had him blubbering inside of
ten minutes. But it takes a man with a strong character to
do something like that. Why, when Father Kaspar's mother
and sisters come to see him, you'd think he was first cousin
to the archangels the way they hover around him, yes
Florian this, and yes Florian that; it just goes to show you
how much respect they have for him. But with Father Cournane it's just the opposite; that whole family of his walks all
over him.

So when he walked out of my kitchen and left me
there with my salad and that dinner to get, I says to myself,
if it isn't good enough for them, they know what they can
do. Because I'm not going to kill myself trying to put a
fancy dinner on the table with everything else I've got to do
here today, and if that Mrs. McGrath wants to turn up her
nose at it, let her do it. Coming back to my kitchen and
poking her nose into everything—just let her try *that* on me
again. I don't care who she thinks she is, with her fur coats
and her marcel waves; she's not telling me how to run my
own kitchen.

They were all supposed to be coming about half past
six, so when the bell rang at quarter after I thought, well,
for once in a way somebody in that family's going to be on

time. But it was only Walter Kittredge, said he wanted to see Father Cournane a minute.

"You picked a fine time for it," I says. "Don't you folks eat dinner at your house?"

"Thressa," he says, "if you look this glad to see me every time I come here, I'm going to suspect you of harboring a secret passion for me. Now you run along and tell the reverend Father I'm here."

That's the sort of thing he picks up, hanging over the counter in that jewelry store of his, talking to every old salesman or policeman that walks down the street. They all know him; it's "Hi there, Walter," and "How's the boy, Ed?" with every one of them, but that doesn't stop him from making a good profit out of them the next time they want a diamond engagement ring or a brooch or necklace for their girl friends. Laura Dennehy says he charged that Heinrichs boy a hundred and fifty dollars for a little bit of a diamond, wasn't much more than a chip, says she was downright sorry for the girl when she brought it to the Young Ladies' meeting to show it around. Grinning at you with those big false teeth of his all on show, and then adding another couple of dollars to the bill. What a man like Father Cournane, thinks he's so well-educated and all, sees in him I'll never know. Oh, he wouldn't have Francis Jaeger or Leonard Dennehy running in and out of here like they owned the place, but it's all right for Walter Kittredge. Well, the Holy Name found out they could do without him these last two years, gave their picnic without him being there running the whole show, and I'll miss my guess if the Married Ladies' Sodality doesn't see the light tomorrow and give Mrs. Walter Kittredge her walking papers too.

So I called upstairs to Father Cournane, said, "Walter Kittredge is here; do you want to see him?" With everything else I had to do, I wasn't going to go waltzing up

those stairs for something like that. And Father Cournane
says he'll be right down, and Walter stands there grinning
at me.

"Thressa," he says, "I have an idea you're going to be
voting on the wrong side tomorrow morning. Correct me
if I'm wrong."

"I think it's the right side," I says. "I've known Mrs.
Milligan ever since she came into this parish, and if you
ask me it's about time she got a little reward for all the
work she's done for it."

"Well," he says, "you may be right."

"Thanks for nothing," I says. "I know I am."

"Some people like having all their problems settled for
them," he says. "You ought to be nice and peaceful over
there at the Married Ladies' Sodality for a change when you
get Mame Milligan in the driver's seat. I don't suppose
she'll be calling for much help in running the show."

"Well, she won't be sitting up there shilly-shallying, if
that's what you mean," I says.

Like some other people I could name, I says to myself.
It would have served him right if I'd let him have one for
that wife of his, old biddy sitting up there smiling at everybody with her hair under that net, hasn't changed the style
of it in thirty years. Acts like a kindergarten teacher the
first day of school—"Now, ladies, shall we take a vote?"
And getting deafer every year, having her long confidential
conversations with the nuns and half the parish hearing
every word that's said. But Father Cournane came downstairs just then, so I had to go off without saying any more.

I left the kitchen door open an inch or two when I
went back, though, just in case I could catch a hint about
what was going on. And as luck would have it they stood
there in the hall, instead of going on into the study, so I
managed to get pretty nearly the whole thing. At first,

though, it was only something about the celebration; the fuss Walter Kittredge was making over it, you'd have thought it was the Pope instead of Father Cournane that was having his twenty-fifth anniversary. Like now: making arrangements to have photographers there tomorrow to take his picture on the church lawn with his family, and then with the first-graders, and then with I don't know who all else, the people who were here when St. Cyprian's parish was started, and all the past presidents of the Holy Name, and the prefects of the Married Ladies' Sodality. Who's going to pay for all that, I'd like to know? As if it wasn't bad enough, taking up a collection to buy new vestments for him, and then all that money for refreshments—ice cream and cake and coffee for everybody that's got nerve enough to step up and ask for it. The way I say is, if Walter Kittredge wants a lot of fancy goings-on like those pictures and imitation-silver paperweight souvenirs for everybody in the parish, let him pay for them himself. He makes plenty out of that store of his.

So, anyway, they stood there in the hall talking about it, and Walter Kittredge saying how the school children were going to present Father Cournane with a spiritual bouquet, a scroll made out with a list of all the prayers they were saying for him, and how he was going to have to be prepared when they gave it to him because Sister Antonius had picked the littlest boy in the first grade to make the presentation speech and no matter how much she drilled him at it he still got it mixed up sometimes and said, "Dear Father, reverend parents, ladies and gentlemen," instead of the other way around. I wasn't paying too much attention by that time, because as far as I was concerned he could say the whole thing backwards and it would be all the same to me, but then I heard Walter Kittredge begin talking in a lower voice and I pricked up my ears again. It was something about "the Boss"—well, I knew who that was, the Cardinal. Not that Father Kaspar would ever call him that, but the rest of those priests, when they get together, it's never anything else but "the Boss," and Walter Kittredge has been around them so much he's even picked up some of their expressions.

Anyway, it was something he said about the Boss maybe coming tomorrow that made me start to listen again.

"I suppose he won't be too happy about that last financial report of yours," I heard Walter say, and Father Cournane says no, he doesn't suppose he will be. Then nobody said anything for a while, and then Walter says, "Would you like me to have a talk with him? I know the situation here in the parish, and as a businessman—"

"Well, the Boss is a pretty good businessman himself, Walter," Father Cournane says. "I suppose he knows the situation here as well as either of us does. The thing is, he expects me to manage a little better—"

"You can't manage money you haven't got," Walter says.

Just like him, trying to make excuses for him. And Father Cournane says something about maybe that was true but still another man might be able to do better, and then something about the Boss thinking of dividing the parish, starting another church out near that new subdivision. Well, that was the first I'd heard about *that*. Wait till I tell that to the girls tomorrow, I says to myself—if that Mrs. Walter Kittredge doesn't get there before me. That ought to take His Nibs down a peg or two, and believe me, if the Cardinal puts a man like Father Kaspar out there it'll be a sad day for Father Cournane, because he'll show him how this parish really should be run. Now you have to say that for the Cardinal: you think when you live in a parish like this he's sitting up there and doesn't know a thing that's going on, but he's got his eyes open all the while.

I was itching to hear more about it, but as luck would have it the doorbell rang just then, some of those Cournanes, so they had to break it off and Walter left. Father Cournane opened the door for them, so I didn't go out, but I looked around the corner of the door and it was Mrs. John Cournane and Mrs. Clohessey and Amy Cournane, Amy Gilman now, with her two kids. I'd hardly have known that Amy Cournane, skinny as ever but she'd calmed down a lot from the way she used to be, let her hair grow too from that short bob, looked like she'd been around, I must say, and knew how to take care of herself. They say that husband of hers isn't much account. And just as blond as ever, but they can fix that too out in Hollywood. And in Atlanta, Georgia, as far as that goes, if you take one look at that Mrs. Clohessey. Now that woman must be every bit as old as I am, but she's got hair on her head as red as fire. And short skirts, high heels—who does she think she's fooling, I'd like to know? Still she's the best of the lot, got nice pleasant ways and that soft little voice, if she wasn't always talking so much. They say she collects bills down in Atlanta; well, what I say is, they probably get so tired of hearing her talk they'll do anything, even pay their bills, to get rid of her.

I could hear her now out there, making a great fuss over Father Cournane; you'd think she was the one that hadn't seen him for ten or eleven years. Amy Cournane just said, "Hello, Father Michael," and kissed him, and then says, "These are my kids; what do you think of them?" As cool as that, like she'd just walked over from across the street.

Well, if she'd asked me about the kids, I'd have said the boy's all right, but what are you feeding the girl on? Air? Because she was a skinny little thing like her mother,

with the big eyes in her face like she didn't miss a thing that
was going on. Sharp as a tack, too; she saw me peeking
around the corner of the door and pointed right at me and
says, "Who's that?" So then of course I had to pretend I
was just coming out, and Father Cournane says, "Oh—
this is Mrs. Dawes, Shivaun."

So Mrs. John Cournane says, "How are you, Mrs.
Dawes?"—like she was talking to the hired help, and Mrs.
Clohessey says, "I smell roast chicken. Now, *honestly*, you
oughtn't to have gone to all that trouble."

"Well," I says, "don't get your hopes up, because it's
catch-as-catch-can around here tonight, with all I've got to
do for tomorrow."

As if it would do any good to tell them that. I can just
see any of them offering to turn a hand around here. That
Amy Cournane did start to say, "Can I do anything?" but
her mother grabbed onto her arm and steered her off into
the living room before she could get any farther. Afraid I'd
take her up on it; well, she needn't have bothered. All I
ask is for the whole crew of them to stay out of my kitchen,
and that goes double for Mrs. Thomas Cornelius McGrath.

So I went back to my kitchen, but you couldn't keep
them all out; in about ten minutes there was a knock at
the door, and when I said, "Who is it?" those two Gilman
kids walked in.

"Could my sister have a drink of water?" the boy says.

"I guess so," I says. I handed her down a glass. "You
can reach the faucet, can't you?" I says to her.

"Oh yes," she says. "Thank you very much."

Well, they were brought up to have good manners,
I'll say that. The little girl drank her glass of water and
stood there looking around the kitchen.

"You're a long ways from home, aren't you?" I says
to her.

"Yes, ma'am," she says. "We live in California."

"And how do you like Amorica?" I says.

She looked at the boy.

"We like it all right," he says. "We've got a lot of relatives here. They're all old, though."

I says to myself, you better not let Mrs. John Cournane hear you say that, *or* Mrs. McGrath. Out loud I says, "Well, you've got some little cousins will be here tonight, the little McGrath girls. They're a bit older than you are, though."

"Practically everybody we meet here is a relative," the boy says. "I never knew a person could have so many."

He was going around the kitchen looking at things; he was a good deal bolder than the girl. Reminded me a little of John Cournane—well, that's not surprising. I says to him, on the spur of the moment, "Did you meet your grandfather yet?"

"My grandfather?"

He and the girl looked at each other.

"Your mother's father," I says.

"Oh," he says. "No. But Mother's going to see him tomorrow. That is, if Cousin Mal can find him."

"Cousin Mal?" I says.

Then I remembered—that Mal Cesti, the newspaper fellow, he's related to the Cournanes somehow or other, came around here a couple of times last year when John Cournane was in that trouble about that woman claimed he owed her two hundred and fifty dollars. Big fellow, husky, black hair, looks like he could do with somebody to press his suits and darn his socks. Well, I says to myself, what's he doing in the picture? Unless it's a case of birds of a feather, and Amy Cournane knew the best way to find her father would be to find him first.

"Oh yes, I know who you mean," I says. "And so you've met him too?"

"He drove us to Granny Cournane's house from the railroad station," the boy says. "He's got a green Chrysler. It's an old one, though."

"And what kind of a car have you got at home?" I says.

"Well—a Chevrolet," he says. "But we had a Packard once, when we were in Texas."

"I guess your daddy was rich then?" I says.

"He owned a hotel," he says.

"Yes," I says, "I heard about that hotel."

Because there's very little I miss, if I do say it myself, and if that Mrs. John Cournane doesn't want the whole world to know all her business she oughtn't to talk about it at the top of her voice. Coming around here telling Father Cournane he never should have fixed up that marriage of Amy Cournane's, she'd have been better off no matter how far it had gone, because Irving Gilman was no better than a bankrupt, she could read between the lines of Amy's letters though of course Amy would never complain. I got an earful that day, all right.

So I says to the kids, "Why didn't your daddy come along with you to Amorica?" There's no sense in not finding out what you can when you've got the chance. "Was he too busy?" I says.

"I guess so," the boy says.

"I guess your mother misses him?" I says.

You never can tell—coming all this way out here without him and taking the kids, it might be another divorce in the Cournane family. Anyway, it looks peculiar to me, and I noticed the kids began to get a little cagier too.

"Yes," the boy says, "I guess she does."

"What kind of business is he in now?" I says to him.

I saw the girl nudge him. Neither of them said anything for a minute, and then the girl up and says, "Mother says when people ask us too many questions we mustn't answer."

Just like that—teaching those little innocent children a thing like that! Well, I says to myself, Mrs. Amy Cournane Gilman, you may think you're awfully smart to be so sly, but where there's nothing to hide there's nothing to fear, and don't think other people can't put two and two together and come out with the answer to that. Like father like daughter, I shouldn't wonder, and teaching her own children to lie and deceive so other people won't find out what she's up to. Well, I found out all about it and then some before that evening was over.

The doorbell rang just then in the hall, and I went out to answer it. It was that Mrs. McGrath, of course, with her son and daughter-in-law and the two little girls. They're about nine and twelve; the older one, Janet, a fat husky blonde, looks like her father, so crazy about herself she'll stand in front of a mirror for fifteen minutes at a stretch, admiring herself while she does all that stuff they teach them nowadays at dancing school, wiggling her elbows and tapping with her feet. The little one, Polly, is the wild one; deliver me from having a child like *that* to bring up.

"Oh—Mrs. Dawes," Mrs. McGrath says. I could see her eyes going around that hall like a pair of eagles looking for something to criticize. I can't bear that voice of hers, anyway—stands up there and talks to you like she was the Queen of England with that ugly mouth painted up and big blue eyes, like all the rest of them trying to be young. "I'm afraid we're a little late," she says.

Well, that was no lie; it was quarter to seven by that time, and there were Father Kaspar and Father McBride upstairs, had to get back to the church to hear confessions again by seven-thirty.

"I'll have the dinner on the table in five minutes," I

says, and went over to the stairs to call Father Kaspar. If they want to come in at that hour for a six-thirty dinner, they can't expect to have people waiting around while they take their time taking their hats off and saying hello to each other.

So they went right on into the living room, were all still standing around in there when I called them in the dining room to sit down. The two little Gilmans were off with the McGrath girls, looking one another over the way kids do, and Father Cournane and the other two priests were talking to Dr. McGrath, while the ladies all jabbered together by the door. Amy Cournane and that Mrs. Mc-Grath Junior were the only quiet ones—they tell me Mrs. McGrath Junior can't stand her in-laws, and I must say she looked sulky enough just then; if you want my opinion, she'd probably read the riot act to her husband about having to come here before they ever started out. He may be a big doctor in this town, office down in the Holmes Building and out playing poker on Sunday with that Sylvester Lowheimer and the Marquettes, people like that, but I'll bet I know who rules the roost at home. You can always tell, the way a man looks at a woman, whether he orders her or she orders him. But she's a good-looking girl, I'll say that for her—a little thing, black hair, dresses like something straight out of those Paris fashion magazines. So maybe he figures he's getting his money's worth, ordering or no ordering.

Well, I called them all to dinner and they went in. You know how it is when a family gets together, everybody talking and nobody saying anything except how much the children have grown and Polly looks like her mother and it's too bad Irving didn't come with you when it's been so long. I thought to myself, well, they could have saved that till tomorrow and not put me to all this trouble of getting a big dinner on the table tonight when I've got enough to do around here anyway to keep any two women busy. I couldn't even keep track of the conversation, what with running in and out of the kitchen, but I guess that's just as well. That Mrs. McGrath was running the whole show as usual, and if there's one thing I can't stand it's a woman who'll sit there and lay down the law when there're priests present, just like she knew more about parishes and religion than they do.

I'm not saying anything about Father Cournane, because he brings it on himself being so quiet, but I can hardly keep still when I hear her talking that way to Father Kaspar: "Oh, do you think so, Father? Now in *my* experience —" He didn't like it, I could see that, but he's too much of a gentleman to say what needs saying to her because after all she is the pastor's sister. And besides he had that Mrs. Clohessey sitting alongside of him, and when she starts talking to you, good night. It takes a brass band to shut her up. She was telling him about when she and Mrs. McGrath and Father Cournane and Mr. John Cournane were all kids together over on West Haley Street—as if that would interest anybody but herself. But like I say, some women like to hear themselves talk even if they haven't got anything to say.

So the ate the dinner—roast chicken, sage dressing, mashed potatoes, canned peas, tomato and lettuce and cucumber salad, and if you want to look picky over that, Mrs. Thomas McGrath, I says to myself, you just go right ahead, because I've got better things to do than to be beating every last lump out of those potatoes or shelling fresh peas at the price they are these days anyway. When I brought on the dessert she took one look at it and says, "None for me, thank you," because it was only brick ice cream from the drugstore, I suppose, not fancy enough

for her. And Mrs. John Cournane says none for her either,
she's on a diet, and didn't eat her potatoes either, I noticed,
so I just stood there with the dishes in my hand and said,
"How about the rest of you?" Because I wasn't going to be
trotting back and forth from that kitchen bringing ice
cream nobody was going to eat, but that Amy Cournane
says, "Oh yes, please, the children love it," and then Mrs.
Clohessey says she adores ice cream too.

Well, they could take it or leave it as far as I was concerned; I can give what's left to that crowd tomorrow, because thank the Lord they won't all be Cournanes and too
particular to eat good food when it's put in front of them.
Even that biggest McGrath girl, Janet, turning up her nose
at it like her mother, thought I didn't hear her but I heard
all right: "Mother, I don't have to eat this, do I?" And her
mother says, "Oh, all *right*, Jan," without even looking at
her, and Dr. McGrath starts to fuss over her then, thinks I
can't hear that either because he talks so low, says to me
finally, "I wonder if Janet could have a glass of milk. You
know how children are; it's been a little warm today, and
Jan's appetite is usually poor in summer." Well, if that's
how she looks with a poor appetite I'd hate to see her with
a good one, because she's got a behind on her now like a
forty-dollar cow. Takes after her father; he doesn't look
like any of those Cournanes, so I suppose it must be the
McGraths they both favor.

Anyway, Father Kaspar and Father McBride had to get
back to church to hear confessions, so they didn't stay sitting at the table very long, which was one good thing, because if there's anything I hate it's people sitting around a
table when the meal's over and I'm waiting to get my dishes
cleared off in the kitchen. The rest of them went on back
to the living room and sat down, all but the kids; the Mc-
Grath girls got the notion they wanted to play outside, and

they took the two little Gilmans along with them. I could hear them screaming and giggling out there while I did up my dishes—a fine sight for a priest's back yard. And after a while the little McGrath girl, Polly, got into a fight with the Gilman boy; well, I can take just so much, so I called out the window to them, "Here now, you kids, if you can't play quiet, I'm going out and tell your mothers how you're behaving."

"We aren't doing anything," that Janet McGrath says, as bold as you please—might just as well have said it to me straight out, "Who do you think *you* are, butting in on us?" For two pins I would have marched straight out to the living room, said to that Mrs. McGrath, both of them, "You think you're so high-toned, well, come and see how those *high-toned* kids of yours are acting." Not that it would have done any good; that Mrs. McGrath Junior couldn't be bothered if they climbed all over the house like monkeys, and Dr. McGrath would be sure to make out somehow that it was me who was doing wrong, not them.

All that while the grownups were jabbering away, thirteen to the dozen, out in the living room, and when I finished my dishes I opened the door a ways and sat down with the paper to see if I could catch anything while I read it. The first I heard was something about the celebration, Mrs. Clohessey still talking about when they were kids, says, "Oh, Michael, I never can get over it when I see you sitting there in that Roman collar, do you remember when we lived on West Haley Street, *you* were always the one organizing the whole neighborhood into battalions of soldiers, and always the general, of course, so earnest about it, you'd be furious when Jack would get bored, hide off somewhere with a book or just swinging himself in that big old swing—remember?—so everybody always said *you* were going to be a soldier or a politician or something like that,

and Jack was going to be an actor, and of course I wanted to
be an actress too, we used to do *Ingomar* by the hour, I
could remember it now if I had to, 'Two souls with but a
single thought, Two hearts that beat as one,' and see how
it's all turned out, you celebrating your twenty-fifth anniversary in the priesthood, me collecting bills down in Atlanta,
and poor old Jack, I don't think he ever really wanted to be
a politician and he was right, after all: look what it did to
him—"

And Mrs. John Cournane says, "What happened to
poor old Jack had nothing to do with politics, Dolly, but
if you're feeling sentimental, don't let me be the one to
stop you."

A bit on the sharp side; she wasn't enjoying herself any
too much, I imagine, with Mrs. McGrath and Mrs. Mc-
Grath Junior both lording it over her with their fancy
clothes, and besides I don't think she liked that talk about
"poor old Jack"; when she talks about him herself, you'd
think he had horns and a tail. And Mrs. Clohessey says—
I could just see her, that way she has of shrugging up her
shoulders like a Frenchman or a Jew, she's a little bit of a
thing, but that doesn't stop her from giving as good as she
gets—says, "Well then, I *am* sentimental; I've never been
ashamed to admit it—after all, why should I be? We're
human beings, aren't we? Not adding machines. And it
just *does* occur to me sometimes, Rosemary—just a *tiny*
little thought comes creeping into my mind, you know—
that if you'd been a *little* more sentimental yourself at a
certain period which shall be nameless—"

Mrs. John Cournane blew up like a firecracker; I never
heard her sound so mad. Said she knew very well all the
Cournanes blamed her for what had happened to Mr. John
Cournane, but if they'd been in her place they'd have seen
it was no bed of roses being married to him, and what was

she supposed to do when he told her straight to her face he was in love with another woman. And Amy Cournane says, "Oh, Mother, please, that's all over and done with years ago," and Mrs. John Cournane says you're darn right it's over and done with and she was sick of living with the legend of *poor old Jack* hung around her neck, she'd like to see any of them living with him drunk or sober, and Father Cournane says, "All right now, Rosemary. That's enough."

But of course he said it so quiet that none of them paid any attention to him. That Mrs. McGrath had to get her two cents' worth in then, said something about Jack has a brilliant mind, of course he's difficult to live with but after all that's what Christian marriage means, self-sacrifice, especially on the woman's part—I'd like to know where she found *that* out. And Mrs. John Cournane says, "Yes, you've always been so damned good at that, haven't you, Una? You ought to have asked Tom for a letter of recommendation when he died."

By that time they were all talking at once, Amy Cournane trying to calm down her mother and Dr. McGrath trying to calm down his, and that Mrs. Clohessey never stopped talking at all; she was still going at it when Father Cournane says, "Rosemary—Una—this is too bad," and they all stopped except you could hear Mrs. Clohessey running down like a clock that needs winding: ". . . always said to Gus, I remember just as well because it was exactly three days—" And then she stopped too, and for about a whole minute nobody said a word.

Then that Mrs. McGrath Junior pipes up, like it was an afternoon tea party, and says, "I wonder where the children are; Tommy dear, don't you think it's time we took them home?" Trying to act like nothing was wrong; well, she could have saved her breath, because I'd had an earful by that time. High-toned is as high-toned does, and if that's the kind of people that's going in the society pages these days they might as well put anybody in.

So Dr. McGrath got up to go look for the children, went out the front door and a minute or two later I heard him out in back with them, wanted them to come in so they could say good-by and go home. But that little Polly McGrath says, "I want to stay and play with Stephen." Fighting with him one minute, and the next minute arms-around-the-neck friends; you can't beat those kids. And that Janet McGrath says, "Come on, Poll, I want to go home," and pulled her by the braid, and the little one after her like a wildcat. Dr. McGrath had to pull her away himself. I know what I'd do with kids like that, but no, that's the way they raise them nowadays, let them tear down the house if they feel like it.

They'd all calmed down in the living room by the time he got back with the kids, but there wasn't much conversation going except what Mrs. McGrath Junior and Amy Cournane were keeping up between them. And as soon as Dr. McGrath came in that broke up too, and Mrs. McGrath Junior said if Mrs. McGrath Senior didn't mind they ought to go now because it was time the children were in bed. Mrs. McGrath said oh no, that was fine with her, and they all went out to the hall and Father Cournane with them. I heard that Mrs. McGrath talking to him low out there, something about the sage dressing; she can't keep her nose out of anything, that woman, and knows how to do everything better than the next fellow, to hear her tell it. Well, I says to myself, you just come on back here with your sage dressing, Mrs. Thomas Cornelius McGrath, and I'll give you a piece of my mind you won't forget in a hurry, I don't care if you are the pastor's sister and your picture's on every society page in town.

But I guess Father Cournane must have quieted her

down, because she went away with the others after a minute. And then Mrs. John Cournane started, she wanted to go too, wasn't going to sit there in that room with Mrs. Clohessey if she could help it, I suppose, after what Mrs. Clohessey'd said about her. She had her own automobile there but she didn't offer very hard to take the others home, out to West Haley Street, that is; they're all staying with the old lady there. Anyway, Mrs. Clohessey says oh my no, they could take a taxi, and didn't have to say it twice, and then she went off herself with the two Gilman kids, because Amy Cournane said she wanted to stay awhile and talk to Father Cournane.

It was good and quiet in the house after they'd all gone. You know how it is on a summer night after it gets dark, feels like something's going to happen, everything peaceful outside except for the automobiles going by and you hardly hear them either at the back of the house. That Amy Cournane was in there talking to Father Cournane about her father; I couldn't catch all of it, but she sounded upset. Said she was going to see him the next day, and Father Cournane says, "Does he know you're in town?"

"No," she says. "Mal promised to find him for me." Says after a minute, "You don't see him any more either, do you, Father Michael?"

"He calls me up once in a while," he says.

"For money?" she says.

He didn't say anything, and after a while she says, a little faster, like she was going to cry, "Father Michael—"

"Yes," he says.

"Father Michael," she says, "what's wrong with us?"

"With us?" he says.

"Yes," she says. "With all of us. With Father and Aunt Una and Aunt Dolly and Mother and Tommyo and —all of us, especially with me."

Well, I could have given her some answers to that,
but Father Cournane only says, "There's nothing at all
wrong with you that I can see, Amy. You look to me like a
young woman who manages her life very successfully."

"Do I?" she says. "That's nice. Because I'm more
mixed up than any of them. At least Father knows what
he wants."

"And you don't?" he says.

"No," she says. "Yes." Then she says, "Oh, I'm crazy;
I can't talk about it to you—to anyone—"

I couldn't hear what happened next. Father Cournane
was trying to talk to her but she said, "Don't, don't," I
don't know if she was crying or not, and then he says something to her about that Mal fellow, Mal Cesti, and that's
when I started to see the light. Well, I might have known,
those kids of hers being so cagey and all; like I say, if you've
got nothing to hide there's no reason to make a secret of it.
And I must say it looked fishy to me from the beginning,
her coming all this way out here from California without
her husband. You can say what you like, but when a man
marries a girl twenty years younger than he is himself he'd
better be prepared for trouble and a lot of it too, because
that's just exactly what he's going to get.

So I was listening then for all I was worth, only to hear
what she was saying to him, whether she wanted to leave
her husband for this Mal fellow or what was it all about.
But there was an old truck going by outside, there ought to
be a law against them on the streets, rattling and banging
along till you can't hear yourself think, and when it was past
there was only Father Cournane blathering away, something about all of us being lonely in America, says, "We're
the loneliest people on earth, Amy, and so we drive ourselves to all sorts of expedients to hide it from ourselves,
social ambitions, sex, the getting of money, even ruin and

despair, because there is always companionship to be had in ruin and despair." And she says, "Well, I haven't tried that yet, so I suppose I still have something to look forward to," and he says, "You haven't really tried any of them," and she says, "You don't know," and he says, "No, I don't know, but whatever it is, you will find out that you will still be lonely."

Now I ask you—with her practically telling him straight out that she was mixed up with another man. He ought to have given her holy Ned, but no, talking to her about being lonely of all things. Well, it's no wonder he's lonely, if that's what he means, shutting himself up in that room of his when he ought to be going around mixing with people and taking an interest in what's going on. And as for that Amy Cournane, any woman who's got a husband and two children to look after hasn't got time to be lonely if she looks after them right, hasn't got time to be thinking about other men. Why, I says to myself, I wonder where she's been meeting him, maybe out in California, for all I know, because he hasn't been in town here very long, and mixed up with Mr. John Cournane, you know what that means, coming around here, I forget the whole story, but there was two hundred and fifty dollars in it and he was trying to get Mr. John Cournane out of some trouble. I'm going to take a better look at him the next time he comes; you couldn't exactly call him good-looking but he's tall, got that black hair, a kind of cool way of looking at you, doesn't talk much. Well, all I can say is, you can never tell about women, because if I was that Amy Cournane, had the fellows raving about me the way they say she had, I think I could have done a little better than that for myself.

So she was trying to make a joke of it now, said something about her misspent life, and Father Cournane says, "It's a sad thing about life, Amy; all lives have been misspent in some degree except Christ's." And she says, "Not yours," and he says, "Mine more than any."

"Oh," she says, "how can you say that, Father Michael?" And he says, "We've specialized in failure in this family, not just worldly failure because Una is well-to-do by all the world's standards, but she is and probably always will be a dissatisfied woman, looking for someone to dominate because she is insecure of everything else, and Dolly scatters herself as wildly as any Roman candle, and there is Jack, who had to be what he was not, and I, who have to be what I am not. And celebrate it too, after twenty-five years. So you see you are not the only one." And she says, "Oh, not you too, Father Michael," and he says, "Yes. If the courage and brilliant talent and honesty that were born into this family could somehow have been channeled in the right direction we could have been proud—no, not proud, humble—before our own achievements. Instead—"

He stopped talking then, heard Father Kaspar and Father McBride coming in from the church, and I says to myself, yes, well that's one time you hit the nail on the head, because if you ask me there's neither you *or* this parish has anything to celebrate tomorrow. Like I say, I wouldn't object if he'd gone in a monastery or to the Chinese missions, but to saddle a parish with him is another thing. You take the debt on this church alone; there isn't a pastor in the diocese that couldn't do better than he's doing at getting it paid off. Why, Father Kaspar says to him one day, says, they've hired some professional fund-raising people out there at St. Rose's, went around and told everybody in the parish just how much they had to pledge, made a big publicity campaign out of it so of course nobody wanted to say no. Expected His Nibs to take the hint, I suppose, but no, all he says is something about giving freely to God. And Father Kaspar says, "Well, Father Falmeyer's had a great success with it," and His Nibs says, "Father Falmeyer has to do what he thinks best for his parish and I have to do what I think best for mine." Which includes running it right into the ground, I suppose, because that's just exactly what he's heading for.

But like I say, you never can tell him anything. That business of having thirteen at the table, for instance—he might have known it wouldn't turn out right. Well, my conscience is clear; I put a good dinner in front of them, and if only I'd known beforehand about those potatoes there wouldn't have been any of them left over either. But I can always fry them up again tomorrow, because with everything that'll be going on around here then it's not likely I'll have time for any fancy cooking. Fried mashed potatoes and eggs, that's what they'll get, and if anybody wants to complain about it they can complain to somebody else but me.

June 12, 1938

MORNING

Miss Laura Dennehy, wearing her new green crepe with the artificial rose on the shoulder, and the beige straw hat out of Trexler's window that she'd bought for Easter and had hardly had on because rain might ruin the cherries, came through the arched Gothic doors of St. Cyprian's Church and looked up at a fresh blue noonday sky. Cleared off beautifully; glad I wore it after all. Sitting just two pews behind me, by good luck. He's never seen me in it; did he notice? The salesgirl at Trexler's said it gave me a very youthful appearance.

She stepped through the doorway, smiling absently at the people streaming out behind her. A lovely crowd there; Father Cournane ought to be pleased. I like a Solemn High Mass when it's not too hot, the organ playing, and all those candles. Now who were those priests assisting Father Cournane? Must ask Thressa Dawes; she would know. The one such a big handsome man, going iron-gray. If Mr. Schneider was to use a little of that Pinaud's on his hair, growing so thin and I don't think after all he's a day over sixty.

She smiled agreeably at Miss Lizzie Clemens, who came hurrying through the church doors, straight as a ramrod in that old-fashioned black gabardine coat-suit she wore winter and summer, carrying a gold-handled umbrella against nonexistent rain. Miss Lizzie Clemens stopped, greeting her.

"How's your mother and father, Laura?"

"Just fine, Miss Lizzie." Miss Laura Dennehy looked, laughing, at the gold-handled umbrella. "And I suppose you're the one who's keeping the rain away from us today," she said.

Miss Lizzie Clemens acknowledged that she supposed she was.

"I'd carry more than an umbrella to make sure Father Cournane had a good day for the celebration," she said. "As a matter of fact"—she came closer, whispering in Miss Laura Dennehy's ear—"I made a novena for him. Nine first Fridays. It never fails."

She went on, moving stoutly through the crowd. Never guess she was in her eighties. Still, those clothes. And it isn't as if she had to; her father left property over on the West Side, and her sister's husband had that Ford agency; they have plenty to go on. One of these days she'll simply have to step down and then I . . . prefect of the Young Ladies' Sodality . . . if Mr. Schneider doesn't. Now where did he go? I was sure I saw him coming behind.

Smiling, she greeted Mrs. Edward Milligan, who was in a great hurry, on her way to the school for the Married Ladies' Sodality meeting. She had time, however, to grip Miss Dennehy's hand tightly for a moment in her own.

"Well, Laura, aren't you going to wish me luck?" she asked.

"Oh, you don't need it," Miss Dennehy said. "I'm just as sure of that."

Mrs. Milligan shook her head, foreboding. She wore a paisley print Bemberg with a black straw hat; now isn't that new? Husband makes good money when he's working, paper hanging, painting, that old Ford truck with the ladder on it. She drives it too when he's not using it. But he doesn't appreciate. Treasurer of the union, spends all his time in that little office of his upstairs or out drinking with those men. Cookie Milligan they call him; I wonder why. Off on a three-day toot one time and sent her a telegram: *Look for Cookie.* Luckily Mr. Schneider doesn't. Except for a glass of beer now and then.

She followed with her eyes Mrs. Milligan's rapid progress down the steps to the walk, till she was distracted by the sight of three young girls in light summer dresses, white hats, and high-heeled white pumps, clustered together a little to one side below, rotating slowly on heels, conversing with one eye on the moving progress of the crowd. Looking for some boys to pick them up, walk them home. Louise and I never. Always with Papa and Mama to the seven-thirty. Of course Papa was right and Joe never did amount to anything, hanging around playing the piano every night till all hours and Papa'd say, I've got to get up in the morning, I've got a bakery to run here, Laura, now you tell him to get out and go home or I will. Postcard he sent me from Hollywood, California: "Dear Laura This is sure some place wish you were here I could show you a fine time in this burg remember me to your folks Yours sincerely Joe." Out

West somewhere now; Papa says a rolling stone gathers no moss.

She greeted coolly Mrs. Walter Kittredge, who, accompanied by Mr. Walter Kittredge in a new checked suit, also emerged from the church on her way to the Married Ladies' Sodality meeting at the school. Mr. Walter Kittredge, unabashed, paused beside her to extract a cigar from the leather case he carried in his breast pocket.

"Well, Laura," he said to her briskly, "how's tricks?"

"Oh, just fine, Mr. Kittredge," she said without enthusiasm.

"You tell your daddy," he admonished her solemnly, "that he sold me a set of stale Parkerhouse rolls last Tuesday. Darned near ruined my upper plate. Tell him I'm going to send my dentist's bill to him."

"Oh, Mr. Kittredge," she said.

If he thinks I'm going to laugh at that. Save his jokes for those old salesmen who come in his store. The one selling flour; I was only sixteen and Papa said, Laura, if I ever catch you again. Wanted to make a date with me. None of those old salesmen are any good but that lovely mustache. I wonder how it would be to kiss.

On an upper floor of a second-rate hotel on Madison Street a radio voice confidently announced that once you had tried Leader's Cough Remedy you would never use any other kind.

Miss Laura Dennehy moved on slowly down the steps of St. Cyprian's Church, wondering what had become of Mr. Schneider. Talking to that Mrs. Madigan with her rouge and that hair not natural of course anybody can see. Drove one man to the grave and now looking for another. Never trust a widow, Mama always says. But I suppose when they're as old as Thressa Dawes. Priest's housekeeper; must be queer living in the house with them. Father Cour-

nane looking so uncomfortable when you go to the parish
house for a spiritual bouquet, and Father Kaspar like St.
Michael the Archangel. Sometimes looking out the window
on a dark Monday when there's nobody in the shop, so
lonesome, see him go by, strong, healthy, clean. Poor Mr.
Schneider suffers from asthma.

She greeted disapprovingly a pair of small boys who
rushed down the steps behind her, found her blocking their
way, and surged out on either side of her. Now. There's
manners for you. That Polish gardener's boys. No respect
even for the nuns. If I. Black veil and that starched white
bib, what do they call it? Sister Angela, I always thought
if I did. Then it wouldn't matter if Mr. Schneider. Thressa
saying, Oh, Laura, you don't know when you're well off,
every night and every night with that old business of theirs,
and then worrying every month till you come around again.
She had two children: both dead. One drowned in the lake,
one with lockjaw. Then the miscarriages, she said, even
worse.

At the foot of the steps she stood watching Mrs.
Thomas Cornelius McGrath and Mrs. Augustus Clohessey,
Father Cournane's sisters, dressed respectively in beige
crepe de Chine and green georgette, get into a taxicab before the church. That Mrs. McGrath a little too heavy but
dresses in the most exquisite taste, a hat just like that,
thirty-five dollars down at Lane's. Her nose in the air, all
that family alike, Mrs. John Cournane at the Christmas
entertainment when they lived on Johnson Avenue and I
played the piano for Mr. Pflaum. But the Mayor. Yes. Such
a handsome man, and so polite. "Miss Dennehy, you're a
real Paderewski." Won't be here this afternoon, but I'd
love to see him again. Poor man. They say he . . . I don't
believe half.

Blinking off into the sun, she saw Mr. Schneider, his

balding head glancing bright in the June sunlight, raise his hat in greeting to Miss Lizzie Clemens as he walked slowly down the street beside Mr. Francis Jaeger, the president of the Holy Name Society. Missed him; now isn't that provoking? But how could I possibly? The side door, probably. Now isn't that the most unlucky?

She stood, a little flustered, trying to appear unconcerned. And me with my new hat and all. But maybe this afternoon.

From around the corner, the bells of Our Lady of Divine Grace Church rang a pair of melancholy notes into the stale Sunday-morning quiet of the room. Mal Cesti lay on the bed with his arms under his head, looking up at swaying shadows on the stained plaster of the ceiling. The shadows above him, which were the optical effect of sun and breeze on the leaves of a tree of heaven growing in the alley outside his second-floor window, and filtered through not recently cleaned glass and net curtains limp with city soot, made a bright pattern on the ceiling. He lay looking at it without moving. Through the open window a radio voice preached gratingly till someone turned a dial and with a startled squawk another voice said hastily, " '. . . cing in the Dark,' with Jackie Prince and the Four Dukes," and insistent music flooded the room.

Except for shoes and coat, he was fully dressed. The bed had a red-and-green plaid cover thrown over it, a surprising island of color in the middle of a silent sea of ancient hotel-walnut, threadbare Axminster, and faded paper. On the walls two framed eighteenth-century figures, demure male-and-female silhouettes behind spotted glass, faced some kind of framed testimonial from a former Balkan king, with the name *Malachi Cesti* in large black letters in the center and a blob of red sealing wax at the bottom.

Along one side of this, three small oblong white business cards were stuck into the frame.

From the next room the announcer's confident voice predicted that once you had tried Leader's Cough Remedy you would never use any other kind. Outside the window sparrows chirped monotonously in the tree of heaven, and through the net curtains Mal saw one of the females, who had just been covered, scratch her head unconcernedly, fluff her feathers, and dart away. He reached over to the table beside the bed, took a cigarette out of a crumpled pack, and put it, unlit, between his lips. Someone came down the hall and knocked at the door.

"Mal?"

"Come on in."

The door opened and a tall young man with close-cropped fair hair and a friendly, eager, homely face came briskly into the room.

"Hey, Mal," he said, "up and at 'em, kid. On your feet. I've just been on the phone, and you know that little blond number, the one I was introduced to last Sunday—" He broke off, his enthusiasm dropping, and looked suspiciously at the figure on the bed. "What's the matter with you?" he asked. "You sick?"

Two miles away Rae Jacowski Cournane, Mrs. John Cournane, walked quickly along Adams Street, carrying a brown-paper package, and turned in at the long flight of iron-balustraded steps leading up to the front door of the brownstone house in which she and Mr. John Cournane lived.

"No, I'm fine," Mal said.

The young man came a step closer to the bed.

"You don't look like it," he said. "You were out pretty late last night, weren't you? Big evening?"

"I was looking for somebody."

"Well, you sure must've found her."

"Him," Mal said.

"All right, him. Don't worry, kid; I'm not trying to horn in. All I want to do is to fix you up with a date with a gorgeous blonde. How's a picnic at the beach sound to you, and after that—"

"Sorry," Mal said. "I've already got a date."

The young man pushed the suggestion away with both hands.

"So you've got a date," he said. "So you break it. I'm giving you the straight goods, Mal; this is a gorgeous little lady I'm dealing you. She's Marie's cousin, and if I didn't go for Marie myself—"

Mal shook his head.

"No dice, Buzzy. I'm leaving in two minutes."

The young man's face fell.

"Well, that's a fine thing," he said. "I thought I could count on you. Now what am I going to do with two dames on my hands?"

"That's your problem. I've got my own."

"You're in a helpful mood, aren't you?" The young man thrust his hands into his pockets, frowned indecisively, and looked, still faintly hopeful, at the figure on the bed. "Your cigarette's out," he offered.

Mal looked at it and tossed it, still unlit, into the wastebasket beside the bed.

Rae Cournane came into the flat, dropped her purse on a chair, and laid the brown-paper package she was carrying on the gas-ring behind the patterned screen in the corner. She put her head in at the open door of the adjoining bedroom.

"Hello," she said. "You up already? I didn't think you'd even be awake."

John Cournane, in trousers and shirt, emerged from the bedroom, drying his face with a towel.

"Not only awake," he proclaimed, "but fully clothed and presumably in my right mind." He dropped the towel to a chair. "May I add, my sweet," he said politely, "that you look ravishing on this bright and sunny Sunday morning?"

He kissed her lightly on the forehead as she ran her hands disapprovingly down her slender flanks encased in a tight-fitting brightly striped cotton dress—then more seriously, embracing her, on the mouth. Her arms went up and clung around his neck.

"You look awful, Jack," she said. "Where were you last night, you beast?"

"At Henry's." He tried an innocent look. "It wasn't so late, was it?"

"Only three-thirty; that's all." She ran a finger under the circles beneath his eyes; the sagging lines made a caricature of his still handsome face. "I wish I'd known you when you were younger," she said. "Before all this damn booze. I'd have made something out of you, you crazy oaf."

He smiled tolerantly.

"My dear, I was a very dull fellow when I was younger. I don't think you'd have cared at all for me then." Willing to leave the subject, he glanced at the brown-paper parcel behind the screen. "I see you've been scavenging in the delicatessens again," he said. "And what has my little garbage collector brought back this time?"

She tossed a lock of dark hair impatiently from her face.

"Only some sausages for breakfast—lunch—whatever you want to call it," she said. "Don't tell me *you're* hungry, after last night."

"You really have the most amazing faculty for reading my mind."

He turned back into the bedroom again, while she stood looking thoughtfully after him.

"Jack—" she said, after a moment.

"Yes, my dear?"

"Jack," she said, "you might as well tell me. I *can* read your mind, you know."

"Tell you what?"

He emerged innocently from the bedroom, putting on his tie.

"You know," she said. "Whatever it is." She sat down on the arm of a sagging overstuffed chair, slip-covered in faded flowered brown-and-red. "Something about last night —is it?" she said. "I want to know what you're trying to prove, getting all dressed up like a bridegroom this early in the day." She kicked at his ankle with the toe of her slipper. "Usually I can't drag you out of your robe and slippers before four P.M."

He shrugged, examined himself for a moment in the darkened glass of a narrow wall-mirror as he finished with his tie, and grimaced irreverently at what he saw.

"Then I should think," he said, "that it would please you to see the first dim glimmerings of a reform in my behavior—"

"Jack," she cut him off.

"Yes?"

"There *is* something the matter. Damn it, anyway, do you want me to nag it out of you?"

"You never nag, my dear," he said gallantly. "That's why I married you."

"You married me because you were drunk and you couldn't keep your hands off my breasts," she said. "Let's not play games, Jack." She got up off the arm of the chair. "Is it that wife of yours—Rosemary?" she said.

He turned away from her carefully.

"I thought we'd agreed not to discuss Rosemary," he said. He jerked open a table drawer, rummaging inside. "My God, aren't there ever any cigarettes in this house?"

In silence she reached into her bag and tossed a pack across to him.

"Matches on the table," she said.

She watched him while he took a cigarette from the pack and lit it.

"Pretty shaky, aren't you?" she observed, after a moment.

"Let's not make personal remarks—there's a good girl."

She looked at him darkly from under her brows.

"You might as well tell me," she said, at last. "Who were you with last night?"

"Oh"—he waved the cigarette airily—"some old friends."

"I'll bet. The Mayor, I suppose—and the Board of Aldermen."

"My dear, it may surprise you to know that a good many aldermen find their way into Henry's at one time or another." John Cournane sat down rather wearily in the brown-and-red chair. "You have entirely too much respect for the governing classes."

She laughed shortly.

"Oh, I know," she said. "They're all like you, aren't they? You're no worse than any of them. That's why they're so anxious to have you run for mayor again."

He did not say anything.

"What in *hell's* the matter with you this morning?" she said. "Are you going to tell me?"

As he did not answer, she reached over suddenly for her purse and started swiftly across the room toward the door.

"Where are you going?" he called after her, in surprise.

"To Henry's. I'll find out who you were with last night."

"Don't be absurd now; Rae—come back here."

She paused at the door, looking around at him, waiting.

"Well?"

He sighed.

"Is there a woman alive who isn't an inquisitor at heart? If you must know, I ran into Mal Cesti last night, and he gave me some rather disturbing news—"

"You're not in any trouble?" Her manner changed; she came across the room and took his arm. "Jack, you fool —you're not in any trouble?"

"Not in the least; what on earth makes you imagine that? It's only— Well, the fact is, he told me Champ is in town."

"Champ?"

"Amy. My daughter. She told Mal she wanted to see me, and—as a matter of fact, she's coming here today."

"Coming here?" Rae's eyes swept quickly over the room's disorder; she turned to him fiercely. "Oh, look at this place! Why didn't you tell me? *When* is she coming?"

"I imagine she'll be along any time now. Mal's bringing her."

"Oh, damn Mal! I don't care what he sees, but I won't have anybody from your damn family—a strange woman—"

She moved about the room furiously, picking up stray objects, straightening cushions, sweeping dust from table tops with the hem of her slip.

"It's not a strange woman, you know, my dear. It's only Champ, and I doubt very much if she's a good housekeeper herself."

"I don't care what kind of housekeeper she is. I won't

have her coming in here, turning up her nose— Why the
hell does she have to come here, anyway? She managed
well enough all these years without seeing you."

He stood looking at her as she continued to move
swiftly about the room.

"And look at me, too—this dress," she said violently.
"And I haven't even combed my hair this morning—"
She ran both hands through it, then paused suddenly and
turned to him. "I suppose what you'd really like me to do
is to go across the hall to Mother's," she said. "Is that what
you were working up to?"

"Not at all, my dear. You do just as you like."

"Well, I don't want to meet her; I don't want to meet
any of your damn family," she said. "I may have been born
over on the West Side, but I have better manners than to
go barging in where I'm not wanted." She came across the
room and stood closer to him. "I'll go over to Mother's, all
right," she said, "but listen to me, Jack—and don't you
forget it—nobody's going to take you away from me. Not
Champ, or Amy, or whatever her name is, or Rosemary, or
your brother with the Roman collar—"

"I doubt very much if any of them would want me,"
he said. He smiled, and put his arms around her briefly.
"Why don't you stay and meet Champ?" he said. "And
then, if you like, you can go over to your mother's."

She looked up at him.

"Do you want me to? Stay, I mean—"

"Yes."

She continued to look at him; her brows drew together.

"You're afraid, aren't you?" she asked him suddenly.

"My dear," he said quietly, "I'm scared as hell."

Miss Laura Dennehy, on her way home from High
Mass at St. Cyprian's, saw at the end of the block before

her Mr. Schneider's neatly straw-hatted head bobbing un-
attainably on as he continued up the street beside Mr.
Francis Jaeger.

His Eminence John Cardinal Shanagher eyed appreciatively, on an array of chastely gold-rimmed plates before
him, two eggs, round yellow glistening islands in a circle of
crisp-edged white, lightly browned toast, and a pat of his
favorite marmalade.

"A fine morning," he remarked encouragingly to Monsignor Damminger. "A fine day it will be, if the breeze
keeps up."

Monsignor Richard Damminger, secretary to His
Eminence, regarded, across the table, his own toast, eggs,
and marmalade, and agreed.

"And the Cathedral was nicely filled," the Cardinal
said.

He ate appreciatively, with deft movements of plump
white hands, his fork moving with rapid precision between
plate and plump pursed lips. Across, Monsignor Damminger's healthy, ruddy, handsome face expressed more matter-
of-fact concern for the necessities of furnishing an athletic
frame with a sufficient number of calories to carry it through
several succeeding hours. Eating, they discussed with cheerful sobriety matters of greater or lesser ecclesiastical and
temporal interest, including His Holiness the Pope's latest
encyclical, the poor state of repair of Our Lady of Divine
Grace Church, and the probability that the Yankees would
win the pennant.

On Madison Street Mal Cesti got into the green
Chrysler he had bought, secondhand, three weeks before
from a used car dealer on Atlantic Avenue, stepped on the
starter, put the car into gear, and turned it in the direction
of West Haley Street.

"And, by the way," the Cardinal remarked to Monsignor Damminger, gently wiping his shining, satisfied lips with his napkin, "there's Father Cournane celebrating his twenty-fifth anniversary out at St. Cyprian's today. You might drop around there this afternoon and convey my best wishes. They're having some sort of observance, I believe."

"A reception," Monsignor Damminger said. He looked at the Cardinal across the table, his ruddy, handsome face noncommittal. "Yes, of course," he said, and asked after a moment, "What ever became of his brother—the Mayor?"

The Cardinal shook his head regretfully.

"Ah, he's still in town, I believe," he said. "But a ruined man—ruined. The old story—" The round, intelligent head, with its wide-awake blue eyes, shook again, more slowly. "It's a sad thing for Michael Cournane," he said. "An able man, he was, but that business shook him badly. Lacks force now—well, you've only to look at that parish—"

Monsignor Damminger said that he would go out to St. Cyprian's that afternoon. And he added respectfully that, in his opinion, His Eminence was very wise indeed in what he was planning to do about the parish.

Mr. Walter Kittredge, wearing his new gray checked suit and surrounding himself with a lazy ambience of good cigar-smoke, strolled along McKinley Boulevard on his way home from High Mass at St. Cyprian's Church. Footsteps approached rapidly behind him.

"Friend or foe?" Mr. Kittredge inquired, half turning his head.

Mr. Edward Milligan, known as Cookie, panted up beside him.

"You know me, Walt," he said. "Let the women battle it out among themselves; that's good enough for me."

"And may the best man win," Mr. Kittredge propounded. He sighed, looking amiably at Mr. Milligan's round bulk in decent blue serge, and at his round domed head half-crowned with bristling black hair. "They seldom do," he said. "I remember one sad day in 1927 when I thought Dempsey would knock out Tunney—"

"And didn't he?" Mr. Milligan said argumentatively. Reminiscently, he added, "I lost twenty bucks on that fight myself," regarding meanwhile Miss Laura Dennehy entering the Dennehy family dwelling by the side door of Dennehy's Bakery.

They walked on for a moment in easy silence.

"As far as I'm concerned," Mr. Kittredge said presently, "your *gute Frau* is welcome to the job. It's hell's own nuisance around the house."

"And what isn't, when there are women mixed up in it?" Mr. Milligan asked philosophically. He glanced skyward for a moment. "Ah, but I pity Father Cournane if Mame gets the place," he said. "He'll never have a moment's peace. She has grand plans for turning the whole parish upside down."

Mr. Kittredge tactfully forbore to comment.

In the home of the McGrath family in Silver Woods Polly McGrath, aged nine, listened to the voices of her mother and father in bitter argument as they passed into the house, returning from Mass.

Mr. Edward Milligan said reflectively, into the silence, "Father Cournane is a fine man, but no hero, I'm afraid. Isn't that a fact, now? I've often thought to myself that if I was a priest I'd make it a rule of the parish that no woman was to open her mouth above a whisper on church affairs. Begod, they keep them out of the sacristy and off the altar, but they can't keep them out of anywhere else—and they can't even keep them out of there when there's no performance going on."

Mr. Walter Kittredge smiled benevolently up at a bright blue sky.

"Did you ever hear the story of Father Cournane's sister and the Bishop of Columbiana?" he asked. "Wait till I tell you—I had it from Father Mulcahy over at St. Anthony's. You know that Mrs. McGrath—"

"Ah, don't I?" Mr. Milligan said, shaking his head. "Mame and Thressa Dawes would like to drink her blood."

"Well, it seems she gives the Bishop the benefit of the same sweet personality down there in Columbiana—" Mr. Kittredge broke off suddenly, nodding to a stout, elderly, gray-haired, immaculately turned-out gentleman across the street who was leading a daintily pink-clad little girl of five by the hand. "My worthy brother-in-law," he said.

"Your—?" Mr. Milligan looked, nodded also.

"He seems in fine fettle," Mr. Kittredge said, regarding Mr. James Heffernan's beaming smile and pouter-pigeon walk retreating across the way.

"And why not?" Mr. Milligan said. "He's got a gold mine—hasn't he?—in that mausoleum of his, does hell's own business over there. I wish I was in that line myself. Your customers can't tell you they've made up their minds to let that little job go till sometime next year, the way they do with papering the parlor."

Mr. Kittredge smiled, savoring the joke in the remark.

"Now about the Bishop—" he said, after a moment. "Where was I? Oh yes—it seems our friend Mrs. McGrath came to him one day last year with a proposition to form a committee to bring some glee club or choir—I forget what it was, some big Catholic college—to Columbiana for a church benefit. The Bishop said, 'Fine'; he knows better than to say anything else to that sweet lady. 'And I want you to know, Your Excellency,' she says to him, 'that there'll be no squabbling among the committee members this time over who is to get what publicity in the newpapers.' 'Oh?' the Bishop says, hopeful but not really believing; he's been Bishop of Columbiana for fifteen years, but he's never managed that little trick himself with a committee of so-called ladies. 'Is that so, Mrs. McGrath?' he says. 'Yes,' she says, looking him straight in the eye, 'that's so, Your Excellency. Because—I intend to have all the publicity myself.'" Mr. Kittredge blew a thoughtful smoke ring. "End of story," he said. "And do you think she didn't?"

He and Mr. Milligan, exchanging broad smiles, strolled on pleasantly through the bright June day.

"I could have told him," Mrs. Cournane said, "how it would turn out." Amy, waiting, listened for the car to drive up outside. The room's shuttered dimness sank softly around her on the black gleam of furniture, the watery breathings of green ferns on marble stands—a museum of Midwestern Victorianism. "Putting the three of them in the same room together," the rusty voice said, "is like tying a set of Kilkenny cats up in a sack. Una couldn't get along with her patron saint if she was to come down to earth and speak to her, and Rosemary's very little better. Then Dolly—I remember when she and Una were girls in this house, Una as high-handed as the Queen of Persia, and Dolly ruining what little peace we had left with that tongue of hers—"

"Really, it wasn't as bad as that, Gran," Amy said. She listened to the cheerful sound of her own voice, thinking, *How do I do it? Face washed, hair slicked back, fresh green-and-white dress, parading an innocence I left behind when I was fourteen. For what? Aren't you the girl who wanted the little second hand to flick around fast, so it would all be over, quietly dead and you could say, It's the past now, and now I don't even have to remember it any more? You've got to have some reason for wanting it to be here again.*

*Father, is it?—Mal?—both lost, ghosts, and you trying to
make them real again—*

The old woman's veined hand fumbled a round, hard
peppermint from the dim little glass bowl on the marble-
topped table.

"You needn't tell me," the rusty voice said, through
the sweet. "Ah, Mother of God, I lived with them all right
here in this house. Jack with his moods, and Father Michael
with his plans and his organizations, and Una, and Dolly,
and the father—I was out of my good senses, I tell you, the
day I took that whole tribe on. I'd sit there at that table"—
her head nodded slowly toward the round mahogany table,
crochet-draped and artificial-flowered in the dimness, beyond the archway—"saying my prayers to the Sacred Heart
to give me patience. *Oh, Sacred Heart, help me!*—whether
it was Una cutting her hair off with the kitchen shears, or
Jack scamping out of school for a whole week to go down
to the Strand Theater and run errands for those actors, or
Dolly wanting to marry that fire-insurance salesman when
she was fifteen—"

"Now, Gran," Amy said. "You know you wouldn't
have missed a minute of it. You were having a perfectly
splendid time."

The clock on the mantel kept on ticking—*and if it
would stop,* she thought, *if everything would only stop and
we could sit here forever, not even communicating in spite
of the voices, peacefully embalmed in the dim amber of a
Midwestern June noon, forgotten here in this quiet room
for the rest of time, and never have to move again, decide—
Because when you married Irving Gilman you thought
deciding was all over, but it never is, as Father discovered
when he met Ermina Marlow one fine November day,
and I didn't even have to meet anyone, Mal there waiting
all the time, and when he looks at me now, waiting—*

"A set of bedlamites," Mrs. Cournane said. "And your

father worse than any of them. I don't know what you expect, going to see him like this; if he'd wanted his family, he'd have come around here now and then, wouldn't he? He and that blackguard of a grandson of mine—two of a kind, that's what they are."

In the eighth-grade room of St. Cyprian's School Mrs. Walter Kittredge tapped with her gavel on Sister Antonius's desk, facing the rows of ladies gossiping across the aisles with one another in their Sunday bests of figured voile and crepe de Chine, and in a mild voice called the meeting of the Married Ladies' Sodality to order.

Father Michael Cournane, having divested himself of chasuble, stole, maniple, cincture, alb, and amice, the vestments of his priestly calling, took the arm of Monsignor Francis Hawk, his deacon during the just celebrated Mass, and led him through the passage which ran from the sacristy of St. Cyprian's Church to the parish house.

"That's a fine lot of youngsters you have there in your choir, Mike," Monsignor Hawk said to him heartily.

His voice betrayed the uncomfortable attempt at cheerfulness of a man unaccustomed to not speaking his mind; he cleared his throat slightly as he ended his sentence. His tall, burly figure and hair growing iron-gray presented him as the picture of the soldier-priest, admired by Miss Laura Dennehy's observing eyes.

Father Cournane, walking, smiled slightly, a little bitterly.

"Say what you think, Frank," he said. "The church—for a new church—is looking shabby; the choir is ragged and badly trained; the whole tone of the congregation is listless. Since when have you stopped speaking out to me?"

He dropped his guiding grasp on Monsignor Hawk's

arm, but Monsignor Hawk himself renewed the contact with a friendly hand laid on Father Cournane's shoulder.

"You do a better job of it than I could do," he said. "Let up on yourself, Mike; you can't change the world, you know—not even your little piece of it here."

"The Cardinal," Father Cournane said, "seems to think I can."

He pushed open the door to the parish-house hall, which led them at once from the cool echoing monastic silence of the passage, faintly acrid with the smell of incense, into the hot bright daylight of the parish house, rich with the commonplace odors of Mrs. Dawes's cooking. Inside, Father Cournane stood looking about him for a moment, his forehead wrinkling suddenly with mundane thought.

"My housekeeper's at the Married Ladies' Sodality meeting," he said, "but I suppose I can rustle up something in the kitchen. Do you still like your tea strong enough to walk out of the cup on its own black legs?"

"The only way to take it," Monsignor Hawk said, rubbing his hands together in anticipation. His eyes, as he followed Father Cournane toward the passage leading to the kitchen, lit on a framed photograph on the wall. "What's this?" he asked, halting, peering closer. "Seminarian Francis Hawk, Seminarian Michael Cournane—Myer—Ryan—Zabinski—I've got one of these somewhere myself—haven't seen it in years, though."

The two paused, tranced, before a representation of serious, cassocked young men, their faces hopeful, unlined, full of the bland arrogance of youth.

"Ryan—" Monsignor Hawk said unbelievingly. "Rabbit Ryan. Died in France—Château-Thierry, I think. Did you ever see a more unlikely-looking candidate for a hero?"

"You can't tell by the looks," Father Cournane said.

"I suppose that's one lesson every priest learns soon enough. The heroes never look like heroes, and the villains are apt to look like angels."

"At least when they're as young as we were then," Monsignor Hawk said, nodding at the frame on the wall.

Shivaun and Stephen Gilman, swinging on the iron gate in front of their step-great-grandmother's residence on West Haley Street, watched a green Chrysler stop at the curb and identified with pleasure Mal Cesti's broad shoulders and rather battered Panama hat inside it.

"When I think," Monsignor Hawk said, considering, marveling, his own quarter-century-younger visage on the wall, "we were bold enough, at that age, to throw ourselves on the world as priests! You were the only one of us who knew enough to wipe his own nose when it needed it. Do you remember old Father Trifani in canon law class? 'This young man *thinks*; what do the rest of you do with that noble instrument of cogitation a generous God has endowed you with?' "

Father Cournane half smiled, still with lingering, remembering bitterness.

"That's one time he was wrong," he said. "I wasn't thinking in those days; I was feeling—following an impulse as blind as any love-sotted adolescent's or drunken tyrant's." He turned to look suddenly into his friend's slightly troubled face. "How hard do you suppose it is for a boy brought up in the way I was brought up to mistake a love of power, of authority, of achievement, for a love of God?" he demanded then. "I can answer that for you, Frank. It's not hard at all."

Monsignor Hawk shifted uncomfortably, still eying his companion's fine youthful pictured face on the wall.

"Ah, Mike, don't be so rough on yourself," he said.

"We're none of us saints; you should know that as well as I do. We do the best we can with what's given to us."

Father Cournane did not move. He too was looking now at the photograph on the wall.

"There was no humility in me then—there's the long and short of it, Frank," he said simply. "I was going to conquer the world with the sword of God. Oh, I suppose if I'd been born into a family with a military tradition instead of an old-fashioned Irish religious one, I might have tried to do it with a different kind of sword—and probably with no greater success. But at least then my failure would have been one that left my conscience clear."

Having said too much, as he thought, he moved on again toward the kitchen. Pausing on the threshold, surveying Mrs. Dawes's domain, he felt Monsignor Hawk's hand lightly on his shoulder.

"You had great things before you in those days, Mike," Monsignor Hawk said quietly. "And have still, believe me—and have still."

Father Cournane shrugged slightly, the smile fixing, then dying, on his face.

"Now where in the name of all that's holy would she have put the teapot?" he inquired.

Shivaun Gilman watched a tall man in shirtsleeves, benevolently balancing a round belly before him, amble past Number 33 West Haley Street.

"Going to church," she said, and Stephen said, "Don't be silly. He hasn't even got a tie on."

She and Stephen were both a little cross. It was hot, and the Captain was too old to play, and there was nothing to do but swing on the gate and watch the people going by. When it was afternoon they could go out to Father Michael's house again and there would be a party, but first

Mother had to go someplace with Cousin Mal. Shivaun could hear Cousin Mal's voice through the parlor window now, talking to Mother and Granny Cournane. He sounded as if he knew a lot of things but wasn't going to talk about any of them unless somebody made him. Mostly Cousin Mal didn't talk much; he just looked at Mother. She bet he was in the parlor looking at her right now.

She could hear Granny Cournane's voice through the window, sounding excited, and then the front door opened and Cousin Mal and Mother came out. Cousin Mal looked black but cool, and Mother looked upset.

"Oh, Mal," she said, "you shouldn't have said that. You really shouldn't."

"All right," Cousin Mal said.

"She's getting so old," Mother said.

"All right," Cousin Mal said. He said it louder this time. "All right. I'm getting old too. Old and as damn virtuous as a tabby cat when it comes to getting what I really want. What the hell right has she to say that to me?"

He saw Shivaun and Stephen standing there by the gate and stopped. Mother stopped too. After a minute she said, "Oh—Shivaun. Why, I thought you and Stephen were back in the kitchen with Josie."

The Captain got up and went over to her and she reached down and patted him on the head.

"We came out here," Shivaun said. "It's hot in the kitchen."

"Show me someplace where it isn't," Cousin Mal said. His face cleared up and he looked at Stephen and said, "You're going to be right at home in the African jungle after a couple of weeks in this burg."

In the flat on Adams Street Rae Jacowski Cournane slipped into a fresh mandarin-collared black cotton dress,

ran a comb furiously through her dark hair, and sketched
her lips quickly in bright-red lipstick, all in a single con-
tinuous movement.

"Where are you going with my mother?" Stephen said.
"Are you going to see her father?"

Cousin Mal looked at Mother.

"Yes," Mother said. "Now you and Shivaun behave
yourselves while I'm gone; don't give Josie or Granny Cournane any trouble. And stay out of the street—do you hear
me, you kids?"

"We hear you," Stephen said, resigned. He looked
after her and Cousin Mal as they went through the gate and
out to the car. "Why can't we go too?" he called to them,
after a minute.

Mother shook her head and smiled and waved.

"Isn't he a relation of mine too?" Stephen said. "I get
to see all my other relations."

The car drove on down the street.

"I'll bet he's a gangster," Stephen said. "Like Dillinger.
I'll bet he holds people up—like this." The benevolent
shirtsleeved man was ambling back down the street carrying some bottles in a paper carton. Stephen pointed both
his index fingers at him and said under his breath, sharply,
"Stick 'em up!"

"What I can't understand is why we have to spend
the whole afternoon out there," Marian McGrath said.

"It's not the whole afternoon," Dr. Thomas McGrath
said. He looked at his plate, empty, swimming in syrup.
"Bessie make any more of these hot cakes?" he asked.

"You've eaten too many already; it's simply terrible
how you've taken on weight this past year. You're going to
be just like your mother in a little while."

"Can't we for God's sake just leave my mother *out* of it for a while?"

"Don't talk to me in that tone of voice, Tommyo; I won't stand for it."

"All right, I'm sorry. Just forget about my mother and let's have some more hot cakes and a little peace in the family for a few minutes."

Polly McGrath exchanged glances across the table with her sister Janet. Bessie brought in the hot cakes, and while she was in the room the two grownups sat sulkily at the table without looking at each other. Then, as soon as the swinging door closed behind her, they started up again.

"You're always implying it's *my* fault," Marian Mc-Grath said, "that things are so upset around here, but let me ask you, darling—did you ever try to get along with your mother for twelve or fifteen hours at a stretch? *You're* off at your office or the hospital, having a lovely, peaceful time with people's tonsils, but I have to sit right here and listen to her—"

"Oh, for God's sake, Marian, she brought me up, didn't she? Of course I know what she's like to be with for twelve or fifteen hours at a stretch."

"I'm not so sure of that. To hear *her* tell it, she's been running the social life of the whole town *and* the diocese down there in Columbiana for the past thirty years; she can't have had very much time for you."

"She had time enough to teach me that a person has to be willing to make a little sacrifice now and then for the sake of his family—like showing up at your uncle's twenty-fifth anniversary celebration when he's a priest of God and a respected member of the community—"

"Oh, for heaven's sake, Tommyo, don't make any of your Knights of Columbus speeches to me. You know as

well as I do, Father Cournane's stuck out there in that
dreary parish with those hopelessly dull people who're going
to spend the entire afternoon gawking at the furniture and
cataloguing what his relatives are wearing."

"It's not as bad as that and you know it. You needn't
be such a snob."

"*I'm* a snob? And what about your own mother, darling—and your aunt Rosemary, if we're really getting down
to cases? She's so impressed by the idea that she was once
the Mayor's wife, she has to bring it into the conversation
every quarter hour; it would be unbearable if it weren't so
ridiculous. And, speaking of your uncle Jack, do you suppose he feels the same sense of family responsibility that
you do, and will think it's his duty to show up at the reception this afternoon?"

Polly McGrath leaned her chin on one fist and began
making a dike with her fork out of the left-over fragments
of her hot cakes, trying to dam up the syrup on her plate.
In the peaceful breakfast room, with the furniture and
decorating that looked as if they came straight out of
House and Garden, the angry voices went on and on. She
thought about Stephen Gilman and about wrestling with
him in the early dusk on Father Michael's lawn the evening before. She liked Stephen and he liked her. And his
mother smiled at him and said, "Stephen, you scoundrel,
what have you been up to?" Her mother was prettier than
his mother, because nobody was prettier than her mother,
but she wished her mother would say to her, "Polly, you
scoundrel, what have you been up to?" the way Stephen's
mother said it to him. Her mother said, "Oh, for heaven's
sake, Polly, do whatever you want to do; can't you see I'm
busy?"

Marian McGrath said, leaning across the table a little
to speak to her husband in a lower voice, "And, by the way,

darling, since we *are* on the subject of your family—what's this interesting rumor I've been hearing about Amy? Is she really leaving Irving Gilman? Your aunt Rosemary was dropping hints like mad all evening."

Dr. Thomas McGrath wiped his mouth with his napkin with dignity.

"Marian," he said, "the best advice I can give you is to let gossip like that alone. *Strictly* alone."

Mr. Edward Milligan, known as Cookie, unlaced with relief, in the front bedroom of his house on Pilsudski Avenue, the black shoes he had worn to church, and thrust his feet into a dilapidated pair of Dr. Bassett's Guaranteed Comfort Slippers.

"Now, ladies—" Mrs. Walter Kittredge said. "Ladies— Ladies— If I may have your attention, please—"

She tapped gently, apologetically, with her gavel on Sister Antonius's desk, her mild, flat voice carrying unexpectedly, with the impervious insistence of the deaf, through the clatter of female voices assailing the bare walls of the schoolroom. Mrs. Thressa Dawes, planted solidly behind an inadequate eighth-grade-size desk in the first row, flicked with emphatic scorn an imaginary particle of soot from the crocheted jabot of her new flowered voile. Well, we'll be rid of *that* in ten minutes, she told herself. With satisfaction she looked at the pile of folded slips in the wire collection basket on Sister Antonius's desk, calculating the probable majority of them bearing Mrs. Edward Milligan's name.

"We're about to count the votes now," Mrs. Walter Kittredge's mild voice continued. "Mrs. Dawes—Mrs. Heffernan—if the tellers will just come up here to the desk—"

With unhurried dignity Mrs. Dawes disengaged herself from her narrow chair and stepped up on the platform beside Mrs. Kittredge. An insult to ask me to serve with that Mrs. Heffernan. Dyed red hair, thirty years younger than her husband if she's a day. Imagines people can't remember back six years, when she was parading around here with a child in her belly and no wedding ring on her finger. But she'd better try none of her tricks on me.

She stared, in solid challenge, at Mrs. Heffernan's flower-decked straw hat, her blue crepe de Chine, and her flaunted white silk gloves.

"I'll leave you two ladies to take charge now," Mrs. Kittredge said, and of course Mrs. Heffernan had to giggle a bit and put on the girlish act, pretending to be sinking under the responsibility.

"Now, Mrs. Heffernan," Mrs. Dawes said firmly, "will you count or shall I?"

She pulled the basket slightly over to her side of the desk; it wouldn't do to let anybody like that one get her fingers in among the votes first. Sly as a fox; wouldn't put it past her to drop a few of them by accident on the floor or into a drawer. Then play the innocent if anybody found them. Going around asking everybody to vote for her dear Minnie, sisters-in-law, of course the Kittredges both of them solidly behind the Heffernans during that trouble.

Majestically, Mrs. Dawes dipped her hand into the basket, picked out a folded slip, opened it, read—"Mrs. Edward Milligan"—in a loud, clear voice, and handed the slip to Mrs. Heffernan for confirmation. Let her find anything wrong with that one. Behind, a meek little scorer, Della Klispie, just married and new in the sodality this year, made a large anxious chalk scratch on the blackboard beside Mrs. Milligan's name.

The clattering schoolroom, with its long blackboarded walls and rows of desks, became suddenly quiet as the reading of the votes progressed. Hot June sunlight streamed in through the open windows; a statue of the Virgin, with flowers before it, presided silently in one corner, with an elaborate chalk scroll on the blackboard behind it warning appropriately: *Man proposes, but God disposes.* Mrs. Walter Kittredge, her mild gray eyes fixed nearsightedly on the clock on the wall above Sister Antonius's desk, seemed to be studying out the correct time on its face. At the other side of the room Mrs. Milligan's face showed a sterner appreciation of the vital issues dependent upon the outcome of this election.

"Mrs. Edward Milligan!" Mrs. Dawes read the last slip out triumphantly.

It was hardly necessary to wait while the scorer totted up the long row of chalk scratches beside Mrs. Milligan's name on the blackboard, and the visibly shorter one beside Mrs. Kittredge's. There was a scattering of hand claps in the room, and a buzz of conversation broke out as if a stone had been thrown suddenly into a beehive. Mrs. Milligan, her austere expression relaxing only slightly, allowed herself to be congratulated by the ladies immediately around her; Mrs. Kittredge smiled her bland, invariable smile. Into the rising hum of confusion the Angelus bells rang.

Mrs. Kittredge rose and made her way without haste to the front of the room.

"Now, ladies, ladies," she said, cautioning them silent with an admonitory finger. She turned her nearsighted eyes blandly on Mrs. Milligan. "Shall we have our new prefect lead us in the Angelus?" she asked.

Thressa Dawes, standing, heard from her victorious candidate's lips the first words of the Angelus—"The angel of the Lord declared unto Mary"—and made response as if challenging the roomful of them to say that she, Thressa Dawes, had not won her battle.

In the kitchen of the parish house of St. Cyprian's,

Father Michael Cournane, innocent of impending evil, poured strong dark tea for Monsignor Francis Hawk and sat down beside him to break his fast.

"Well?" Mal said.

Amy Gilman looked from the car window at the long flight of iron-balustraded steps leading up to the door of the brownstone house on Adams Street.

"Do you want me to go in with you?" Mal asked.

She looked at Sunday-morning quiet, the summer suck and fall of curtains at blank open windows, an abandoned newspaper blown gently down the street beside the curb.

"Will she be there?" she asked.

"I don't know," Mal said. "Probably."

"What did he say last night?"

"He didn't say much of anything. You usually don't when something hits you right between the eyes."

"I don't want to hit anybody between the eyes. Mal, I want—I just want—" *to go back, she thought, make it yesterday, two weeks ago, Irv in California saying, Why, yes, Amy, sure, if you want to go, and I would say, No, I don't want to, I don't want to see any of them, Mal, Father, any of them, I won't go, I'm going to stay here—*

She opened the door of the car and got out, not waiting for Mal to come around. At the top of the steps the door of the house was open. It was dark inside after the bright street, and there were a dozen names penciled or inked in over the smudged mail boxes: "Mr. and Mrs. R. M. Stirbinder, Jack Smith, Opie Winkle, Delie Carruthers"— *Pink paper, she thought; always a semi-pro whore or two in a place like this*—"Mr. and Mrs. John Cournane"—

Mal came up behind her.

"Look, Champ," he said, "be reasonable now. You don't have to go through with this."

"I do. I do."

Below "Mr. and Mrs. John Cournane" it said "Apartment 1B." She walked across the hall to a brown-stained door and knocked. There was a long silence; then the door opened abruptly. A handsome, dark, slightly sullen face looked out at her from above a black mandarin-collared dress.

"Hello," the husky voice said. "You must be Amy. I'm Rae. Hello, Mal; I haven't seen you in ages. Where've you been keeping yourself?"

"Here and there," Mal said.

She held the door open and they went in. John Cournane, rising from an armchair with a splendid show of perfect ease—*Why shouldn't he?* Amy thought. *Once a politician, always a politician; just smile, smile, that's all there is to it, and be sure to remember their names*—said, "Well, well, well—what have we here? Champ, you beautiful creature, aren't you going to give your old father a kiss?"

"You look marvelous, Father, just the same as ever."

When she kissed him she smelled the whisky, morning courage: she closed her eyes so she wouldn't see the veins reddening the classic nose, the heavy pouches beneath the eyes. He stood there with his arm still around her, addressing the other girl with that dreadful show of ease.

"What did I tell you, Rae?" he asked. "Isn't she a real champion? And we're to believe that this gorgeous young thing is the mother of two infants—?"

"Seven and nine," Amy said. "They're not infants at all. Stephen comes almost up to my shoulder already."

"Really?" Rae said. "Jack always talks about you as if you were just out of hair ribbons yourself; I'm afraid he's a little behind the times when it comes to his family."

Amy smiled. *But what good does it do*, she thought,

the two of us pretending when she'd like to scratch my eyes out? Younger than I am, quick, sullen, frightened, and Mal looking at the two of us—Mal, Mal's girl—was she once? The way they looked at each other when we came in— Don't let her have been Mal's girl, don't let her—

She watched him standing there looking at her and the other girl with the completely detached expression of a man observing a pair of women going through an act that he knows is a fake.

"Why don't you two sit down?" Rae asked. "I just stayed to say hello; I'm going across the hall to Mother's in a minute, and then you and Jack can talk as much as you want to."

"Oh no," Amy said. "Don't go. Please." She plunged in desperately. "We really ought to get to know each other; after all—"

"After all, I'm by way of being your stepmother—is that it?" Rae said. She sat down on the arm of John Cournane's chair, swinging one foot gently, sullenly, back and forth. "Look," she said suddenly, "let's not kid ourselves, shall we? I may be married to Jack according to the records down at the courthouse, but as far as you're concerned it's strictly no sale; you think I'm living with him, with a wedding ring on my finger for window dressing—"

"She didn't ask for that, Rae," Mal said. *But he's saying it wrong, Amy thought, because no man talks that way to a woman, assuming a right, a familiarity, unless he once had that right, so no wonder he didn't want me to come. Aunt Dolly saying, You know Mal always has some girl on the string—Well, what did I expect? Only not this one, not Father and Mal too, not both of them to that dark secret haven—* "Maybe that was a good idea of yours," Mal said, "about going over to see your mother—"

"Don't you butt into this, Mal," Rae said, her hand

resting lightly on John Cournane's shoulder. "She walked in here on her own two feet, and if she wants to stay, she can take care of herself."

"Rae, you unreasonable little vixen," John Cournane said, "will you tell me what the point of all this is? Amy hasn't said a word—"

"She doesn't have to." Rae stood up, turning on him bitterly. "I wasn't born yesterday," she said. "Why do you think she came here in the first place? It was to work on you, you sentimental Irish slob—and the rest of your damned family is probably sitting there at home holding their breath, waiting for her to report—"

Mal said, "Shut up, Rae." Then he took her arm and without a show of force except for her own futile reaction to the movement brought her a few steps away and spoke quickly in her ear. She just listened, then pulled her arm violently free.

"Why don't you mind your own business?" she said. She looked across the room at Amy. "The two of you," she cried. "Why don't you just mind your own damned business?"

Then she was gone, and only the frantic slam of the door echoed in the stale quiet of the room. John Cournane, with one hand over his eyes, began to weep suddenly.

"Amy—" he said. "Amy—my little girl—"

To a mellow sound of Sunday bells Mrs. Edward Milligan, Prefect-elect of the Married Ladies' Sodality of St. Cyprian's Church, emerged from the door of St. Cyprian's School and strode briskly down the steps into the warm June sunlight. On one side she was escorted by Mrs. Thressa Dawes, housekeeper to the Reverend Michael Cournane, pastor of St. Cyprian's Church, and on the other by Mrs. Francis Jaeger, wife of the President of the St. Cyprian

Holy Name Society. A throng of ladies less prominent in the affairs of the organization of which she was the newly elected head followed admiringly at her heels. The supporters of the defeated Mrs. Walter Kittredge were still gathered in whispering knots in the corridor above, but several of them, already conscious of the vulnerability of their position, had slipped quietly away to join the triumphal procession below.

At the door Mrs. Milligan took counsel briefly with her lieutenants. She spoke in firm, self-assured tones of the changes that would be necessary in the management of parish affairs, of plans concerning the school, the altar, the parish house. Mrs. Dawes vehemently, Mrs. Jaeger piously, agreed. The less-favored ladies hung discreetly near, treasuring each syllable overheard. Then, at a signal from Mrs. Milligan, a brisk—"Well, girls, I'll see you all this afternoon"—the group broke, each going her separate way. Mrs. Dawes and Mrs. Jaeger briefly lingered, congratulating each other on the victory, perhaps waiting to enlarge their triumph by observing the emergence of the defeated from the building.

Mrs. Edward Milligan, alone, strode briskly across the deserted schoolyard, taking the short cut, with her customary directness, to her home. In her mind she reviewed, with a general's eye for the strategic detail, a variety of subjects, including her plans for the future of the parish, the probable (discounted) opposition of Father Cournane, the undoubted (not discounted) approval of Father Kaspar, the possible (completely discounted) disapproval of Mr. Edward (Cookie) Milligan, and the probable state of the roast which she had put into the oven in the kitchen of her house on Pilsudski Avenue on her leaving for church some two hours before. Mr. Edward Milligan and the two young Milligans, aged eight and twelve, had received specific instructions to look at said roast in her absence, but her family was not addicted to the same stern sense of duty that she was, and she counted, with the indifference of the victorious general for minor losses, on burnt meat for dinner that day.

She strode on, black-straw-hatted, paisley-print-Bemberged, past Dennehy's Bakery, closed and shuttered for the day, past the grave door of the Heffernan Funeral Home, where there reposed, she was aware, the body of Mr. Henry Strieter, awaiting the last ceremonies of the Church and a trip to St. John's Cemetery on Monday morning, and turned up Pilsudski Avenue toward her own home. On her way she noted the youngest Flynn child squalling in a playpen on the Flynn front porch, the deplorable state of the walk in front of the Merowski house, Mrs. Waner's roses, and the decidedly shabby appearance, in respect of paint, of her own domicile, and resolved to set Mr. Edward Milligan to work on it on his next free day. As she marched up the steps to her front door, the expected odor of burnt pork drifted out to her nostrils, and she entered the house on a strong note of protest, calling loudly for the culprit to reveal himself.

Mr. Edward Milligan, in shirtsleeves and Dr. Bassett's Guaranteed Comfort Slippers, ambled unhurriedly after her into the kitchen and surveyed, with the philosophic gaze of a man accustomed to overdone meals, his wife's vigorous efforts to salvage what was salvageable of his ruined dinner.

"Well, Mame," he inquired, "did you get it, now?"

She turned around to him emphatically, fork in hand.

"You bet your sweet life I got it," she responded. "Hand me that wet dish rag, Cookie—that's right. And *now* you're going to see some changes made—"

AFTERNOON

Mary Ann Milligan

Because there is no gratitude in this world: that is the first thing you learn when you labor to help your fellow man in this vale of tears. As who should know better than me? —seeing how it happened in the P.-T.A. over at St. Rose's, where it was "Mrs. Milligan, this" and "Mrs. Milligan, that" whenever they wanted anything done, and then to be turned out when they had no further use for me. I know what Cookie says, that I ought to have been satisfied with running things as long as I did, but I will always say to my dying breath that it was not for my personal glory but all for the good of those children that I did it, worked and slaved harder than any other woman in that parish. Then to be turned out. But I said to Cookie that same night, "We're going to move," I said; "I won't stay around here to watch another woman ruin all the work I've done." And so we bought the house over in St. Cyprian's, where I've been content, let anybody say any different if they dare, to be a humble laborer in the vineyard for four long years.

So I should have known how that would turn out, too. You might think it would be different with a priest of God, but no, I could see for myself, the minute I walked into the parish house this afternoon and set eyes on that old crowd planted there already, gathered around him like they meant to hold onto what they'd got, no matter who was elected prefect of what, that I couldn't look for any gratitude there. He was polite, because he always is polite, I will give him that, but I knew that if he had his way it would be Minnie Kittredge sitting up there still at Sister Antonius's desk on Sunday morning with the gavel in her hand.

"I'm sure the sodality will be in good hands with you at the helm, Mrs. Milligan," he said to me, but I could see Walter Kittredge and Miss Lizzie Clemens standing right there with the look on their faces like "We know what we know," and I knew they'd all been talking out of a different side of their mouths not five minutes before. Thressa Dawes says she was in the dining room, seeing to getting the cakes cut up for the refreshments, when they came in, the Kittredges and the Heffernans and the Pflaums and Miss Lizzie, and they all had their heads together, talking low, so she couldn't hear them, till the very minute Cookie and I walked in the door. Well, let Walter Kittredge say what he pleases, I know my rights and I know my own conscience, and if everybody else's in that room was as clear as mine, my name isn't Mary Ann Milligan.

So I had to go up then and say hello to Father Kaspar, and as luck would have it he was talking to Monsignor Hawk, that friend of Father Cournane's that came out to assist him in the Solemn High Mass this morning. He has some big parish on the North Side, one of those priests that looks like his Roman collar is off as much as it's on, while he's out playing tennis or golf with his rich parishioners. And *too* polite by far, if you know what I mean. Birds of a feather flock together; I felt that the minute I laid eyes on him, and I've surely had no call to change my mind since.

He was standing there, listening to Father Kaspar congratulating me on the Married Ladies' election and smiling that self-satisfied little smile he has, when who should walk in but old Mrs. Cournane and one of Father Cournane's sisters, Mrs. Clohessey from down in Atlanta. And then, of course, there had to be a great fuss made over *them*. You would think a priest of God, who is required to give up father and mother and brother and sister, as the Bible says, would be ashamed to make more of them than he does of his own parishioners, his brothers and sisters in Christ who are assisting him in his holy work, but it never stops Father Cournane. She is only his stepmother, but he had her out in the reception hall for fifteen minutes, looking at all the presents that were spread out there, while the rest of us cooled our heels in the parlor. And then she had to have the best chair in the place, just beside him, where she could watch everybody coming up and congratulating him all afternoon long.

They had the children with them, too, Father Cournane's niece's children from California, and that's another thing—bringing children in a crowd like that. I had told Minnie Kittredge and told her again, it ought to have been in the school hall, where there'd have been plenty of room for everybody, but she said Father Cournane wanted it in his own home, not like a circus in a public hall, and of

course that was the end of that. I said to Mrs. Clohessey—
I've met her before, and she seemed to know all about *me*,
I guess from her sister, that Mrs. McGrath—I said to her,
"Where's their mother?" because she wasn't at the church
this morning either, and she said, as careless as you please,
"Oh, Amy'll be along a little later."

With that Mal Cesti, I suppose, I said to myself, because Thressa Dawes gave me an earful about *that* this morning. If they have any more scandals in that family, somebody
ought to take it up with the Cardinal; it's a disgrace to the
good name of the parish, is all I can say. I have my own
cross to bear in my married life, the Lord above knows, but
I would scorn not to lift my burden and walk the road of
life a faithful helpmate to my husband.

As I have told him myself time and time again. The
time he went off on that three-day toot when I was in the
very midst of getting ready for the P.-T.A. euchre, and how
I ever got through it except for the strength of the Lord
nobody will ever know, the chicken patties sent out to St.
Rose of Lima's by mistake and me on that telephone all
morning trying to track them down, till Western Union
finally gave up trying the number and sent the telegram out
by messenger. I held it in my hand and I thought, He's dead,
gone off somewhere and been killed in an accident, the way
he always said he would when he took too much, sitting
there crying about the good old days and Micky Finnerty
or whoever, that old crowd he used to go around with, one
worse than the other if you want my opinion. All I could
think of was the funeral expenses and those chicken patties
going to waste over there at St. Rose of Lima's; it was like
the Lord had struck me down. Then I opened it and there
it was, in black and white: *Look for Cookie.* Wasting good
money on that in his drunkenness.

Still I did my duty by him when he came home, climbing into bed with me as hangdog as you please, as if that was going to make it all up again. "Well, I can do without you," I said, "if you can do without me three nights away from your own bed and home"; but he can be so limber and jolly when he pleases, a different sort of man altogether from when he's going off on one of those sprees. My mother warned me when I married him, "He's a spree-drinker, Mame," she said to me; "all those Milligans are spree-drinkers; he'll be steady enough and then one day he'll be off and all the Newfoundland dogs in the city couldn't find him for you till he's got it out of his system." But I took up my burden, and the Lord Himself knows I have never lagged in trying to win him from evil ways.

So I was standing there talking to Mrs. Clohessey, and more people coming in by that time till the place was crowded already, the ladies' committee with their hands full in the dining room and kitchen, trying to keep the ice cream and cake going. I was not asked to help because that was all Minnie Kittredge's doing and if I set my foot inside that house in any way I am interfering, even if it is to get down on my hands and knees and scrub the floor. But I could see well enough it would run to trouble before the afternoon was out, slices of brick ice cream an inch and a half thick on those plates, the next thing would be Walter Kittredge trotting off to the drugstore and not even getting it wholesale because he'd have to rob every store in the neighborhood, Catholic, Protestant, and Jewish, and the bills coming in for the Holy Name to pay. But I stood there eating mine and never saying a word about it except to Thressa Dawes, when I noticed Mrs. John Cournane in the parlor talking to Father Cournane, and Thressa said, "See if she goes up and talks to Mrs. Clohessey; they had it hot and heavy last night, and I want to know if they've made it up."

Well, I have as much curiosity as the next one, so I went out to the parlor again. Sure enough, they were speaking, but it was stiff enough that you could have cut it with a knife. Mrs. John Cournane was looking around when I came up, and after a minute I heard her say to Mrs. Clohessey, "Where's Amy?" And Mrs. Clohessey says, "Why, didn't you know? Mal took her out to see Jack. They hadn't come back yet when we left."

That Mrs. Clohessey looks like a good-natured woman, but she isn't above getting in her little jab too, because she knew as well as anyone else how Mrs. John Cournane was going to like that, her daughter going off to see her ex. I was watching her—Mrs. John Cournane—and she colored up as red as fire.

"To see Jack?" she said. "Are you sure?" And Mrs. Clohessey said, "Of course I'm sure. Mrs. Cournane told me all about it when I came home from church this morning. Mal came to the house to get her, and he and Mrs. Cournane had another spat—"

"He's going to have worse than a spat with me when I see him," Mrs. John Cournane said. She looked like she'd be glad to have the chance that very minute. "What the hell business is it of his, taking her over there?"

In a priest's own house—those were her very words. And Mrs. Clohessey didn't even look shocked, just said, "Well, it wasn't *his* idea, Rosemary; Amy *asked* him to take her. After all, it's only natural for her to want to see Jack; he *is* her own father, and it's been years—"

"And I suppose it was *only natural* for her to want to meet his new *wife*, too," Mrs. John Cournane said. She looked mad enough to bite a penny nail in two. "I do think she might have consulted me, at least considered for a minute how *I'd* feel—"

"I don't see why you should feel any way at all about

it," Mrs. Clohessey said. "Amy's a grown *woman*, Rosemary, with children of her own; of course she's going to do
as she pleases." Then she looked up and saw somebody
coming in the door across the room, and said, "Oh, there's
Una, and Tommyo; I'll just go over and say hello."

I suppose she was glad to get away, because from all I
hear, Mrs. John Cournane is more than a match for her.
They say Mayor Willis thinks twice before he crosses her
himself. Cookie went down there once about what was it—
something about that everlasting union, two years ago it
must have been, because we were living here—and she was
as high-and-mighty as if she was the Mayor herself, "Do
you have an appointment, the Mayor can't see you till
four," and all that sort of thing, looking him up and down
till he was afraid to tell her he knew Father Cournane or
even open his mouth, do anything except sit there and wait.
"Well," I said to him, "you should have had me down
there, Cookie, because I will defy any woman like Mrs.
John Cournane to stare me down; I'm a respectable married
woman, making a good home for my husband and family,
and that's more than she can say for herself." All I can say
is, they had better not come looking for trouble with me,
any of those Cournanes, because I am not Minnie Kittredge, doesn't know or care half the time what's going on.
I know my responsibility, and there is no one, in this parish or out of it, going to tell me what to do.

So when that Mrs. McGrath came in, in a bright green
chiffon dress and garden hat, looking like she owned the
place and everything in it, I said to Laura Dennehy, she
was standing just beside me, "You come on over with me
while I speak to her, and be sure to tell her about the election this morning." Because the sooner she knows about
it, I thought, the better; she won't like it, but that's none of
my concern.

"What do you want me to say?" Laura said.

She was a little timid about it; well, what can you expect, cooped up there in that bakery all her life, selling bread and coffee cake over the counter? I said to her just last week, "Laura," I said, "you've got to make up your mind now, either Mr. Schneider or Prefect of the Young Ladies' Sodality; you can't have them both, you know, and you won't have either one if you don't roll up your sleeves and get to work." Not that it did any good; she just isn't the kind of girl to set her sights on something and go out and get it with the help of the Lord.

So she said, "What do you want me to say?" and I said, "Why, nothing, Laura; listen, don't you go making a big thing out of this. All I want you to do is just let it drop into the conversation that the ladies elected me prefect this morning."

If I'd had a minute to think, I'd have looked around for Georgiana Jaeger to do it instead, but I couldn't see her in that crowd, and Thressa Dawes was busy in the dining room with the refreshments. I took hold of Laura's arm and brought her over to the door where Mrs. McGrath was standing with her son and his wife and those two girls of theirs. Mrs. Clohessey never had gotten over there to talk to her; the way I thought, that was just an excuse to get away from Mrs. John Cournane.

She saw me coming, all right—that Mrs. McGrath, I mean. The last time I saw her was a year ago, when she and Thressa Dawes had it together about those chops, not fit for a priest's table, she said, and Thressa said, "I do what I can on what money's put into my hand," she said, "and if you're meaning to insinuate that a single red cent of the food money that's spent in this house goes into my pocket—"

That was when I just happened to have been waiting in

the kitchen to talk to Thressa and couldn't help overhearing, both of them raising their voices to each other, of course. And knowing what I do about Thressa's troubles in that direction, Father Cournane insisting on dealing at Martin's instead of the chains, though Thressa has told him time and again Jimmy Martin adds every cent of that discount he *says* he gives onto the price of the meat, naturally I came out and said what I knew was the truth about the whole business. I know my duty when there's an innocent person, my own friend, being falsely accused. And *she* had the gall—Mrs. McGrath, that is—as much as to tell me to mind my own business. That is a lesson she could learn herself, as I'd have told her if Father Cournane hadn't come in just then. She went off into the parlor with him, shut the door, but you could hear her gabbing away in there. I asked Thressa if she wanted me to stay, but she said, "No, I can take care of this." Told me later Father Cournane never opened his mouth about it to her afterward. She had to bring it up herself, because she wasn't going to stand for that kind of talk going around about her and her saying nothing, asked him point-blank if he believed what Mrs. McGrath had said, and he said, oh, she mustn't put too much emphasis on the whole thing, it was only a tempest in a teapot. "Emphasis, my foot," Thressa says to me. "I'll *emphasis* her if she comes nosing around my kitchen again."

So when I went over to her with Laura, she looked at me like she wasn't even going to say, "How do you do," to me. But I spoke up and said, "Good afternoon, Mrs. Mc-Grath," and then, of course, she had to speak too.

"You remember Laura Dennehy?" I said, because she'd met her once too, though the way she looked at her, you'd never have known it.

"Oh yes," she says, in that cool way she has—like Thressa says, trying to wipe West Haley Street off her face.

Well, West Haley Street is where she came from, and there's nothing she can do about that, even if she's written up on every society page in the country.

Laura said, "How do you do," looking scared; if there's one thing I can't stand, it's a woman who's afraid to face up to another woman because she's got more money and fancier clothes than she has herself. I've told Laura time and time again, the Lord sees the inner woman, not the outward show, and He's no respecter of persons, as the Bible says. But she is weak, and I knew right off I wouldn't get any help from her. She'd be able to tell me every stitch Mrs. McGrath *and* her daughter-in-law both had on when we'd finished talking to them, and that was all. Anything that needed saying I'd have to say myself.

So I made some remark about the reception first, just to be polite, but the answer I got would have frozen rainwater in July. Well, I says to myself, if that's the way you want it, Mrs. T. C. McGrath, it's all right with me. I've done my best to be civil, and if you won't have it that way, the fault isn't mine. And so I said it to her straight out, "I suppose you've heard about the election this morning," I says to her.

She just looked at me for a minute, like she didn't know, or didn't want to know, what I was talking about. And that seemed to wake Laura up, because she said all of a sudden, in a hurry, "Oh yes, the ladies elected Mrs. Milligan prefect this morning." And then stopped talking, the minute she'd said it, like she was frightened to death by the sound of her own voice.

But Mrs. McGrath never even looked at her, kept right on looking at me.

"Elected *you?*" she says.

"Yes," I says. "I'm the new prefect. It's a big responsibility, but with the Lord's help I'll do my best."

She didn't say anything at all for a minute. Well, she didn't have to say it; if looks could kill, I'd have dropped dead on the spot.

"I suppose I must congratulate you, Mrs. Milligan," she says finally.

"Don't bother," I says. "It's the Lord's work; I take no credit for it."

She never paid any heed to me.

"I suppose you *do* realize," she said, "the responsibility of your position? Mrs. Kittredge understood her place so well—in relation to the parish work, I mean. She deferred in every respect to Father Cournane."

Trying to teach me *my* place—well, I have worked for the church as long as she has, and if I don't have the knowledge of my responsibilities now, I will never learn it from a woman like her.

So I said to her, "Mrs. McGrath," I said, "I know my duty to Father Cournane and to this parish, and I know which of them comes first. I've had a sacred trust put in my hands, and nobody, whether they're a priest or not, is going to make me turn aside from the path."

She never colored up; she's not that kind. Those china-blue eyes of hers just got bigger and bluer, and that big ugly painted mouth of hers straightened out in a hard line.

"Mrs. Milligan—" she says, beginning.

"Or a priest's sister," I said to her. "You may have some say down in Columbiana, if all I hear is true, but this is not Columbiana, and you have no call to come in this parish and try to tell us what we ought to do here."

I said that to her, straight to her face. There are some things that are better off out in the open, and she might as well learn now as any other time that she is not dealing with Minnie Kittredge any more. Because I do not expect gratitude in this world, but I do expect to do my duty without interference from a woman like that. So she may as well know now. I am not Minnie Kittredge, that will take her words, or Father Cournane either, who will let her do what she pleases without rebuking her in the name of the Lord.

Father Kaspar came up; he could see there was something going on. It's a comfort to me in the trials before me to think there's a true friend of the right in that house.

"Why," he says, "is something wrong? Mrs. McGrath —Mrs. Milligan—we aren't going to have any disagreements marring this happy occasion?"

A true friend of the right. And she knew it, because she never said a word. She just looked at him standing there beside me, and her face went the color of batter, but she never said a word to either of us. She just turned around to her son, and "Tommyo," she says to him, "we haven't spoken to Michael yet. Do come along."

And off she goes, with her marcelled hair and her big painted mouth, as if we were dirt under her feet and she wouldn't demean herself by exchanging words with us. Well, she will find out, is all I have to say. If the Lord gives me strength, she will find out a good many things, because I know my responsibility and I know my true worth as a humble laborer in the vineyard of the Lord. And if there is any justice, so will she. I don't expect much, but I do expect that. Even in this world, I do expect that.

Shivaun

Aunt Una was talking to the lady in the black straw hat, and they both talked fast, and then Father Kaspar came up and said something to them and they stopped talking. Stephen said, "Come on. They've got ice cream and cake in the dining room."

"Can we?" Polly said. "Mother? *Mother?*"

Aunt Marian said, "Oh, Polly, for heaven's sake, don't bother me. Just run along, and do try to behave yourself."

"Where's *your* mother?" Polly said.

"She went to see somebody with Cousin Mal," I said. "She didn't come back."

"Isn't she ever coming back?" Polly said.

"Of course she is, stupid," Stephen said. "Come on, let's go and get some ice cream."

The house looked different with so many people in it. The windows were all open, but it was hot, and you could smell all the flowers and the ladies' perfume. Everybody was talking and you couldn't go anyplace without pushing in between them. Stephen made a game out of going first and we had to follow the leader. Jan didn't want to play; she stayed with Aunt Marian. Aunt Marian is not really our aunt because she is our cousin by marriage, but Mother said it would be polite for us to call her that. But I don't think she likes us to call her Aunt Marian. I don't care if she isn't my aunt because I don't like her very much either.

Stephen went roundabout through the room because we were playing follow-my-leader, and he didn't bump into anybody but I did. It was a man in a checked suit with shiny black hair that was combed over the top of his head but didn't nearly cover it all. He said, "Hold up there, soldier. Where do you think you're going?"

"Excuse me," I said. "We're playing follow-my-leader."

"Well, you picked a pretty bad place for it," he said. "Next time why don't you try to find someplace where there's a crowd?"

He was smoking a cigar and he looked like he belonged

in the house because he wasn't talking like everybody else but just standing there watching.

"I know who you are," he said to me.

"Do you?" I said. "I don't know who you are."

"You just call me Walter," he said.

"Are you a relation of mine?" I said.

"Not that I know of," he said. "Haven't you got enough of them around here today?"

"I like most of them," I said.

"I wish I could say the same for mine," he said.

Father Michael saw him talking to me, and he stopped shaking hands with people and said, "Who's that you've got over there, Walter? My young niece?"

Walter and I went over and Father Michael smiled and said, "Well, Shivaun, weren't you going to come over and say hello to me?"

He smiled at me but he didn't look happy. He didn't look happy last night either, and when we got home Aunt Dolly said to Granny Cournane, "I do pity Michael with those two awful prigs of assistants and that woman's cooking."

"Congratulations and best wishes," I said to him. "Mother said I was to say that to you."

"And very nicely said, young lady," Walter said.

"Now don't flatter her, Mr. Kittredge," Granny Cournane said. She was sitting next to Father Michael in a big black chair. "She's having her head turned enough with everybody in the family making over her," she said.

"Aah, you—you're jealous," Walter said. "You're used to being the belle of the ball yourself, Mrs. Cournane."

Granny Cournane nodded her head up and down.

"I had my day," she said. "And she'll have hers, like her mother before her. Much good it will do her, men being what they are."

"Well, we're a bad lot, sure enough," Walter said. "But we're the best on the market, so you'll just have to make do with us."

"My mother—God rest her!—used to say to me, 'If you have to have a man, Pegeen, try to get one that cleans easy,'" Granny Cournane said. "They're a dirty lot, the Lord knows, but I was lucky enough to get two of the right kind."

"The Gold-Dust Twins," Walter said to Father Michael. He said it so low that Granny Cournane didn't hear. He said, "Guaranteed sparkling and sanitary from top to toe."

Father Michael looked as if he was going to smile, but he stopped, and then a man and lady came up and he smiled in a different way.

Walter looked at me.

"I have it on reliable authority," he said, "that they're giving away ice cream and cake absolutely free in the dining room. Are you interested?"

"Yes," I said. "That's where I was going when I bumped into you."

"Well, don't let me keep you," he said. "They might run out, you know. You never can tell."

I looked for Stephen and Polly. I didn't see them because there were too many people, but I saw Aunt Dolly talking to Aunt Una, and the lady in the black hat talking to Father Kaspar. They didn't look like they were at a party, and there were some other people talking to them too, and none of them looked like they were at a party.

I went between the people and I was in the dining room, but I still couldn't see Stephen and Polly. The dining room was full of people too. The table had some big cakes on it and there were ladies cutting them and giving pieces to people. And there were other ladies going in and out of the kitchen door carrying dishes and more cakes, and they were all laughing and talking to each other. I didn't know any of them but Mrs. Dawes. She was standing at the table giving out pieces of cake and telling the other ladies what to do.

I went up to her.

"Excuse me," I said. "Did you see my brother?"

She put her hand over her heart.

"For pity's sake," she said. "You scared me out of a year's growth, child. *Don't* come sneaking up to a person's elbow like that."

"I'm sorry," I said. "Did you see my brother?"

"Well, I should say I did," she said. "He and that cousin of yours just marched out of here with four pieces of cake between them, two devil's food, two marble. They thought I didn't see them get that second piece."

A lady in a flowered dress came up and said to her, "Thressa, we're running out of cream. Shall I tell Minnie, or—?"

"Don't you do anything of the kind," Mrs. Dawes said. "She'll just send Walter out, and you know what *he*'ll do—we'll have ice cream running out of our ears here for the next three weeks. Let Francis Jaeger take care of it; after all, the Holy Name is the one that's going to be footing the bill."

The lady said something else in her ear, and they both looked at a gray-haired lady in a blue dress across the table, and Mrs. Dawes said out loud, "Then let her lump it." The lady in the flowered dress giggled and went away. Mrs. Dawes looked down at me.

"There isn't any more ice cream," she said. "You can have a piece of cake if you want it."

She put a piece of coconut cake on a plate and gave it to me. I don't like coconut cake.

"And don't go around the table and try to pick up another piece like your brother," she said.

"No, ma'am," I said. "I won't."

I asked her where Stephen was, and she said he was out in back with Polly. I went through the kitchen and out the back door. The ladies were all laughing and talking and running around with their aprons on in the kitchen. One of them smiled at me and said, "Is that one of the little Mc-Grath girls? Now isn't she a pretty little thing?" And another lady said no, and whispered something in her ear, and they both stopped smiling and looked at me.

I went out the screen door and Stephen and Polly were sitting on the back steps, eating cake.

"What happened to you?" Stephen said.

"I was talking to a man," I said. I sat down on the steps with them. "I talked to Father Michael too," I said. "You know what Mother told us. We have to congratulate him because he's twenty-five years old."

"Twenty-five years old," Stephen said. "Listen to her. That's all she knows."

"He is too," I said. "Mother told me."

"He's probably fifty years old," Stephen said. "He's been a priest twenty-five years, stupid; that's what you're trying to say."

He was being smart-aleck because of Polly. He had a piece of marble cake on his plate. I said, "Do you want to trade?"

He looked at my cake.

"All right," he said.

We changed plates. It was hot on the steps and you could hear the ladies talking and laughing in the kitchen and the whole house was full of talking and laughing. Polly had a piece of devil's food cake on her plate but she wasn't eating it. She kept crumbling it up with her fingers and then she tried to feed some of it to the ants on the sidewalk but they ran away. She had her head down almost between her knees, watching them. All of a sudden she said, "My father and mother had a big fight before we came here."

"That's nothing," Stephen said.

"Do your father and mother ever fight?" Polly said.

"Not much," I said. "Do they, Stephen?"

"Not much," Stephen said.

"I wish mine didn't," Polly said.

She tried to push some of the ants over to the cake but they wouldn't go. Then she straightened up. Her face looked red.

"My father makes a lot of money," she said. She looked at us. "Does yours?"

"I don't know," I said.

Stephen didn't say anything.

"I'll bet he doesn't," Polly said. "I heard my mother and father talking. Your mother has to work."

"She likes to work," I said. "She writes things in the newspaper. She likes it."

"I'll bet she has to do it because your father doesn't make any money," Polly said. Her face looked redder and she looked like she was going to cry, but she was being mean and so I didn't care. "My mother says maybe your mother's going to leave your father," she said. "She says that's why she came here and brought you with her. You're not going back."

I looked at Stephen and Stephen got red too and said, "Your mother doesn't know what she's talking about. I'll bet she doesn't even know my father."

"She knows your mother," Polly said. She got up off

the steps and stood there looking at us. "She knows all about her," she said. "And she says maybe she's never going back."

Stephen pushed her and she hit him and a lady came to the screen door and said, "Children! Children! If you can't play like little ladies and gentlemen back here, I'm going to have to tell your parents." Stephen and Polly were fighting and the lady changed her voice and opened the door and said, "Now you stop that right now. Do you hear me? The very idea."

Stephen stopped and then Polly stopped. Her hair ribbon fell off and she picked it up and tied it back on and then she looked down at the ants that were all eating the cake now and stepped on them as hard as she could. She stepped on all of them she could find.

"Come on," Stephen said to me. "We don't have to stay out here."

We went on in the kitchen again. The lady who'd talked to us out the door said, "My, my, my!" and clicked her tongue at us, but we didn't pay any attention to her.

"What are we going to do now?" I asked Stephen.

"I'm going to see if Mother's come yet," he said. "I'm going to ask her myself. I'll bet we are going back."

"I'll bet we are too," I said.

I followed him through the dining room. Mrs. Dawes was talking to the gray-haired lady in the blue dress, the one she and the other lady had looked at when they'd said, "Then let her lump it." They didn't look like they were at a party either. I wasn't having a very good time and I wished Mother would come and take us back to Granny Cournane's.

We went into the front room. When we went in everybody was talking and laughing so it almost hurt your ears, but then all of a sudden the noise stopped and everybody looked at the door and I looked too. There was a man coming in. He looked just like everybody else, but all the people were looking at him. He was a kind of old man, older than Mother. Aunt Dolly looked at him too and then she went over to him and said, "Jack—Jack—why, just imagine this. Why, Jack, I didn't *know* you were coming—"

He looked at her and smiled a little and patted her arm, and then he looked around at all the people and they stopped watching all of a sudden and started to talk again. And Walter went over and shook hands with him and said, "Well, Mr. Cournane, this is just fine and dandy; I'm glad to see you here today."

"Who is that?" I said to Stephen. "He called him Mr. Cournane. Is he a relation too?"

"He's Mother's father," Stephen said. "Didn't you hear Aunt Dolly call him Jack? That's what Cousin Mal called him yesterday."

"He doesn't look like a gangster," I said. "He looks just like anybody else—doesn't he?"

"So do gangsters," Stephen said. "You can't tell just by looking. You'd have to see his gun."

Father Michael came over and said, "Well, Jack." I thought he would say something else, but he didn't. He and the man stood there looking at each other. Aunt Dolly was there, and she kept talking, and looking over her shoulder, and I looked where she was looking and there was Aunt Rosemary. She was talking to Aunt Una, only they were both talking at the same time, and then Aunt Una tried to take hold of Aunt Rosemary's arm but Aunt Rosemary walked away and walked over to where Father Michael and the man were standing. The people all stood aside for her to pass. Everybody was watching but they were trying to act as if they weren't.

Aunt Rosemary walked up and said, "Hello, Jack," and the man turned around and said, "Rosemary."

"Well, don't look so surprised, for heaven's sake," Aunt Rosemary said. "You surely knew I'd be here today." Then Father Michael said, "Rosemary," too, but Aunt Rosemary kept right on talking. "Why, Jack, you're looking splendid," she said to the man. "I've been hearing reports—somehow they didn't do you justice."

She was smiling but the man didn't smile, and he said something to her in a low voice that I couldn't hear. Aunt Rosemary kept right on talking.

"You've seen Amy, I hear," she said. "That must have been a touching reunion. She's looking well, don't you think? A little strained, of course, but then under the circumstances—"

Father Michael said, low, "Rosemary, if you don't mind, I think Jack would like to talk to me in private—"

"Of course I don't mind," Aunt Rosemary said. Her voice sounded as if she was having a good time at a party, but her face didn't look like it. "After all, who am I to mind?" she said. "Go right ahead; don't pay any attention to me." Her eyes went all around the room in jerks, as if she was trying to look at everybody in it at one time, and then she saw Stephen and me standing there and she came over fast and grabbed both of us by the arm.

"Oh, but wait," she said. "You mustn't go before you've met these kids. These are Amy's kids, Jack—your grandchildren. Don't you at least want to say hello to them?"

She pushed us over in front of the man. He looked down at us and I got behind Stephen and the man said to me, "You aren't afraid of me, are you? Shivaun. Isn't that your name?"

"Yes," I said.

He looked a little like he was going to cry, only men don't cry. He put his hands out and I went over and he lifted me up and kissed me. He smelled like the whisky in the cut-glass bottle that is on the sideboard at home and when people come at night Daddy pours some out for them. I didn't know why but all of a sudden I liked him a lot and I kissed him back. He didn't put me down for a minute.

"Shivaun," he said. He looked at Father Michael. "She looks like Champ," he said. "At that age—those same skinny little arms and legs—"

"And this young man," Father Michael said, "looks like you, Jack."

He put his hand on Stephen's shoulder to bring him closer but Stephen just stood there. The man put me down and looked at Stephen and said, "Well, thank God, I can't see it. I hope he takes after his own father instead. A finer man never wore shoe leather."

He wanted to shake hands with Stephen, but Stephen backed away and Aunt Rosemary laughed.

"He's spoiling your little scene, isn't he, Jack?" she said. "Stephen, don't be a naughty boy, now; shake hands with your grandfather. You're ruining everything."

Stephen just backed away. He is like that sometimes. Mother says, "Stephen, sometimes I can't do a thing with you," but he doesn't care. He backed away and then he ran out to the dining room and pushed open the kitchen door and almost ran into a lady with some dishes in her hand and ran into the kitchen.

"Oh, dear," Aunt Rosemary said. "How unfortunate for you, Jack. Just when you were doing so splendidly, too."

Everybody was watching and Father Michael said, "Come on, Jack, we'll go upstairs," but Aunt Rosemary wouldn't stop talking. She said, "By the way, Jack, you really shouldn't have come alone, you know. We've all been dying of curiosity; we hear she's younger than Amy but not *quite* so young as Shivaun—"

Father Michael took my grandfather's arm and the people stood aside and they walked out to the hall together. My grandfather doesn't look like a gangster; I don't care what Stephen says. And Aunt Rosemary said, "Well, I like that. I *like* that." Her face was all red and Aunt Una came up and said to her, "Rosemary, for heaven's sake, try to get hold of yourself." Aunt Una didn't look mad because she is too polite, but you could tell she was anyway, and Aunt Rosemary looked like she was going to slap her. But she didn't. She just looked around at everybody watching, and then she said something low to Aunt Una and her voice was shaking. It sounded like, "Damn you. Damn all you damned Cournanes." Then she walked out of the room.

Aunt Marian came up and she and Aunt Dolly started to talk to Aunt Una. They all smiled and tried to act as if everything was all right, but I felt like crying. None of them paid any attention to me. I stood there and wondered where Stephen was and then Walter came up and looked at me standing there.

"Shivaun Gilman," he said to me. "You look to me like a little girl who needs another piece of cake. What do you say we go back to the dining room and see what we can wheedle out of Mrs. Dawes?"

He took my hand and we went in the dining room. I like Walter. And I like my grandfather; I don't care what anybody says. And when he picked me up he kissed me and said I looked just like Champ.

A lady in the dining room gave Walter and me each a piece of devil's food cake and Walter asked her if she made it and she said, "What was that going on out there?" Walter looked at me and said, "Laura, I don't know a thing." We ate the cake. It was good cake. Walter laughed and talked to me and the ladies all the while.

Father Michael Cournane

He walked into the room before me and, as if he had flung the whole terrible emotion of the moment like a handful of charged dust into the air, the summer atmosphere, priestly, quiet, in the room above the gabble of voices below seemed to become suddenly too heavy to breathe. We stood there, our lungs laboring at it, avoiding each other's eyes. Then he said, "Mike."

"Yes."

"I'm sorry," he said. If I could only believe him, simply, cleanly, I thought, as I believed him when we were children because he would not lie to me. To anyone else but not to me. "I'm sorry," he said. "I didn't realize—today —all those people. I simply thought, 'I've got to see Mike—'"

"Yes," I said. "Sit down."

He sat in the chair beside the bed, the one that is never used because when that door is shut it is shut on them all and there is no one. He looked strange in that room. He brought life into it, warm, rotting life. I looked at his fine marred profile and thought that what he was showing me in it was a map of life. The black secret nights, the days full of sad revelry, and all they had left him was a network of lines tracing the corners of the mouth, the sag of jowls, underlining the pouches beneath the eyes. This is Jack, I thought, the brightest, the wildest, the most brilliant of us all. He sat in the chair beside the bed and wept.

I sat too, slowly, in the well-worn leather of the chair

at the desk. Now, I told myself. He is coming to you, like
a thousand others, for wisdom. To a bankrupt priest, a
most unsuccessful shepherd of a dissatisfied flock. And
you—oh, you will give him words, as you have given them
to all the others, fine, dead, high-sounding words for a man
who is already dead himself, who walks in and out of his
grave daily, remembering, forgetting. He will ask you for
bread and you will give him a stone. Because you do not
know the answers any more, either, because you are as dead
inside as he. Because you have forgotten how to be alive.

He wiped his eyes with his handkerchief, furtively,
ashamed of his tears, and I looked away so I would not seem
to notice.

"I'm sorry," he said again.

"It's all right."

"Walking in on you like this, in the middle of something like this. I just forgot, I didn't realize—"

"It doesn't matter." I could look at him now, across
the quiet, priestly room. "I'm glad to see you any time,
Jack," I said. "You know that. I only wish that you'd come
oftener."

It is worse than useless for us to talk, I thought. We
have nothing to give each other but the dry ashes of our own
despair, and so we pretend, we say the conventional words
to each other, realizing all the while that we are two figures
mouthing phrases on an empty stage before an audience of
two—ourselves.

"You must think I've gone balmy," Jack said. He was
trying to smile now, a flash of the old lightness in his voice.
"But, Mike"—then he shook his head, and the light, fading
quickly, died out of his face—"Mike, I tell you, I don't
know when anything's ever hit me like this—"

"Like this?"

"Like Amy's coming—like seeing her, those kids. My

God, Mike, it came over me, I realized, 'I'm her father, *her father;* how can I sit here and let her see me like this?' "

He sat there, brooding, as wonder-struck by his own paternity as if now, for the first time in how many years since his seed had struck home in Rosemary's waiting womb, he had become aware of a relationship that should have been by this day as much a part of his identity as his own name. Like myself, I thought, that is what it is, because I too have a piece of identity that I cannot fathom, Michael Cournane as Father Michael Cournane, the shock coming each time I hear the title, after all these years. I am not your father; I am nobody's father, nobody's wisdom, nobody's infallible guide; we are children together in the dark.

Jack said, "When I saw her standing there this morning, all I could think was, 'What kind of man *am* I, to bring her here to something like this? What kind of man—?' "

He struck the chair arm with a loosely clenched fist. In the spinning sunlight in which he sat I could see, as if half obscured in the golden radiance, my own father, making that same gesture half a century before. He was not Jack because Jack is himself, the mayor, the lawyer, the grand success whom Patrick Cournane admired and distrusted and certainly never understood, but Patrick Cournane too was a living reality in that room because we both carried him with us wherever we went. Into the confessional and into the brothel. I saw his face, stern, collected, aghast at the company we had brought him into, like a veronica hung above Jack's face on the wall. As he sees it above mine, I thought. Father. Brother. There are no more terrible words in the language.

I said to Jack, "I know. I know how you feel." And he looked at me, strongly shaking his head.

"Not you, Mike. No," he said. "You're the only one of

us who's done anything really decent with his life. You're
the only one of us without regrets. You don't know what
it's like to sit where I sit and look back at one damned,
foolish, pitiful act of weakness after another, all of them—
or most of them, anyway—your own fault—"

He was a little drunk. You would hardly have realized
it if you had not known him as well as I do, or if you were
not a woman used to suspicion, used to the moment's
shrewd inspection of an erring mate. The recollection of
Mrs. Milligan's pale, outraged face floated back to me on
the faint flurry and hum of voices from below, no laughter
now, only the concentrated buzz of fruity gossip. A dull
afternoon it might have been for them if the pastor's
brother hadn't walked in to enliven it. But he is used to an
audience, I thought, so he will not mind. He will not mind
when they stare at him as he leaves as they stared at him
when he came. I have seen him stand in a courtroom, gaily
facing down a hostile crowd, drawing them, turning them
over in the palm of his hand. Then, turning to his neighbor:
"Well, Joe—or Paul, or Jim—how did it go? No tar and
feathers for me today."

"I had to come here this afternoon, Mike," he said.
He was so terribly in earnest that in spite of myself I was
attentive to what he was saying. "Listen," he said. "Listen,
Mike, is it ever too late? I mean—damn it, it's all in the
Gospels, the prodigal son, the lost sheep—damn it, you
know what I mean—"

I knew what he meant. Why is it that it is always the
most brilliant, the most sophisticated, who come to you in
their crucial moments with the naïveté of a child, as if they
were actors who had stepped out of their well-conned roles
and returned to their own fumbling devices of conversation?
I did not know what to say to him: "No, Jack, it is never too
late; God forgives—only will you forgive, will your body

forgive, forgetting all its old habits, old desires? It is not as charitable as God; after all, it has been a long time and it remembers in the very lines of your face, the sag of an eye pouch—"

But instead I said, "No." I didn't have to make the words up because I had said them so often. "No, it's never too late, Jack. You know that."

He sat there; I doubted if he even heard me. He was wrung in some terrific inner struggle of his own, the mortal conflict of everything he had become with everything he would have liked to be. He looked at me, his eyes unseeing.

"I tell you, Mike," he said, "I tell you, when I saw her standing there—You don't realize, you go on from one day to the next—"

He raised the fierce unseeing eyes to me. If only I had not seen it so often, I thought, if only I had not sat patiently through so many scenes of sad repentance, the drunkard, the adulterer, the petty thief, the embezzler of family funds, all weeping, all swearing by their God to give up their fault, all—or almost all—creeping back in a day, a month, a year, to the same dirty round of human infirmities. I did not want it to be Jack sitting there in that place. I wanted him to not-be what he was by some single fierce eagle-sweep of wings that would beat him upward into the sun of what he had been.

"Listen," he said to me. "Listen, Mike. I've made up my mind."

"Yes?" I said.

"To leave her," he said. "Poor kid, it's not her fault— but she'll be better off. You were right about that, you know; you always are."

"Leave her?" I said.

"Rae," he said. "My God, I don't know what I was thinking of—yes, I do. She put it in a nutshell for me only this morning."

I saw her only once, a proud low-bred passionate Assyrian face. "Don't you come here trying to interfere," she said, "with your Roman collar." A duty call, paid because of that same Roman collar.

"You see, Mike," he said, with a wretched attempt at a smile, "I'm not a high-class character, like you; I never have been. All day today I've been seeing myself as I haven't seen anything for years—the boy who married Rosemary because it was the easiest way to satisfy everybody concerned, the lawyer who went into politics because he liked being the center of attention and the hell with how he got there, the careless father, the unfaithful husband, the tired romancer of young girls—"

"Jack," I said. "Shut up. Shut up. Do I have to shut you up myself?" He looked at me, surprised by my vehemence. "I'm not your confessor," I said then, more quietly. "I'm your brother. I was that first, before I was a priest."

I am tired, that is it, I thought, too tired to go through it all again. So I said it to him, brutally, to put an end to it now, "You're a little drunk, Jack. This is going to wear off." And I saw his head jerk back a little and then steady, his eyes looking at me again.

"No," he said. "No, Mike, you're wrong. This isn't going to wear off."

Saying it to me steadily, eye to eye, the steel of purpose under the debauched sagging flesh, the small flame of hope keenly in the eyes. And I wanted to say it, too: "Jack, Jack, do you know what you just did? You made me realize, acknowledge purpose and hope, only for this moment but if for one moment why not for two, three, a year, a lifetime—?"

But all I said was, "All right. We'll see. You show me."

It was gone already but I knew it had been there. I did not even have to believe him to know it had been there, and something lifted off me, some stone of despair. How could I sit there disbelieving and still so peacefully delivered from doubt? I disbelieved him now as I had before, but if I could believe for one moment— It was like believing in God, because if you could say, "I believed for one instant," He could never disown you; He would have to be because of that instant. You would create Him if He had not already created you. So I had created the Jack I once knew out of a moment of belief, and even if he never— He would not. I knew that. But even if he never—

You could hear them talking downstairs, the tight lowered hum, and then something else, a stir of arrival in the hall. We sat there peacefully, talking, and after a little someone mounted the stairs and tapped discreetly at the door.

Walter Kittredge

When I saw them putting their heads together with that look on their faces, I said to myself, "Well, brother, we are in for it now." That bunch of hens had been spoiling for something like this ever since they'd walked in the door, and they weren't going to let this chance go by; you could bet your bottom dollar on that. I gave Cookie Milligan the high-sign while I was fixing the little Gilman girl up with a piece of cake, and when he came over I said to him, "Cookie," I said, "I guess you saw that little act?"

"Didn't I?" he says. "I had both my ears open and my eyes dropping out of my head. Why did he come here, if that's a fair question?"

"I wouldn't know that," I said. "But he should have charged admission; that's one thing sure."

"The wife slammed out of here like a bolt of lightning," Cookie said. He looked almost as uneasy as if he'd been struck by one himself, and yet there was a light in his eye. It can get pretty dull for a man, standing around a whole afternoon drinking coffee and engaging in light conversation about Holy Orders with the women, and there comes a point where any form of excitement is gratefully received. "She's a looker," Cookie said, "for a woman her age, but still I can't say I blame His Honor the Mayor. If she'd had her way just now, she'd have had him where the collector had the butterfly—neatly pinned, through and through, for any and all to admire."

"Yes," I said. "I know her of old. He had a merciful deliverance the day she walked out on him—or vice versa."

"It was very much vice versa, the way I hear it," Cookie said.

"That may be," I said, thinking that if Cookie had a little more of what separates the men from the boys, he'd do the same. He's got a bitch of his own I'd match with Mrs. John Cournane any day.

But it's a ticklish business to try to talk to a man about his wife. All I wanted to say to Cookie was, "Tell that *Frau* of yours to hold her horses; she'll be in the saddle soon enough without trying any shenanigans here today." But you know how it is; you have to go all the way around Robin Hood's barn with a thing like that or the next thing you know you've got somebody down on you for life. I'm a peaceful man, and I'm in business, so I went about it the easy way.

Well, to make a short story long, I started by hinting around at that little run-in his wife had had with Mrs. Mc-Grath a bit earlier in the afternoon. "After all," I says, "it's Father Cournane's anniversary, and if he recruits a whole regiment of certified red devils out of that family of his and brings them in here this afternoon, it's up to us to make them welcome, at least until the party's over."

He looked at me kind of funny.

"Walter," he says to me, "you're right. But if you mean Mame—"

"Not only her," I says. "Look at them all over there by the door, now—Thressa Dawes, and Georgiana Jaeger, and the three Dennehys, God bless their floury little souls—"

He just stood there shaking his head and looking around at them over his shoulder.

"Walter," he says, "I know what you mean. But I'd sooner walk into a den of lions than try to crash that hen party with some well-meant advice. Get Jimmy Heffernan; he's used to handing out platitudes in a properly hushed voice."

"He ain't married to one of them," I says, and Cookie looks at me and says, "Well, that's another advantage he has; he won't have to take it to bed with him." And backed out of there fast. I guess I should have known better than to expect it of him. He's a great friend of mine, Cookie is, but I'd be the last man to claim that he's a hero.

So the next one I thought of was Father Kaspar. It's my private opinion somebody slipped up somewhere the day they let him inside the seminary gates, but half the women in the parish think he's first cousin to an archangel —Mame Milligan among them—so I thought if I could put a bug in his ear it might do some good. He was standing out in the parlor next to old Mrs. Cournane's chair, where Father Cournane had been standing himself to greet all the company—trust him to grab the steering wheel if you ever let go of it for one split second. But before I could get over to him, there was some kind of commotion in the hall, and the next thing I knew there was Monsignor Damminger, the Cardinal's secretary, walking into the room.

Well, you'd have thought it was His Holiness the Pope himself to see those women fluttering about. He's a big brute of a fellow, has it in the upper story, I suppose, or the Cardinal wouldn't have him around, but he wouldn't look out of the way stripped to his pelt in a prize ring. Of course he looked around, first thing, for Father Cournane, and of course there was no Father Cournane on view. Father Kaspar was over there beside him like a shot out of a gun, and Monsignor Hawk not far behind, and you could see the two of them making with the explanations. I turned around and saw Francis Jaeger standing there beside me, swallowing once or twice and his eyes gleaming like a pair of two-hundred-dollar diamonds behind his glasses, like he was just rehearsing his speech of welcome before he went over too.

"Somebody'd better go up and tell the reverend Father he's got company," I said to him. "I mean A-Number-One company—"

Francis started out of his trance.

"Why, yes, Walter," he said. "Why, yes. You're absolutely right. I'll get Mrs. Dawes."

She was right at his elbow; he didn't have to go far. Trust her not to miss anything; I'll bet if you could make a phonograph record of that brain of hers, you'd find you had every word of gossip spoken in that house this afternoon engraved there and ready to come blaring out the minute anybody took the trouble to wind her up. Why Father Cournane puts up with her is more than I know, but of course she'd turn the whole parish upside down if he ever tried to get rid of her; it would be like trying to fire your grandmother.

Anyway, there she was, right at Francis's elbow—but did she go on up, like a decent Christian soul, and warn Father Cournane he had a bigwig in his parlor and he'd better come down? Not Thressa: that was much too simple for her. She says to Francis, as soon as he slipped the word in her ear, "Yes, I'll go right up, but first—now listen here, Frank, let me ask you this—" And then there was a buzz of whispering in his ear. I couldn't catch what it was, but Francis looked more serious than ever behind those owl eyes of his.

"Maybe we'd better talk to Father Kaspar," he says, looking across the room at the reverend Father uncertainly.

"Somebody ought to tell him," Thressa says. She didn't look uncertain at all, but then if Thressa ever is uncertain about anything, I wish they'd sell me a ticket so I could have a front-row seat to watch it. "It'd be a disgrace," she says. "What would the Cardinal think?"

"About what?" I says. If you don't take the bull by the horns, you'll never get anywhere with that lady.

"About the pastor's brother coming to his twenty-fifth anniversary celebration drunk," she says. "Now don't tell me you didn't see—"

"Thressa, they ought to have you on the police force," I said. "I wonder how they ever do without you."

She tossed up her head.

"Now listen here, Walter," she says, "I don't want to hear any of your old jokes. This is a serious business. I'm going to get Father Kaspar."

So she sails off across the room—the Cournane women had moved in on Monsignor Damminger by that time, so she could get Father Kaspar away without much trouble—and I said to Francis, "What in the name of the twelve Apostles has that woman got on the brain now?"

Francis looked at me with his owl eyes.

"Walter," he says, "she's right; this is serious. What

kind of an impression is it going to make on Monsignor Damminger if Mr. Cournane comes down here in that condition?"

"So?" I says.

"So somebody ought to tell Father Cournane," Francis says. He had the grace to look uncomfortable about it; I'll say that for him, anyway. "His brother could stay upstairs till Monsignor Damminger leaves," he says, "or— or—"

"He could climb out the back window, too," I says. "Father Cournane would like telling him to do that."

Well, that is human nature, I suppose, and there's no use being upset about it, but if everybody would mind their own business once in a while it certainly would be a nice change for all concerned. There were three or four people in that room, though, that didn't have the same idea, because when Thressa got back she not only had Father Kaspar with her, she had Mrs. Milligan and the Dennehys too. The old man and his wife, that is. Mrs. Dennehy is one of these little pious women that lets her old man do all the talking, so I suppose they let her come along just as an audience. Anyway, the five of them got their heads together with Francis, and I was near giving them all the slip and going upstairs myself to tell Father Cournane to come down and bring his brother with him, the hell with all of them, only Min came over about that time and said to me, "Walter, don't you get mixed up in this."

"What do *you* know about it?" I says. "Did they broadcast the whole thing over the radio?" And she says, "No, but I was standing right there when Thressa Dawes spoke to Mrs. Milligan. They want Father Kaspar to go up and tell Father Cournane not to have his brother come down here till Monsignor Damminger's gone. And you're not going to get mixed up in it, Walter. All you'll do is cause more hard feelings."

Minnie's a great one for peace; it's been one of the blessings of my married life, but there are times when I wish she had more of the spirit of the Gael.

Anyway, I says to her, "Well," I says, "they'd better make up their minds to do something, is all I have to say, or the party will be over before they start. That man of the Cardinal's has a look on his face like the mourner who went to the funeral and found the corpse hadn't bothered to show up."

She said, "Sh-h-h." Minnie has the reputation for being a little deaf, but I think myself it's because she found out a good while ago that what you don't hear can't cause any battles; she does pretty well when she puts her mind to it. She was doing that now, listening to Thressa Dawes and Mrs. Milligan jawing away with all the triumph of women who've really pinned one on you and are aching to make a public example of you. And there was Francis Jaeger saying, "Yes, exactly—exactly," and Father Kaspar trying to look judicial about it all even when that little moist underlip of his was glistening like a kitten's that's just tasted cream. He'd have liked nothing better than to go pussyfooting up there and give Father Cournane a knock like that, only he's never the one to take any chances, and I suppose he was weighing the consequences. There wasn't any doubt in my mind, though, how it was going to come out. With Mame Milligan and Leonard Dennehy and Francis Jaeger squarely behind him, there wasn't much he could lose, and after a few minutes he said all right, he'd go up, it was a most unpleasant mission but he could see it was necessary. And off he goes, looking like the executioner when they bring on his Number One enemy and tell him it's his sad duty to chop off his head.

Well, I stood there and waited, and that posse of women stood there and waited too, watching the door to the hall so they'd be sure not to miss the minute when

Father Cournane walked in. Myself, I didn't want to see it; I like Father Cournane, and the thought of that gang of human hyenas enjoying themselves over his carcass didn't appeal to me so much I didn't want to miss the sight. I turned around instead and pretended to be interested in an engraving of the martyrdom of St. Peter on the wall, and then Min grabbed my arm and said, "Walter—" and I looked around and there was Father Cournane coming into the room with John Cournane big as life beside him, and Father Kaspar following along behind, as red-faced as if he was practicing up for a case of sunstroke. There was one gasp out of the females, but I didn't wait to hear their remarks; I wanted to get over where I could have a ringside seat for the main show.

Well, I got there just in time to hear Father Cournane welcoming the Cardinal's man as calm and serene as if he entertained the Cardinal himself in his front parlor every day of the week. Monsignor Damminger, naturally, didn't know what this was all about, but there was something about the petrified way everybody was watching that must have given him an idea all was not as it should be, because he stammered a bit over the little speech he made to Father Cournane about being the bearer of the Cardinal's felicitations. Father Cournane just stood there with his head a little bent, listening to him like there wasn't another soul in the room but the two of them. And when he'd finished, he—Father Cournane, that is—thanked him and then said, in that same calm voice, "By the way, I don't believe you know my brother. John, this is Monsignor Damminger—"

That was about the time Father Kaspar seemed to get over whatever kind of shock he'd had upstairs enough to push his way into the conversation. I don't know what he thought he was doing, except in the state he was in all he could think of was that whole roomful of people was watching him and waiting for him to do something, and so he had to do it. He kind of babbled something about refreshments, and grabbed John Cournane's arm, and then Father Cournane turned around and said something to him. I can't say what it was, because he said it so low I couldn't hear it, but if Father Kaspar'd been red before I don't know what shade to say it was he turned now. He dropped John Cournane's arm like he'd been scalded, and backed away, and barged straight into Lizzie Clemens's plate of cake, which she'd been holding a bit neglectful because, like everybody else, she was straining her ears to hear what was going on. The blessed cake plumped down on the floor like a shot of lead, some woman's Sunday-best chocolate frosting all over the parlor carpet; you could hear Thressa Dawes screech from one end of the house to the other. I almost felt sorry for the poor man, with Lizzie and Thressa matching insults inside a split second over whose fault it was, and him right in the middle of it. He actually got down on his knees to try to help Thressa pick the cake up, and the sight of the two of them, Thressa all gussied up in her best corset so she could hardly bend at the waist, and him scrambling around in chocolate cake like a choirboy, struck me so rich that I had to turn out into the hall so they wouldn't see my face.

Well, it just goes to show that you never can tell about people. I've been watching Father Kaspar taking over this parish for the past four years, and Father Cournane not doing a single thing about it except looking a little quieter and grimmer every year, and then, all of a sudden—wham! I'm only sorry I missed Mame Milligan's face when her favorite reverend Father was scrambling around with the chocolate cake; that's one part of the performance I'd like to have seen.

When I went back to the parlor again, there were

Father Cournane and his brother engaging in light chitchat with the Cardinal's man like they were all a set of prize scholars at a Sunday school. As a matter of fact, it was John Cournane who was doing most of the talking; oh, you could tell he was a bit more elevated than he'd ever have gotten on Thressa Dawes's coffee, but he's one of those Irishmen that's only improved with a drink or two, and even the Monsignor looked like he was enjoying the conversation. I said to Cookie Milligan, who was standing close enough to hear, "What are they talking about?"—and Cookie says, like he didn't quite believe it himself, "Enclicklicals."

"What?" I says.

"Enclicklicals," he says. "You know—those things the Holy Father sends out—"

"Encyclicals," I says. "Now what in the name of all the saints would John Cournane know about encyclicals?"

"He knows a hell of a lot more than I do, anyway," Cookie says, with a look of reverence on his face.

Cookie's a drinking man himself, and he has a natural respect for anybody who can walk into a situation like that with a snootful and carry it off like he'd never associated with anybody under the rank of Monsignor in his life. He wasn't left to his admiration very long, though, because his better half came up just then with a full head of steam on and grabbed his arm and said, "Cookie, we're leaving. Right *now*. Come on."

"What's the matter, Mame?" I says, and she gave me a look like the better class of martyrs must have put on just before they burned them at the stake.

"Walter," she says, "you can stay here and watch this disgraceful exhibition if you want to, but Cookie and I are going home. Did you hear what *he* said to Father Kaspar?"

"No," I said. "I didn't. But I'm willing to listen if you'd like to tell me."

"I wouldn't repeat it," she says. "Come on, Cookie."

And off she prances, in that black coal-scuttle hat of hers, with poor old Cookie following behind like a dog on a leash. That's the trouble with women; they get one man well-trained like that, and they think it's their duty to try to do the same with everything else in trousers they come across. But I think that sweet lady has a job cut out for her with Father Cournane; one swallow doesn't make a summer, but he's made a start in the right direction, and there's no telling how far he'll go now. Father Kaspar, for instance, never opened his mouth the rest of the afternoon except to say yes or no when somebody asked him a question; it was Thressa Dawes who had to beat the drums at the indignation meeting she and Leonard Dennehy and the Jaegers were having over in a corner by themselves. He's a prudent man, is Father Kaspar, and if he sees the big guns moving to the other side, it won't be long till you'll find him there himself, singing hymns louder than anybody, like he'd never been anywhere else in his life.

Like I say, you never know about people. And maybe I have got too big a hope for Father Cournane, but it was a grand sight anyway while it lasted. He'll have that to remember the rest of his life—Kaspar and the chocolate cake, and John Cournane discussing encyclicals with the Cardinal's man like the two of them were a pair of delegates to the Council of Trent.

What I'd really like to hear, though, is that Monsignor's report on the whole business to the Cardinal. Did he smell for himself that John Cournane was drunk, or was he too dazzled-blind by that show he was looking at to walk out of there with a true view of the situation to report back to the powers-that-be?

Now that is one thing I would certainly like to know.

June 12, 1938

AFTERNOON– EVENING

Mal

When we left Adams Street it was after two and I said, "Do you want to stop somewhere and get some lunch?"

"Looking like this?" she said.

She'd been crying, but it didn't show much. Only every time she tried to talk her voice would start to shake and then her shoulders would shake too because she was trying not to cry again. I could have taken Jack Cournane and laid him out cold. Because I've known Jack a long time, and if there's one thing I know for sure it's that he's never going to get off the bottle. He's fifty-six years old, for

God's sake; even St. Augustine wouldn't have made it if he'd waited that long. There's a time when you can do it, and you know it; you know you can say yes or no to yourself and make it stick. But when you're like Jack you're just playing around with it. You're at stage center and you're having one hell of a great time keeping the audience on the edge of their seats, but you know that when the curtain goes down you're going to be right back where you started from. I knew Jack when he was the greatest man in this big cold city, and I'd do as much for him as I would for a brother or a father, if I had one, but I can't look at what he's doing to Champ and not see red.

So we drove right on back to West Haley Street. I tried to talk to her, but it wasn't any use; all she would say was— "Mal, don't, please don't"—just sitting there with that look on her face. I don't know what in hell she expected. Maybe that the last eleven years were just going to never be and everything would be back the way it was that last year she was at Ste. Marie's, with Jack still mayor and her a kid who hadn't found out yet what the excitement was all about. She knew better than that. Champ's a smart girl, and she's been around, and she knows as well as I do about the little hands on the clock.

I stopped the car in front of the house. The windows were all closed and it looked deserted, and I could feel my heart beginning to go all of a sudden like when you're runing a hundred-yard dash and you're thirty-two years old and you know if you don't hit that little white tape now you're never going to have the chance again.

"I'll go in with you," I said. And tried to make it casual. But she knew it wasn't casual. She turned those big steady gray eyes of hers right on me and looked at me for a minute. And then she said it, very slow and grave, as if she were telling me something I didn't know.

"I think they're all gone," she said. "I don't think there's anybody home."

"I don't think there is, either," I agreed.

"Well, then—" she said. And waited.

"Well, then," I said, "I'll come in anyway. Look, you're an old married woman, aren't you? Are all the old married women this careful in California?"

"Oh, Mal—" she said. "Oh, Mal, don't—not now—"

She didn't even look at me when she said it. The way the Bible puts it, there is a season for everything, and a time for every purpose under heaven, and it was pretty obvious that in her book this wasn't the time or the season for what I was trying to lead up to. I should have known that, and maybe I did know it, but I still didn't wait. I was in the middle of that hundred-yard dash, and my heart was going sixty to the dozen, and I couldn't stop any more than you can stop a runner, once you've fired that pistol, with anything short of earthquake or murder. I was bound to say what I had to say.

"Let me come in a minute," I said. "Just let me come in and talk to you."

She shook her head, but she didn't say anything. That is, I told myself, she didn't say no. I sat there, looking out, through the haze of city Sunday-afternoon heat, at that old house where I had lived for almost a dozen years way back when I was a kid in knee pants and had hated its pious lace-curtained respectability the way I've never hated any other place on God's green earth since, and I had a crazy idea. I had a crazy idea that I was going to be happier now than I had ever been in my life, and that it was going to be right there in that house. Because she hadn't said no. She had shaken her head, but there had been doubt and distraction in the gesture, so I looked at the house and thought, This is it. And I thought, By God, if I'd known, I'd have loved that house instead of hating it, I'd have loved every mangy brown wall, every moldy lace curtain, every stick of piously preserved furniture that stood inside it.

I looked back over at her again.

"We can't sit here all afternoon, you know," I said. "This is a respectable neighborhood, and it frowns on mixed parking in broad daylight."

"Oh, Mal—" she said. She tried to smile a little, but it didn't come off. "Don't try to make a joke of it," she said. "I feel so awful—and so happy—"

"It isn't funny to me, either," I said. "Not any of it. Especially what I've just seen over on Adams Street. And if you're trying to tell me that that's what's made you happy—"

"That's part of it," she said. "That's a big, wonderful part of it. Oh, Mal, don't you see?"

"All I saw was a first-class act," I said. "It was a beauty, all right, but it was still an act."

I shouldn't have said it. Women are that way, and she was a woman, sure enough, no matter how much she knew now about getting a job, and keeping it, and seeing that there was enough money in the house on the first of the month to make sure the bill collectors weren't going to walk off with the furniture or the car, and coping with the general bastardy of a cold hard world. She still believed what she wanted to believe. And you can't tell them, you can't prove to them that black is not going to be white just because if it isn't their world is going to come to an end. So I didn't say any more. I just sat there and watched her frown and shake her head and say, "Oh, Mal, you know that isn't so."

"All right," I said. "I know it isn't so. Now can we talk about us?"

"He can do it if he wants to," she said. "He can do anything; you know how he is."

"How he used to be," I said. She looked at me. "Forget I ever said it," I said. I opened the car door. "Come on," I said. "We're getting out of here."

I went around and opened the other door for her, but she just sat there for a minute with her hands folded in her lap, like a good little girl waiting for somebody to give her the word to move. It struck me the way something does that you've been looking at for quite a while without really seeing it, and all at once you do look at it, and you find out there's something different about it that you'd never noticed before. There was something different about her. Maybe it was that pose—because in all the years I'd known Champ I'd never thought of associating the word *serene* with her before, and yet that was the word I was thinking now. She looked as if she'd got hold of something, and maybe it wasn't just what she'd been looking for, but anyway she'd got hold of it—got it tight and hard. I guess I just stood there looking at her. And all at once she smiled and moved to get out of the car.

"You're staring," she said. "Do you know you're staring? It isn't polite to stare."

She got out of the car and the smile was still there, and I followed her around and up the walk to the door and wondered if the smile was for me or for whatever she'd got hold of inside. She had a key, and she gave it to me to open the door, which I considered in the light of an invitation, but it wasn't, because she looked a little surprised when I followed her in.

"Oh, Mal," she said, "you know it's late and I have to change, I have to get out to Father Michael's—"

"Just ten minutes," I said. "Do you realize this is the first chance I've had to talk to you?"

"You talked to me yesterday. And all of this afternoon."

"Yeah," I said. "I talked to you. And to Jack and Gran and Rae and your kids—"

That house—every time I walk into it, it gives me the creeps. I've never spent any time in jail, which may make me more fortunate than virtuous, but at any rate that is the way it has turned out, but if I had, I think I'd feel like that when I revisited the cell where they'd kept me locked up and looked around at the walls and remembered how it was when that had been my permanent address. For it is that way when you are a kid in a house you hate; you can't get out, and you know you can't, and the bitterness piles up inside you till you think you're going to choke on it before you're old enough to walk out and make it stick.

I ran away from that house three times when I was a kid, once right after they brought me there, when I was six, once when I was ten—I got as far as Lakeview that time, and Jack Cournane was delegated the job of getting me out of the clutches of the local constabulary, who had grabbed me when I pinched some apples from a grocery store—and once when I was fourteen and had some fond illusions that people would take me for a man, give me a job, and let me alone. Being brought back that time was the worst of all, and if Gran and Grandpa hadn't been Irish-jealous of any slur on the family name, I'd have ended up, without much doubt, in a reform school. After that I had sense enough to stay put till I was eighteen, when I walked out for good. I can still remember coming back at Christmas that year and doling out presents all around: somehow it seemed to help wipe something out to put them on the receiving end for once in their lives. Gran didn't like it, I remember—and I spent the last cent I owned on a locket for Champ with a blue stone in it.

She stood there in that dim musty hall looking at me now, and she lit the whole place up like the Fourth of July.

It used to be that way when we were kids; she and Jack were the only people belonging to me I ever cared about, and when they came down to West Haley Street it was as if a dark curtain had gone up and you could see the sun for the first time in weeks. She was just a skinny little kid then, with big eyes, but she was as reckless as a Cossack; she'd do everything you'd do and then go you one better. Jack just used to laugh at her; he wouldn't let Rosemary put a bit on her, which he'd have lived to regret if he'd taken the trouble to find out as much about her as I did later. We got along fine, the two of us, had our fights like any other kids, but we always made them up before she left.

Then one day she wasn't a skinny kid any more, but a slick young girl in fur coats and expensive dresses who went out with college boys, and I fell in love with her. I never had the nerve to tell her, because I was just somebody she'd known from the time she was a kid, and I didn't go to college, and I was lucky when I even had a job, but I was in love with her, all right. I was so much in love with her I'd even have gone back to that house on West Haley Street if I'd thought I could have seen her oftener that way.

She stood there in the hall now and said, "Mal, I really do have to change. You know I've got to go to Father Michael's."

"Is that what you want to do?" I said.

Because I had to find out; the time always comes when you have to find out. You can go along just so long hoping and waiting and telling yourself your chance is going to come any day now, boy, just don't be in any hurry. Then something happens and you are in a hurry. You're in such a hurry you haven't even got a day, or an hour, left to find out; you want it now. I'd waited in New York; I'd looked at her and said, "Sure, Champ, sure, you go back to California, because I want you to be sure." And she'd said,

"Oh, Mal, I'll never be sure—don't you know that? Don't you see I never can be sure?"

Well, I had waited then, maybe because I was gut-scared the answer might be no, or maybe because I was being noble, or maybe because I was just used to waiting. But I wasn't waiting now. I stood there and asked her, "Is that what you want to do?" and watched her eyes blink a couple of times, fast, as if I'd hit her with something, and I knew she didn't want to answer it now, but I wasn't waiting. She knew I wasn't. And after a minute she faced up to it and said, "All right. I guess I owe that to you. I guess the least I can do is to talk about it."

She didn't even look at me then; she just walked across the hall and into the parlor and stood there in the middle of the room with her head down, as if she was going to make a speech in front of an audience and was collecting her thoughts beforehand. I followed her in and stood there too. It was so quiet you could almost hear those damned ferns Gran always has on stands in front of the windows sucking the dead air of the room up and using it to grow greener and taller and wirier by the minute. I knocked one of them over once when I was a kid, and you'd have thought I'd practically crucified Christ.

So I stood there, and after a minute, as if she'd made up her mind to something, she turned around and spoke to me.

"Mal," she said. "Mal, I can't."

It was just like that. "Mal, I can't." And I knew the minute she'd said it that that was Jack too, that damned sentimental scene he'd put on over on Adams Street, because how could she walk away from that and then turn around and act like anything but a pillar of nobility herself? I'd picked my time to get impatient, all right, and I'd picked a fine time, the worst time in the world; I should have had my head examined for trying to do as much as even hold her hand right then. But I'd started it, and I had to go through with it. I couldn't just pick up my hat and say, "Well, too bad, see you around"; I had to do the whole thing, and the way I felt then, I was going to do a thorough job.

So I said to her, "You're being pretty definite about something, aren't you? As far as I know, I haven't even asked you to do anything yet. Just what was it you had in mind?"

She looked at me.

"Don't be that way, Mal," she said. "Please don't be that way."

She wasn't mad yet, but I could make her mad. I hadn't known her as long as I had without finding out the things that would get her temper up, and then maybe she'd forget about Jack and being noble enough to match that scene he'd just put on, and admit to me how she really felt. And to herself. Right now we had Jack between us as big as life and as effective as Banquo's ghost; nobody else was going to get any notice as long as he was on the stage.

I said, "I'm not being any way; I just asked you a question. I just wanted to know what you had in mind."

She twisted her fingers together a little.

"Oh, Mal," she said, "I'm sorry I came, I was sorry as soon as I saw you at the station yesterday that I'd ever come, I shouldn't have, it only makes things worse—"

"It would make them a lot worse if you walked out on me again," I agreed. "In fact, it would make them so much worse that I have an idea something would bust wide open and all the king's horses couldn't put it back together again. I've waited a long time, Champ."

"I know you have," she said. "Oh, Mal, don't you think I know it? I've waited too—"

"Yes, you've waited," I said. And watched her standing there with that lost, distracted look in her eyes. "With Irv Gilman and your kids," I said. "With a home of your own— Hell, I know I don't pass for the domestic type, but, hell, I want to settle down sometime too, I want a wife and a home— Do you realize I've never had a home in my whole damned life since I was six years old?"

That wasn't what I'd meant to say. And it wasn't what I ought to have said, either; I ought to have told her how much I loved her, and that I couldn't go on living without her, which was pretty nearly true but not quite, because you go on living no matter what. You go on living even though the light goes out and they close the doors and you are left standing all alone outside, with the thing you've wanted all your life more than anything else in the world locked tight and safe away from you. That is the way things are, but I shouldn't have said it; I should have gone on working her up, getting her mad enough to forget about Jack, and then switching to low gear and telling her how much I loved her and needed her. The trouble was, I was too worked up myself to do it right. Well, I'd wanted a showdown, and that was what I was getting. But it wasn't turning out quite the way I'd thought it would when I'd sat out there in the car and looked at the house in the Sunday-afternoon heat and had that crazy idea about being happy there.

So I said the wrong thing, and she looked at me, not mad, the way I'd wanted her, but only more upset and quiet now, and she said, "Oh, Mal, I know how it is, I know it. But don't you see, it's just because I *do* have a home, because I'm part of something—"

"And I'm not," I said. "Is that it? I'm the fifth wheel on the wagon, the guy who invited himself to dinner—"

"Mal, don't—don't." For a minute I thought she was going to grab hold of me, the way women do when they're trying to tell you something you can't or won't understand. But she didn't; she just pushed her hair back off her forehead and then shook her head and walked away across the room to one of the lace-curtained windows. "You ought to go away," she said, in a kind of muffled voice. "I've told you, I can't—" Then she turned around all of a sudden and said to me, her voice rising higher, "Oh, you're right, you ought to have someone, it's not fair, but it doesn't have to be me, it doesn't have to be because we grew up together and now I'm all mixed up with the past, and you'll never be able to forgive it for being the way it was unless you can make it all up with me—"

It just came spilling out like some sort of phonograph record that somebody had started up inside her; I don't think she'd known she was going to say that herself. She stopped, and a kind of surprised look came into her face, and then she did walk over and grab me and she was crying hard, and I put my arms around her and thought, This is not it. Because she was crying the way a woman cries at a wake, not at a wedding, grabbing hold of something as hard as she can because she knows she is going to have to give it up. That was the way it was; I could feel it. I fished out my handkerchief and said, "Here, for the love of Mike, stop that." And she stopped and took the handkerchief and said, "Oh, Mal, I'm sorry. I don't know what's the matter with me today."

"I do," I said. "I can put it in one word of one syllable. It's Jack."

She shook her head; she was standing there with her face still pretty well covered by my handkerchief, but I could feel the definiteness of the gesture anyway.

"No," she said after a minute. "It's not that. Or it's not just that. Oh, Mal, can't you see"—she looked at me then —"can't you see it's everything, it's just the way things are?

We had our chance, we had one chance years ago and we didn't take it, I didn't take it, it's all my fault, but that's the way it is—"

Yes, that was the way it was. The way it was was that I was out in the cold again, or not again, because I had never been anywhere else, but out in the cold, period. I ought to have known that nothing that happened in that house was ever going to turn out right for me.

Oh, I argued with her awhile longer, but that's all it turned out to be, an argument, with the two of us squared off like a pair of debaters and nothing getting settled except that no matter how convincing I was she wasn't going to play any games with me. I never did get her mad. When we parted, it was more in sorrow than in anger, as the poet says—at least on her side, it was. I was mad enough to go down to Casey's Gym and play some blistering hot handball with the first customer I met and end up with a split finger. Then I went back to the hotel and took a shower and lay on the bed for an hour or so with the electric fan on because it was sizzling in there but not as hot as I was inside. It was a fine way to spend a Sunday afternoon.

It must have been around seven when the phone rang. I reached over and picked it up fast, because for one crazy second I thought it might be Champ. But it was Jack Cournane's voice that came over the wire to me. He said he was down at Henry's, in the back room, and he'd like to talk to me.

"That's a kind of odd place for a reformed character, isn't it?" I said, because he didn't strike me at the moment as the person I wanted most to see. But he only said, pretty humbly for Jack, "Yes, it is—but—well, you see, Mal, I'm at loose ends; I've got to make some plans, and I thought maybe you'd have some ideas—that maybe that hotel of yours—"

"Do you want to come on over?" I said. "You can get a room here all right if you can walk in the front door."

He didn't say anything for a minute. Then he said—he always was that way, he could pull one of those grave, sensitive little acts of politeness on you that made you feel like a peasant for your own crudeness—he said, "All right, Mal, forget it. I'm sorry I bothered you." And hung up. Not angrily, but gently and considerately, which made me feel just that much worse. I got up and put on a shirt and tie and coat and went out to Henry's to look for him.

He was still there when I walked in, sitting in the back room alone at a table with a virtuously half-finished drink in front of him and the mournful expression of a man who has turned over a new leaf and finds the nice clean white page that is staring up at him looking pretty blank. He cheered up visibly when he saw me, though, and asked me to sit down and what would I have?

"I hope I didn't take you away from anything," he said. "I had an idea you were busy when I called."

"Me?" I said. "I wasn't doing a thing. You were just a little too fast for me."

I sat down, and Mrs. Henry, which was the name the politer patrons at Henry's applied to the weary-looking blonde who presided over the back room in Henry's absence, brought me the beer I asked for. There were a couple of other steady customers minding their own business over their drinks; Henry's is pretty exclusive about its back room, and has never yet been known to get in trouble with the police by advertising its disregard of Sabbath decorum.

"What was it you wanted to see me about?" I asked Jack. "Are you and Rae really splitting up?"

He gave that one a full sixty seconds before he answered it. But when he said, "Yes," it was as firmly as if he'd been giving it out in court. Then he shook his head, considering it sadly.

"She'll be better off without me, poor kid," he said. "I told that to Mike this afternoon."

I took that in; I'll admit I hadn't expected *that*.

"To Mike?" I repeated it. "You mean you were out at Father Michael's this afternoon?"

He nodded, smiling suddenly as he looked up at me; he's always had that kind of cheerful way of looking at you when he's pulled a stunt like that, like a devil-may-care kid.

"Mal," he said, "it was a wonderful situation. Mind you, I'm not saying I'd have walked into it if I'd remembered—but there I was, wading up to my armpits in reverend Fathers and pious ladies—" His cheerfulness faded as fast as it had appeared. "I embarrassed the hell out of Mike," he said. "He was fine about it—but there it was—"

"I can imagine it," I said. I could, too; if they ever give Father Michael a martyr's crown, one or two of the biggest jewels in it will have been put there by Jack Cournane. "What did he say?" I asked him. "I mean, about your future plans?"

"Well—" Jack looked at the amber in the glass before him. "Well, it occurred to me," he said, with an attempt at jauntiness, "that he was a little skeptical."

"Is that so?" I said.

"Not quite as skeptical as you are, of course," he said, letting me have it back right between the eyes.

"Maybe that's because I've tried turning over new leaves myself," I said. "I've had personal experience. It's not as easy as it looks."

He considered that; in the process he did away with what was left of the drink in front of him.

"It doesn't even *look* easy to me, Mal," he admitted then. "As a matter of fact, it looks as hard as hell. But it's something I've got to do—for Amy's sake, for those kids' sake—"

I'd been wondering how long it was going to take him to get around to that. He looked over at me as if he thought I might have something to say about it myself, but I was the last man in the world he should have expected to get into a cozy conversation with him on the subject of the effect his sudden conversion was going to have on Champ. Of course he didn't know what had happened just a few hours before back there in the house on West Haley Street; as a matter of record, he didn't even know how I felt about Champ. Jack's always been too absorbed in his own romantic didoes to have much time left for wondering about anybody else's. I remember when I introduced Rae to him; I don't think it ever occurred to him to wonder how she and I had been spending our time before he walked into the picture.

Anyway, he finished his drink, and when he looked at the empty glass the impropriety of sitting there with it that way in Henry's back room probably struck him, and he ordered another one. And maybe I looked surprised, or not surprised enough, when he did it, because his face flushed up a little, angrily or defiantly, as he picked up the new glass and made a start on it.

"Damn it, Mal," he said, "you don't know how it is; you don't know what it's like—after all these years, to try to pick things up and put them together again. But I'm going to do it, I've got to do it, for Champ's sake—"

It struck me about then that he was a little vague on the subject of just what he *was* going to do for Champ's sake; he didn't seem to be in any hurry to get down to business. What he was ready to tell me was what a wonderful girl Champ was, and how he'd met her kids out at Father

Michael's, and how the little girl looked just like Champ when she was that age.

"You remember, don't you, Mal?" he said, and I said sure, I remembered, and then he told me how he used to go up to her room when she was a kid, evenings before she went to sleep, and tell her stories till Rosemary called him to come downstairs, and how she'd come home from school sometimes when he was in the living room with some of his friends, and he'd take her on his knee and show her off to them.

"I was a great man to her then, Mal," he said, shaking his head over his drink, "and she was the dearest thing I had in the world. I must have been a fool, a madman, to give it all up—and if Rosemary, God save her, hadn't been the complete and perfect bitch you know her to be—"

I could have reminded him that a young lady named Ermina Marlow had had something to do with all that, too, and that he'd seemed a little confused at one period of his life as to just who was the dearest thing in the world to him. But he wasn't even talking to me by that time; he was just indulging in the happiest pastime of an Irishman who's had enough whisky to soften him up—remembering the good old days that are gone forever.

Oh, what he was feeling was real, all right, but I've seen a guy who's just pumped four bullets into his wife crying like a baby over her body, and maybe the bank robber walking off with the loot has a moment when he wishes he hadn't done it and was back in the third grade wearing his altar-boy's surplice over his lily-white little soul. If we were marked on what we'd like to be in our better moments, we'd all come up with an A-plus on our report cards—but there's a little matter of doing, too, and what Jack was doing about becoming that lamented ideal father he had in his mind was, at the moment, exactly nothing. He was sitting in

Henry's back room drinking whisky and making grand resolutions, and meanwhile he was getting more than a little
drunk.

I should have tried to stop him. I know that too. But
I am not used to acting, either, like the ideal Malachi Cesti
I would like to be. So I acted like the far inferior grade of
article I am accustomed to foisting on the public, and sat
there thinking morosely about Champ, and only not getting
drunk myself because I had sense enough to stick to beer.
I heard all about Jack's troubles with Rosemary, and about
Champ's running away and getting married to Irving
Gilman, and about how it was never proved in court that
he—Jack—had been guilty of any misconduct in office,
about the men who had been his friends and the men who
had betrayed him—the past, the past, always the past, the
glorious, furious, terrible, heartbreaking, grand old past.
And, hell, I knew that was where I was, too. In the past,
with a guy named Mitch saying, "Take it easy, sonny, it
happens to a lot of girls"; in the past with Champ smiling
at me over a little gold locket with a blue stone in it; in the
past with Gran, with West Haley Street, with Mal Cesti,
Vittorio Cesti's kid, half Irish, half Italian, and never sure
which side he belonged to.

It got on to be nine, maybe ten o'clock. Jack hadn't
made any visible progress in the way of solving the problem
of his immediate future, but he had made considerable
progress on a bottle of Scotch, and it didn't seem to have
improved his mood. I'd seen it happen before, so I wasn't
surprised—the jaunty determination fading, the sentimental
recollections of the past darkening to regrets and recrimina-
tions, till finally he was left staring into the black pit of his
own failure. I guess the thing was that the drunker he got,
the more clearly he was able to see himself; a couple of
drinks could bring him into that state of cheerful euphoria

we are all looking for when we raise the bottle, but an over-
dose of the stuff burned away all the nice illusions from his
brain like raw acid eating at pretty silk veils. He was looking
at Jack Cournane naked, and he didn't like what he saw.
Around eleven he was weeping with his head on the table,
and Mrs. Henry came up and said why didn't I take him
home. They were used to him there, but he was definitely
undermining the morale of the customers.

Taking him home, though, posed something of a problem. As far as I knew, he didn't want to go back to Adams
Street, and when I asked him where he did want to go, all
I got was an obstinate silence. He was still sitting there
with his head down on the table and his eyes closed, but
he hadn't passed out; you could tell that by the way he
was breathing.

"Jack—" I said again.

It might have been a signal; all of a sudden he raised
one fist up and began beating on the table with it as fiercely
as if he'd been beating a drum, and every time it hit wood
you could hear him groaning out under his breath, "God!
God! God!" Mrs. Henry came running up; the glasses were
jumping all over the table, and it was making a hell of a
racket.

"Here, now, you quit that, Jack Cournane," she said
to him indignantly. "What's the matter with you tonight?
Why don't you go home and go to bed?"

He heaved himself up in his chair. I got a good look
at his face, and it looked pretty dangerous to me; his eyes
were glittering like a man's who's a good customer for a
strait jacket.

"I shall go home, my good woman," he said, enuncia-
ting his words with a distinctness worthy of a Shakespearean
actor, "when I am disposed to do so, and not before. Is that
perfectly understood?"

"Perfectly," Mrs. Henry said. "And if you don't behave yourself, I'll have you thrown out. Is *that* understood?"

He stared at her fiercely, but she didn't give way; I guess she'd been through all this before. And after a minute he started to smile; he spoke to me, nodding his head toward her in grudging admiration.

"She's an engaging little trollop, isn't she?" he said. "Quick—very quick—at repartee—"

"She's right, too," I said. "It's time for both of us to be going."

"Mal, my boy, the evening's young!" He looked at me reproachfully, then suddenly leaned across the table toward me confidentially. "I'll tell you what we'll do," he said. "We'll have just one more drink; then we'll go and see Champ."

That was a new idea. I could just see him walking in at that hour of the night at West Haley Street; Gran would have put on a scene to raise the roof. But I couldn't talk him out of it; the more I said, the more he stuck to it. He was going to see Champ, he said, and that was all there was to it. I noticed the dangerous look was coming into his eyes again, so I finally said all right, if he had to see her, I'd call her up and have her come down to Henry's herself. I thought I could stall him that way, but that didn't work either. He insisted on my phoning right off, and when I came back from a pretended conversation with West Haley Street and reported that she wasn't there, he said to me icily, "Mal, lying is obviously not one of your accomplishments," and started toward the door. So I thought, What the hell, and said this time I would really call her, and I did. I figured it wouldn't do her any harm, anyway. She was going to have to find this out sooner or later, and the longer she went on living in a fool's paradise, the harder it was going to be for her when the eviction notice came.

I didn't say much to her over the phone. I just told her I was with Jack at Henry's, and that he wanted her to come. There was too much commotion on the wire, anyway, for me to be very specific; Josie'd answered first, and she had to call Champ, and I gathered that all that woke Gran and the kids; there was a regular ree-raa, as Gran used to say, going on. I don't know how Champ explained it all to them. They probably thought Jack had broken his neck or something equally fatal, and that I was just trying to break it gently over the phone.

So when I'd hung up, I went back to the table and told Jack she was coming. The black mood was back on him again by that time, and he only glowered over at me and said by God, she'd better be.

"Because if she doesn't walk in that door in half an hour," he said, "I will go over to West Haley Street myself, and you nor anybody else is going to stop me." He leaned across the table toward me truculently. "Why shouldn't I see her?" he demanded. "She's my daughter, isn't she? I'm her father. Isn't it natural for a father to want to see his daughter?"

I said it was natural, all right. I was getting pretty tired of the whole business by that time, and I guess he saw it, because all of a sudden his face kind of gave down out of its angry, arrogant lines and I had a moment's very clear view of him, not as Jack Cournane, the great lover, the great politician, the champion of all the witty has-beens, but as a tired, sick, aging man who wanted to go home to his family and be taken care of and live decently and comfortably until he died. And I thought, My God, he's getting old; it came to me with a shock, because there are some people you never figure as getting old, any more than you figure a face on a statue is going to get old.

Well, we sat there and waited. I don't know what he thought was going to happen when Champ got there, but I had a persistent picture of her taking him by the hand and leading him out of Henry's back room to the pious con- fines of West Haley Street, where she would make a new man of him—a picture so out of character for both her and him that I began to wonder if I was a little drunk too. I was beginning to feel as depressed as hell. But we didn't have very long to wait, because maybe twenty minutes, a half hour, after I'd hung up the phone and come back to the table the door opened and Champ walked in. Jack saw her as soon as I did, and he got to his feet, stumbling to- ward her, weeping again suddenly. Her face looked—just white, unbelieving, as it vanished from my sight behind his shoulder when he took her in his arms.

You know how it is: there are moments you don't even like to think about, once they're over, God-awful mo- ments when the bottom just drops out of everything and all you want to do is pretend they never happened. This was one of them. I saw that look on Champ's face, and I wished I'd knocked Jack Cournane over the head with the nearest blunt instrument before I'd brought her down there to see him like that. She didn't say much—he was maun- dering some sentimental blather, and she just let him go on—but you only had to look at her to know how she felt. After a minute she kind of put her arm around him, steadying him, and said in a voice so low I could hardly hear it, "Come on, Father; we'll go home."

"Home?" he repeated it. It was the wrong word; he straightened himself up and looked at her as if she had dashed ice water in his face. "Home?" he said. "I have no home. Unless you are referring to that wretched museum of horrors on West Haley Street—"

Champ looked at me.

"Mal," she said. "Can't you help me get him out of here?"

Maybe it was because she was used to handling Irv

Gilman, and that was how she managed him when he was drunk, if he ever was, or when he was just blind pigheaded, as I guess every man is sometimes, but she sure as hell said the wrong thing that time. I saw the dangerous, black glint coming in Jack's eyes again, and he pushed her away from him, not even gently, and fell back himself against the table.

"And where did you learn that sanctimonious tone, if I may ask?" he said to her, with that overpoliteness he always carried around with him like a weapon. He stood there staring at her till I could see the color coming up in her cheeks, and then all at once the lines of his face relaxed and he began to laugh. "Look at her, Mal," he said, leaning against the table, pointing at her. "Look at her. Look at the virtuous matron she's turned out to be. By God, she has some of Rosemary in her, after all."

I wanted to push his face in.

"He's drunk," I said to Champ. "Listen, you don't have to stand there and take this. Just turn around and go out the way you came in."

She shook her head.

"No," she said. "I'm going to stay." She looked over at Jack; the color had drained out of her cheeks again, and her face was set, so you couldn't tell what she was feeling. "Father," she said to him clearly. "Where *do* you want to go? I'll take you—"

"I am perfectly capable," Jack said, still with that ironic overpoliteness, "of going anywhere I please under my own power, my dear. Contrary to Mal's nasty insinuations, I am not drunk—" He stopped, considering it. "Not *very* drunk— And as a matter of fact," he went on, turning around to the table again, "I don't particularly want to go anywhere at the present moment; I'm very comfortable right here."

And he sat down again and pounded on the table.

"Mrs. Henry," he said. "Mrs. Henry! What kind of service are you providing here for your customers, my good woman? I want a drink."

Champ stood there looking at me. I could see her neck muscles tightening, but she stood her ground.

"Mal," she said, "we've got to get him out of here."

"Why?" I said. She looked as if she was going to hit me then. "Don't you ever give up?" I said to her. "This has been going on for ten years, and you think you're going to walk in on him and in one day—"

"I don't think it will be in one day. I don't. But don't you see he made a start, he wants to— We can't just leave him here like this."

"No, we can't," I agreed, watching Jack, who was engaging in a bitter verbal battle now with Mrs. Henry on the subject of whether she intended to provide him with further liquid refreshments. "I'll go along with you there," I said, "maybe not for your reasons, but I'll go along with you. But if you don't mind my saying it, I think I could handle this better without you. So why don't you just go home and let me—?"

I knew she wouldn't, even before I'd got that far. Because she was proving something to herself, she had to prove it, and she couldn't wait to hear the result long distance. She walked over to the table and put her hand on Jack's shoulder.

"Father—" she said. Mrs. Henry, seeing her about to take over, broke off her conversation with Jack and went to attend to the wants of her other customers. "Father," Champ said then, "I've got to talk to you—really. And I can't here—"

"Why not?" Jack said obstinately. "This is actually a delightful place, in its own miserable way, once you get used to it. I spend the greater part of my waking hours here, or in similar establishments. Mrs. Henry!" he called out, after his departing hostess. "Mrs. Henry! Are you going to bring me that drink or aren't you?"

I didn't think it would do any good for me to get into it, but seeing Champ standing there with that look on her face reversed my better judgment, and I said to Jack, "Look here, you were the one who brought her down here, remember? You were the one who was weeping in his beer half an hour ago, telling me all you were going to do for Champ—"

He stopped me; he struck both his fists down on the table so hard that the glasses almost jumped off of it. All of a sudden his face looked livid.

"Mal—" he said. "Let me alone. Let me alone. God damn it, let me alone! Don't you see I can't—I can't—I can't—I can't—"

Every time he said *can't* he hit the table again. One of the glasses did jump off to the floor and broke, and he stared down at it, and then all at once he pushed back his chair and stood up. He still had his hand on the chair; I thought for a minute he was going to pick it up and hit somebody with it. His face had flushed up, and the sweat was standing out on it in drops, and he stood there, staring around at us, breathing like an animal that the dogs have been chasing for a long time and have finally brought to bay. All that fine control had snapped in an instant. Champ stood there, looking shocked, stunned into immobility—and then the door opened and Rae walked in.

I will say that for women; you never have to draw diagrams for them. She'd probably been hunting for him all over town, and all she had to work on when she walked in was that tableau the three of us—Jack, Champ, and

I—presented to her, but she picked up the dialogue as if she'd been in the middle of it all along.

"Jack, you *fool*," she said. She went straight up to him and eased that chair out of his hand and stood there looking at him as if there wasn't anybody in the room but the two of them. I was watching Champ, and I could tell that hit her—the way Rae didn't even bother to glance at her, as if she wasn't that important. "What do you think you're doing?" Rae went on, to Jack. "Do you know I've been looking all over for you?"

She put her hand on him, touching his arm, and you could just see whatever had been eating him—terror, despair, fury—oozing away like the tension going out of a man when he hits the hot, relaxing, humid air of a steam room.

"Well, my little Sherlock Holmes," he said to her, "so you've discovered me, have you? May I inquire if you used deduction, or only bloodhounds?"

"If I had a bloodhound, I'd set him up in front of the door so you couldn't walk out like this again," Rae said. She had on some sort of narrow dress with black-and-white stripes going round and round, and all that junk-jewelry she liked to wear; I could see Champ taking it in, trying to add it up—Jack and this. Well, that was the way it was, and maybe she would get it through her head now that it *was* that way, and go home and forget about it. "Do you know I've been chasing all over town after you?" Rae said. "Oh, Jack, you moron, going off on a bat because that—because these—"

She did look over at me and Champ then; she didn't waste more than a glance on us, but it was enough to galvanize Champ into action. I hadn't figured she'd stand there and take it much longer. She took a step forward and said, "Father—"

Rae turned around to her swiftly.

"Listen, Champ—Amy—whatever your name is—
haven't you made enough trouble for one day?" she said.
She looked at Champ the way women do when the gloves
are off—about as friendly as a cobra. "I'm going to tell you
something, and I don't want you to forget it," she said, in
that husky, definite voice of hers. "I'm married to Jack, and
I intend to stay married to him, and there's nothing you can
do about it. You've got your own man, haven't you? Well,
just go back to him where you belong and leave us alone."

I looked at Jack; he was standing there shaking his
head and smiling indulgently now, like a man watching a
pair of five-year-olds preparing to do battle.

"Now, now—" he said, shaking his finger at them. "I
want you two children to get along—charming girls, both
of you—"

I'd had enough of it; I grabbed Champ's arm and said,
"Come on. We're getting out of here."

I'd grabbed her arm, but she pulled away; I could feel
her shaking, even those few seconds I had hold of her. She
didn't look at me; she had her eyes on Jack.

"No," she said. And then she spoke to him: "Father,"
she said. "If you don't—If you go with her now—"

His smile got a little more sheepish; that was all. He
was good and drunk, of course, but even he should have
been able to see what this meant to her; even he shouldn't
have been able to deal her a hand like that.

"My dear—" he mumbled, wagging his head at her,
"my dear—my dear—just this once, you see—"

Rae had hold of his arm still, and she didn't let go;
she didn't wait, either, to take any bows over her victory.
She just steered him toward the door, and he went along
with her as docilely as a lamb. I knew why he went, all
right. He went because the steam room is always more
comfortable than the icy plunge, because habit is a cable,

as the copybooks used to tell us smugly, and at last we cannot break it. Maybe I even felt sorry for him a little, sham-
bling out of there under Champ's accusing eyes, but mostly
I felt sorry for her. She had stood there and taken it right
between the eyes, and now everything had come clear and
ugly and true out of the golden mists of memory, and she
was looking at the real thing. Not at Jack Cournane, the
greatest man in town, but at Jack Cournane, a drunk living
off a girl he was still not too old to charm, at Jack Cournane, who could mock and threaten her, but who rolled
over and played dead when the other girl snapped her
fingers.

Maybe I ought to have told her something else, too—
which was that he loved her too much to be able to endure
her seeing him as he really was. But I figured that she would
find that out some day for herself, and that she wouldn't
have believed me if I had said it. It was true, though. I
don't know that it makes him any better, but that much,
anyway, was true.

We didn't waste much time getting out of there ourselves. I paid the tab, which Jack, as usual, had conveniently
forgotten, and then we went outside, to the sights and
sounds and smells of a big-city summer night. In the neon
light I could see that she still looked white enough to
match the white dress she had on. I started to say something, but she cut me off.

"Mal," she said. She wasn't even looking at me; she
was standing there looking across the street as impersonally
as if she was giving directions to a cab driver. "Mal," she
said, "take me up to your place. Now."

I don't know why it hit me that way, but all of a
sudden I was so mad I couldn't see straight.

"Look—" I said. "Look—every time your father does
some damn fool thing, do you have to go off and do some

damn fool thing, too?" She turned around and looked at me then, and there still wasn't any expression on her face, and for some reason that made me madder than ever. "I've got news for you, sister," I said to her. "That is not enough for me. It is not nearly enough. I don't want to play gigolo for you like your friend Mitch."

Even that didn't change the way she looked. She still stood there staring at me through the neon-dark with those wide, fixed, almost impersonal gray eyes, and then she said, "No. Not for me. Only for girls like her, I suppose. Do you think I don't know? Do you think I don't? First you, and then Father—Were you tired of her—is that it?—or was it just that you couldn't compete with him?"

She started to walk on all of a sudden down the street, and I went after her; I took hold of her arm.

"Champ—" I said.

"Let me go. I said, *Let me go!*"

There were people going by, so I gave up and just walked on beside her. After two or three minutes I looked and she was crying, the tears running down her face but her head still up.

"Champ," I said, "I'm sorry—"

She wouldn't answer me. We walked on some more and then I couldn't stand it any longer and I pulled her into a doorway and said, "Champ, don't— Listen, I'm sorry, I said I was sorry—"

I thought for a minute she was going to break away again, but then she put her head down and she really was crying and I could hear her saying, "Oh, Mal, it's not that —oh, you can say it, but it's not the way you think—it's because I can't fight any more—I can't, and oh, you said that—"

"All right," I said. "All right. It's all right. It's all right."

There didn't seem to be anything else to say, because

she was crying that way and I stood there with my arms around her and the hell with anybody passing by, and for the moment it really was all right. Then she raised her head up and looked at me. I could see the tears still there on her face and she looked more beautiful than I'd ever seen her before in my life, and she said to me, "Oh, Mal, you can believe whatever you want, but you've got to believe one thing for me, you've just got to, and oh, I don't even know how to say it, after all these years—" She stood there looking at me, and then she said it. "I love you very much," she said.

June 13, 1938

Dolly

Well, you might have known how it would turn out. Life is life, as I said to Mrs. Cournane this morning, and human beings are human beings, and to expect them to behave as if they were anything different is against nature, and only a disappointment to those who do.

Not that I supposed she would understand. What woman would, who'd married one man for love and another for convenience? I wouldn't say if it had been both for convenience, because a woman who has never known what real love is has a right to manage her life the best way she can, adding up the dollars and cents and making it all come out with a profit. That's all she's ever learned, and so it's her privilege to shop and choose, and if Patrick Cournane has more profits after his name than John Doe, it's Patrick Cournane she walks to the altar with.

But for a woman who's had a real love of her own to settle for worse the second time is a sad thing, I've always thought. When Gus died, I sat by the bed and said to myself, "Well, that's enough. We've had our good life together, and now it's over, but I can never forget it if I live to be a hundred." And I never have, though I must admit I came very close to it once. Just the thought of the way he used to look at me and slip his arm around me when he came home from doing a good piece of business and we'd plan the good times we were going to have is enough to keep me going on many a bad day.

But with Mrs. Cournane it was just the opposite. When she'd had much, she wanted more, not remembering that greediness is bad manners as well as bad morals, and so when Tom Dineen died she set her cap for Pa. I remember I used to see her in church when I was only a little bit of a thing, parading up to the first pew, with Tom Dineen beside her looking like a plucked chicken she was carrying off to market. Poor little man, I always did wonder what she saw in him. But it was a love match, right enough, and when he died nobody thought she'd ever marry again, from the scene she put on at the grave. There she stood, wailing like one of the women from the old country, where she was born, and beating herself on the breast, and would have torn her hat and veil off too, to get at her hair, but her sister slammed the hat back down on her head and threatened never to speak to her again if she didn't behave herself.

Then a year later there she was standing up in the church with Pa and saying, "I do." I was only a girl then and I thought I never would get over it, having a step-mother in the house. But it turned out all for the best, I suppose, for we were all getting a bit wild with nobody to look after us but housekeepers since Ma died. And then she would be nice to the boys and make them gingerbread and chocolate cakes that they dearly loved, and see that their clothes were as smart and decent as any in the neighbor-hood. Jack was her favorite, because she was always a little afraid of Michael; he was too brainy for her, she always said. But she was ready to jump out of her skin with joy when he came to her and said he wanted to study for the priesthood. It was the grief of her life that she and Tom Dineen had never had a boy, so she could have what every Irishwoman wants most in life, a son a priest. And this was the next best thing to that.

That is one reason, too, that she and Mal have never gotten along, and why she was so angry with him this morn-ing. For though he can't help it that he is half Italian, he can help it that he is not a priest, and it makes no difference to her at all that he is as much suited to that life as she is to being the Queen of Spain. I remember hearing her tell her daughter Cathleen, when Mal was born, that she ought to take him to the church and dedicate him to the Virgin Mother, and Cathleen, who was always as rough with her tongue in her way as her mother was in hers, laughed and said, "Oh, holy saints, how do I know what he'll grow up to be? If he's anything like his father, there won't be any virgins in it, I can tell you *that*."

It was talk like that that used to set Mrs. Cournane in a regular fury. She used to say she'd been a decent woman all her life, and she didn't know what the Lord was punish-ing her for in making her the mother of such a trollop. And it's true that Cathleen was always free in her ways. Una could never bear her, said she was vulgar, like her mother, and of course she hadn't been to the Academy like Una and me, but had gone to school with all the tag, rag, and bobtail over on Ferris Street, and then had gone to work in Stoneman's Department Store. That was where she met Vittorio Cesti, her husband-to-be. He had a good job in Deliveries, and there wasn't a reason in the world why he shouldn't have come courting her like any other young man with a girl he fancies, except that of course Mrs. Cournane wouldn't hear of an Italian.

So they got to meeting on the sly, and nature, as they say in books, took its course. In fact, Cathleen was four months gone when they ran away and got married, but nobody knew it, not even her mother, till she had the baby one morning in that flat over on Bank Street, five months to the day after the wedding. That was just like Cathleen— lacing herself in and trying to brazen it out, expecting the Lord would pass some sort of miracle, I suppose, and let her carry the child a full thirteen months so she could pass herself off as having behaved herself in a respectable way. She was always as stubborn as her mother, never seeing what she didn't want to see, and seeing twice as much of what she did. So when the baby was born she and Mrs. Cournane agreed never to speak to each other again, because that seemed to be the only way the two of them wouldn't be shouting their heads off each other every time they met. And I doubt if they would have spoken, if Cathleen hadn't had trouble with her milk and the baby wouldn't take to anything else, and Mrs. Cournane had to go over and take charge of the whole shebang.

She never did get over hating that poor Italian, though. She used to say he'd carve her gizzard some day with a knife, and I wouldn't have blamed him if he had, she made herself so disagreeable to him. He was a nice-looking boy, too, easygoing and hard-working; you couldn't ask for a nicer son-in-law. Finally he got so fed up with it he packed Cathleen and the baby off to St. Louis and got a job there, and all we had from them was picture postcards for four years. There was one of Cathleen, and she'd gotten thinner—it suited her; she was always a lump of a girl, for all her fine complexion—but Mrs. Cournane was sure "that Italian" was starving her. And when Cathleen died in 1912 of erysipelas, Mrs. Cournane wanted to take him to court for neglect. I'm sure it was all Jack and Michael could do to stop her, because Pa just sat there, as usual, saying nothing at all when she ranted on like that.

She didn't forgive the man even when he died too, within the month, and she had to go out and get Mal. I always will say she took it out on the child, though she prides herself to this day on how well she did her duty by him. But *duty* is not all an orphaned child wants, and it used to make me heartsick, when I was married and off myself and came home to visit, to see the boy ordered about like he was dirt in that house, and nothing he ever did praised or spoken of kindly. She may blame him for not coming near her now, but I'm sure he'd have to be a true saint for forgiveness to want to.

I know I could never warm to her myself, though she was a good deal decenter to Una and me than she ever was to Mal, and I never could bring myself to call her Mother or Ma. Jack used to, in some of his wild moments, when he was trying to get around her about something he wanted, but none of the rest of us ever did. She was "Mrs. Cournane" to us, just as if she'd been no relation at all, and I suppose it suited her that way, because she never asked to be called different.

Now that I look back at it, I can see she never considered herself a Cournane at all, as if she'd taken nothing but the name when she came into that house. And I'm not surprised at that, either, because, as I've said, it was more like a business arrangement to her than a marriage when she took Pa. I don't know how I knew that, nothing but a girl as I was at the time, but I realized it even then.

So she is always hard on those poor women who aren't lucky enough to be married to a man they love, as she was with her first, or cold-livered enough to stick by their bargain in a business arrangement, as she was with her second. She never had the weakness of those who, once they have given themselves out of necessity or prudence to a man they don't love, see no reason for denying themselves to another man they do love or even have a fancy for—something that is at the root of dozens and dozens of scandals every year. For, if that act of all others is so important, then no woman should be obliged to be part of it when she has no real love for the man who takes her, for she loses all her self-respect when she does, whether there have been marriage vows given or not. And if it isn't important, then she isn't to blame for doing it where it is so dearly wanted, when she has already done it for money, or a grand name, or any of the other bad reasons that persuade a woman into a situation like that. I have a great respect for religion, but still I can't think a few words said by a priest can make what is bad to begin with any better. And I think that as long as there are bad marriages, there will be bad wives, even though they preach against them from the pulpit every day in the week.

So I wasn't surprised—not *surprised*, but a little vexed with myself for not having seen how things were shaping to happen—when Josie came to my room at the first crack of dawn this morning and told me Amy hadn't come back at all during the night. I suppose she'd lain awake herself all night through, poor soul, waiting for her, because Mrs. Cournane has her so scared for her life if anything out of the way happens in that house, she would worry herself silly over a bent pin. She came in to me—I was half asleep, dreaming about Gus and one spring day we were in Atlantic City together, the sky all cold and blue because it was before the season and the wind blowing to take the breath out of you, but we walked for hours and were shouting-happy all day long—and shook me a little to wake me, and said, "Oh, Dolly, I don't know what to do. I don't know *what* to do. Amy hasn't come back; I looked in her room and there's Shivaun sleeping alone, and *what* am I going to say to Aunt Peg?"

I swam up out of my sleep and looked at her. She had on a pink wrapper over her nightgown, and she looked like a girl sitting there in the half-light with her hair down, even if she is letting it grow gray. Poor thing, she's never had a life of her own, first with that father of hers who was no good at all but to worry the life out of people with his ideas about sanitation and health—he lost a good job at Clarkson's because he insisted on washing his hands every time a customer handed him a bit of money, said he wouldn't be responsible for spreading germs from one person to another—and then here under Mrs. Cournane's thumb. She was nearly crying now, she was so worried, but all I could think of, half asleep as I was, was that Amy had gone to see Jack, and that if she wasn't home yet, she must be still with him.

So I said, "Say she's with Jack," and she jumped at it like a drowning man after a rope.

"Oh, do you think she is?" she said. "Do you really think so? I don't know what to think myself; Aunt Peg kept me awake till all hours last night, she was so angry because I called Amy to the telephone when Mal asked for her, and then she kept saying Jack wasn't in it at all, it was just a trick to get Amy out of the house."

I sat up in bed.

"That's nonsense," I said. "You know Mal as well as I do; if he wanted to come here for Amy, he'd walk right up to the front door in broad daylight and dare anybody to stop him."

Because if there was one thing you could never accuse Mal of, it was being a sneak. He'd been in every other kind of trouble when he was a boy, but even Mrs. Cournane had to admit he'd never do anything behind her back. So if he'd said Jack wanted to see Amy last night, I knew in my own mind it must have been so—only it was queer about her not coming home again. And first I thought something terrible might have happened to Jack, and that was the reason for it, but then, after Josie had gone and I was dressing, I got to thinking about it, and I didn't think it was that at all. Because there is one thing about bad news, it travels quickly, and if Jack had been murdered or dying, or in jail, we'd have heard of it one way or another by that time.

It was when that thought came to me that I had a shock. Because all at once it came up before my mind's eye, like a picture on a wall, the way Amy's face had looked the day she came, when I'd mentioned Mal and that old story about his having had a fight with a young man on the front lawn of her house when she was in high school, just before Jack and Rosemary were divorced. I hadn't thought anything of it at the time, because I was too full of the excitement of her coming, but now it came back to me as clear as day: she'd tried to look unconcerned, and I had put down the rather sharp way she'd cut me off to the care she had as a mother for what her children heard—but now I felt it wasn't that. Or not that alone. She'd had a look in her eyes that I knew—the look of a woman who hasn't made up her mind. And quick as a flash it popped into my head now: "God help her, I suppose she made it up last night."

I won't say I wasn't surprised. I like Mal, and he's the

kind of man who can always get the girls when he likes—
a big dark fellow who doesn't talk too much and when he
does can flatter nicely, though he laughs when he does it
at you and at himself. But somehow I'd never thought it
was serious between him and Amy, not even with that old
story in my head about his being jealous of her, and with
Mrs. Cournane going on all yesterday about the way he'd
looked at Amy when he came to West Haley Street in the
morning to drive her out to see Jack.

"Making calf's eyes at her like he was nineteen years
old," she said. "It wasn't decent, and I told him so."

Well, trust an enemy to find you out any day when a
friend is blind as an owl, I thought. For if you look long
enough for the bad in someone, you're bound to find it,
since none of us has ever been perfect since the world
began. As I know well enough, to my sorrow, though if it
hadn't been for his eyes when he looked at me, as sad as a
spaniel's but as romantic as only a Frenchman's can be, I
would never have given in to him, and I would have saved
myself a good deal of trouble into the bargain.

Part of it was his name, René Duval, and part of it was
being stuck off in that awful little flat all winter long when
I'd lost my job at the Markham Company and couldn't
afford any better, day in and day out coming home to that
mauve wallpaper with the brown streaks in it that you'd
wonder any person in his right mind would ever have put
up on the walls to be looked at. So I went into the best
hotel in town one evening, just to get away from it for
once and have a dinner like Gus used to take me out to, and
there he was. He came up to me in the lobby when that
silly girl in the checkroom had mislaid my good brown coat
and there was all kinds of fuss going on about it, the girl
saying, to cover her mistake, that she believed I had come
in without a coat, and the hotel detective sent for and all.

I was nearly crying, I was so put out, when he came up and said he'd seen me coming in in the coat; he'd noticed particularly because he'd admired it. And I knew when he said *it*, he meant me instead.

They found the coat at last, off in a heap in a corner where that careless girl had let it fall off the hanger, and my Frenchman held it for me to put it on. And of course, with all that excitement, we got to talking and exchanged names as we went outside, and he told me he came from New Orleans, was some big cotton broker there. Which I believed, like the giddy thing I was. For I was past forty then, but still as apt to be taken out of my senses by some new pleasure as any girl, and pleasure had been scarce as gold with me since Gus had died. Then it was such a lovely evening, just turning spring, the air so soft you could almost taste it when you breathed, and the sky as full of stars as a field of daisies. We stood outside the hotel, and he said his automobile was there, and gave me a good deal of talk about how he wouldn't offend a lady for the world, but it was a beautiful night and we were both alone and he would be honored by my company for an hour or two. And the upshot of it all was that I went along with him. I realized at the very moment I did it that it was a risky thing to do, because I knew no more about him than I did of a man from Mars, except what he'd told me, which might be all lies.

But I did it just the same. I thought of that mauve wallpaper with the brown streaks on it, and I went with him as if I'd been used to picking men up in hotels every day of my life.

So for two months after that it was nothing but drives and dinners and flowers and moonlight, for he really did have plenty of money, it seemed—that much of what he had told me was true. And I suppose I thought of marrying him, since it seemed that was the logical thing for all this whoop-te-do to be leading up to, and I would lie awake at night thinking of Gus and feeling like the worst traitor in the world. I didn't love him as I'd loved Gus; I was quite sure of that. But he was pleasant to be with, and I felt sorry for him, somehow, in spite of his being rich and a cotton broker and a handsome man that women would turn around to look at on the street. He was forty-nine and losing a little hair in front, but a Frenchman at that age can be even more attractive than when he was young.

Still, attractive or not, I wasn't in love with him and I didn't think I wanted to marry him. I was always a flighty girl and a flighty woman, but your flighty ones can be touchy when it comes to men, and to come right down to it, I couldn't see myself going to bed with him. Setting his table and seeing to his clothes and sitting with him in the parlor after dinner—yes; but there is more to marriage than that. It wasn't that I disliked him in any way; it was just that I couldn't picture myself, Dolly Clohessey, in bed with a polite Frenchman who called me *Dolleee* and looked as if he'd been born in his clothes. There is something so undignified about that sort of thing, at least all *I* knew of it, the way Gus and I used to romp about, that I thought one or both of us would die of embarrassment, either I because I was jolly instead of romantic, or he because he couldn't bear to make himself ridiculous for any woman. I always thought he looked like a picture out of one of those old novels I used to read when I was a girl, back in the nineties—the kind that were always in evening clothes and an opera cape, with a mustache, and soulful eyes—and you could never imagine one of *them* in his skin.

Anyway, he hadn't said anything yet about marrying me at all. But you could see he was leading up to something, and one fine day it all came out. We'd been for a drive that afternoon—it was a warm June Sunday, I remember—and we'd stopped for some supper at a little country hotel about twenty miles out of town. I thought it was by accident, but it turned out later to be no such thing. It was early when we got there, and we had the place to ourselves, and I was surprised when all at once he began talking to me confidentially, because he had hardly spoken all afternoon. That wasn't like him in the first place, and should have warned me.

At any rate, he began talking to me about how it had been when he had been a boy down in New Orleans. And that was my second surprise, because it turned out he hadn't been rich then, or even well-to-do, but a poor, clever young man with his way to make, though he had grand relations, he said, but they would do nothing at all for him. And then he began to get sentimental and said it was only since he'd met me that he realized what a wasted, wicked life he had had up to now, for the upshot of it was—and he confessed the whole thing to me—that he had made his living since he was a boy in ways that were not exactly honest. I suppose he was what they call a confidence man, though I didn't see it then in that light. The way he told it to me, he had been careless, and a little too clever for other people, but never downright on the wrong side of the law. And he said it was up to me to reform him.

I don't know that I was ever so confused in my life. First he had made me like him, and grow used to having him around, and then to tell me a thing like that. The worst of it was that he cried when he told me, right out there in a public place, with the waitress likely to walk in at any moment. And I, of course—soft thing that I am for anybody's tale of woe—was almost crying too, the two of us sitting there with tears in our eyes on that lovely summer day, with the windows open and the smell of fresh grass and honeysuckle all around, and the sleepy feel of a small town on a

Sunday afternoon. It wasn't natural for anyone to be so sad on a day like that, and before I knew it there I was trying to cheer him up, and getting in deeper with him with every word I said.

I am not trying to excuse myself. I may be a foolish woman, but I know right from wrong, and the man had told me himself what he was. But maybe it was just because he *had* told me that I did what I did, because no woman can ever resist the urge to reform a man who says he loves her. It seems like nothing but criminal neglect to her if she does, because here is a poor soul like wax in her hands, admitting it only wants her love and care to be formed into something useful and new. So she gets to feeling like a missionary looking at a village full of savages, gloriously exalted and excited and a little tipsy with the knowledge of her own power. And the long and short of it is that she usually ends up like the missionary too, a martyr to her own zeal—with or without a ring on her finger. Which, I am ashamed to admit, is what happened to me.

But at the time I wasn't ashamed at all. It seems strange to me when I look back at it now, a woman like me, who had never had but one love in her life, going upstairs in that little hotel that evening as brazenly as any hussy who made her living out of men. The truth is, I suppose, that I was fired up to it. I had gotten used to the idea that I would marry him some day, and then there was that missionary zeal in me, and all my pity for him with his wasted life and his remorse and the tears in his eyes in a public dining room. I felt as if I would have been as hardhearted as Herod to refuse him.

Even afterward I didn't come to myself and seriously realize what I had done. For it was like being a girl all over again, giddy and thinking of nothing but the next hour's pleasure, and the weight of those two hard years of being alone and a widow seemed to roll off me like a stone. Sometimes I would sit at the window, looking out at the people going by on the streets and the golden summer sunshine pouring down on them, and I would think what a miracle it was that out of all those people, who cared nothing at all for Dolly Clohessey, there had been one sent to love me and cherish me above all the world. And then I would think, with a moment's guilt, that we should be married, but whenever he or I would mention that, there always seemed to be something that put us off it.

I think sometimes I was afraid because of Jack and Michael and Una. For though I was miles away from them down in Atlanta, it hardly seemed fair to them—the one a priest, the other a mayor, and the third a great success in high society—to bring a man who was in difficulties with the police into the family. Yes, he told me that too, after that day at the hotel. His name wasn't really René Duval at all, but Charles Schirmer, and there was a warrant out for him in Louisiana. But he swore to me that it was only a technicality, and that when he got his affairs settled he could put it right.

Still I knew how clever Jack was, and how terribly curious Una was, and I thought they would be sure to find it out. So I went on from day to day, and every day my Frenchman would tell me what he was doing to set himself up in a proper kind of business and to see about clearing things up in Louisiana, so that I believed it wouldn't be long before everything would be settled and I could hold up my head as Mrs. René Duval. I even signed over the insurance money Gus had left me, ten thousand dollars that he'd made me promise never to touch except in the worst kind of emergency, because it gave me a little income and was always there for me to fall back on. Well, it wasn't quite ten thousand, because I *had* gone into it a little during the winter when I was out of a job. But, at any rate, I put it all into a joint account, because Mr. Duval said it would help to settle matters if he had it to draw on, only for a few months, till he could liquidate his other assets.

Now, of course, a baby could have told me how *that* would turn out. The next day Mr. Duval was gone, and my ten thousand dollars with him. I couldn't believe it at first; I'd been used to having someone else look after me all my life, first Pa and then Gus, so I didn't half know the wickedness of the world, and even the two years that had gone by since Gus had died hadn't really prepared me for a turn like this. First I cried—cried for days, so ashamed of myself and so furious because I'd let him come over me like that, that I was in a kind of rage that was almost like a fever. But I was too ashamed to put the law on him, so there was nothing for me to do in the end but set my teeth and go to work. And I will say I learned my lesson. I am a flighty woman, as I've said before, but no man has ever pulled the wool over my eyes with a fine tale from that day to this. And the agency says there isn't a better person than me to send out on bills that everyone else has given up hope of collecting. I just close my eyes and ears to them and remember Mr. Duval.

But there was Amy now, who'd married not for love— nobody ever supposed that, because it wasn't only that Irving Gilman was older than she was, he just was not the sort of man a girl like Amy ever would fall in love with—but for comfort or security or something like that, and goodness knew what kind of trouble she'd got herself into now. So I dressed right away and went downstairs, and there were Mrs. Cournane and Josie already down before me, and Josie just at the point of having to admit to Mrs. Cournane that Amy hadn't come home last night. Of course Mrs. Cournane said, "I told you so"; she's not the woman to

drop an advantage like that. She was mad as a hornet, pur-
pling up in the face, though she stayed grim and calm, and
poor Josie started off, "But, Aunt Peg—" trying to settle
her down a bit.

"Don't you *Aunt Peg* me," Mrs. Cournane said. "Get
that young divil of a grandson of mine on the telephone;
that's what you do; and tell him I want to talk to him. The
limb of Satan—that's what he always was and always will
be."

"Now, Mrs. Cournane," I put in, *"don't* you go jumping to conclusions. Amy has a perfect right to stay with her
father all night if he needs her—"

Mrs. Cournane snorted; well, really, that was the only
word for it.

"Her father," she said. "Is it Jack Cournane? It isn't
daughters that one is after." Then she went back again to
Josie. "Are you deaf now, girl?" she said to her. "Didn't
you hear me tell you to get my grandson on the telephone?
The number's written down in the little book—not that he
gave it to me; I had to look it up myself."

Of course Josie had to go out then, and I thought the
best I could do was say nothing at all, and see if Mr. Mal
could do his own explaining. We could hear Josie getting the
number in the hall, and then asking, in such a trembly
voice it's a wonder anyone could understand her, for Mr.
Malachi Cesti. But it seemed he wasn't there, for a moment later we heard her say, "Oh no, I'll call again," and
then she came back to the kitchen.

"He isn't there," she said. "The man said he didn't
know when—"

"And there's ways to make people forget where you are
and what they know, too," Mrs. Cournane said. She sat
there in her chair beside the kitchen cabinet, her face getting redder and madder by the minute. "He ought to be put

behind bars, the young blackguard," she said. "Like his father before him, that divil of an Italian, getting around decent girls with their palaver. And hot as goats, every one of them."

Josie looked shocked.

"Oh, Aunt Peg!" she said.

"I mean it," Mrs. Cournane said. "Mind you, I knew from the beginning how he'd turn out, from the first minute I held him in my arms, with that divil's blood in him as plain as the mark of Satan. His father bringing scandal on a decent house, and Cathleen not even telling me, her own mother, running off to marry him when she was four months gone—" She was working herself up, the way she always did when she remembered anything about Cathleen and her marriage. "And that divil of an Italian standing there," she went on, "facing me down, saying, 'We're married now, so what difference? And it's a fine baby, a boy—' "

Well, of course I had to try to put a stop to it, because there was no telling what kind of state she'd work herself into if she was let be. She was getting old, and old people have too much time to sit and brood and rage over all the things that have gone wrong with their lives, like King Lear in the play. When you have your own little job of work to do, you can't be so particular about the past.

So I said to her, "Now, Mrs. Cournane," I said, "you mustn't go on like this, raking up old tales. Why, they're all over and forgotten years ago, and you know you haven't any right to say those things about Mal. He's a fine young man; Michael says himself, we're all going to be proud of him some day. You've never appreciated him, but it's true."

She reared back at that.

"Appreciated him, is it?" she said. "If I'd given him the back of my hand oftener when he was a boy, it'd be the better for him now." She broke off then, and I saw her looking over at the door. "And what do you think you're staring at, miss?" she demanded all at once.

I looked over too, and there was Shivaun standing in the doorway. Goodness knows how long the child had been there, or what she had heard. She looked as if she knew something was wrong, at any rate, for she'd come downstairs in her nightgown, without even slippers to her feet. And she was standing there looking from one to the other of us, not saying a word, the way children do when they hope to find out something from your face.

I went over and said, "Why, sweetheart, what in the *world* are you doing down here? Breakfast won't be for another half hour, and we like our little girls to come down with their faces washed and their nice clean dresses on."

She just looked at me as if she hadn't heard a word I'd said. She *is* like Amy at that age—quiet as a mouse, with those big, wide-spaced gray eyes, and much too serious for a child. And then she said to me, "Where's my mother?"— bringing it out like a bombshell. Well, I thought, whatever she knows, she knows too much, and that's a fact.

But naturally I had to put a good face on it before her.

"Why," I said, "she had to stay with your grandfather last night, honey. She'll be along in a little while now."

I didn't know whether she believed me or not; you never do, with those quiet ones. But anyway she let me bring her out to the hall and start her up the stairs, and she promised to wash and dress herself before she came down again.

Of course when I went back to the kitchen Mrs. Cournane started up again.

"I don't know what good it does to lie to the child," she said, in that angry, self-pitying way she was in now. "She'll have to find out the truth sooner or later. The pair of them are probably halfway to New York by now, or where-ever they've gone for their wickedness. Well, I told Jack when Amy married that man—'No good will ever come of it,' I said. 'You mark my words, no good will ever come of it. She's a young girl, and a wild young girl; she'll never be tied down to an old man—' "

"Oh, Mrs. Cournane, for pity's sake!" I said. I was vexed out of all patience to hear her talking like that. Because after all, until it's proved a woman hasn't kept her marriage vows, her own people, of all the world, shouldn't throw dirt on her. "You're not going to make anything a bit better by looking on the dark side," I said. "Amy's a sensible girl; I'm sure it's never crossed her mind to leave her husband."

But Mrs. Cournane wasn't to be put off by me.

"It's crossed Rosemary's, then," she said stubbornly. "She told me yesterday in that many words, said, 'Why did she come all the way out here without her husband?' " She began rocking herself slowly back and forth in her chair. "Ah, I don't know what I've done to deserve all these troubles," she said; "I don't, indeed. My own daughter taking up with one of hell's divils, then Jack with his women and his drinking, that brute of a grandson, and two good husbands gone to eternal rest—the good Lord knows I've had my purgatory here on earth."

As I've said, I've no patience with that kind of talk, remembering all the bad times of your life and forgetting the good. For even the unluckiest of us has moments to remember when the cream was thick on the milk and the bed soft to our back. But Mrs. Cournane was always one of those women who take their pleasure in looking on the black instead of the bright, and so she went on, while Josie and I stood there, helpless to stop her, till the telephone rang all at once out in the hall.

Josie, of course, went to answer it before there was so much as a second tinkle, while Mrs. Cournane and I lis-

259

tened with all our ears. We heard Josie say, "Amy? No, she's
not here," and then, "Mal, is that *you?* Why, we've just
been trying to call you; what *hap*pened last night? We
haven't seen Amy since she—"

You know how it is, trying to make out a phone conversation when you can hear only one side. But we didn't have
much time to be tantalized with our curiosity, because in a
minute or two Josie hung up the phone and came back into
the room, her face looking rather puzzled.

"Well?" Mrs. Cournane said. "Was it that grandson
of mine? What does he have to say for himself?"

Josie just stood there in the doorway, looking as if she
was trying to remember something.

"Well, I don't exactly know, Aunt Peg," she said,
after a minute. "He sounded so confused—you know how
people talk over the phone when they're in a hurry, and you
can't stop and ask—and then he just hung up. But Amy's
not with him; I'm sure of that. He wanted to talk to her;
he thought she was here—"

"Ah!" Mrs. Cournane said angrily. "You should have
let me talk to him; I'd have got it out of him. He's slippery
as an eel, but I didn't raise him not to know how to pin
him down. Where was he, did he tell you that?"

"No, he didn't," poor Josie had to say. She looked as
if she was guilty of something terrible not to have found
out more, and indeed Mrs. Cournane's look was enough to
have made anybody feel that way. "I just thought—I
imagined he was at his hotel," she said. "But he did say
something about finding Amy; he said we weren't to
worry—"

Mrs. Cournane pulled her mouth down in disdain.

"Finding her, is it?" she said. "I suppose he knows
where to look, well enough. If she wasn't right there beside
him all the time—"

I saw that she wasn't going to leave the thing, and besides I was worried about Amy, not knowing where on earth she could be if she wasn't with Mal, as I'd suspected, so I made up my mind to have just a bite of breakfast and then to go out and see Michael. For I knew she couldn't be with Jack, or Mal would have known it, and if there was any trouble, Michael would be the one to know *that*. Poor Michael, he lives like a saint himself, but he's always up to his ears in other people's devilment.

So I called a taxi and off I went. It was early still, not eight o'clock, and I do love the streets at that hour on a fine fresh summer morning, the people all hurrying to work, everything busy and new and exciting, as if everybody had his place in the world and was glad to be in it. How different from the way they come home at night, sober and tired and rumpled, only asking for peace and fodder, like the beasts of the field.

So I enjoyed my ride out to St. Cyprian's, even if I did have Amy on my mind. The taxi man was nice, too, an older man, and we talked about the way Amorica used to be and pointed out the old landmarks as we went by. So that I was in a good humor when I went up the steps and rang the bell at the parish house, and it brought me up with a start to see that face glowering out at me from behind the door. Mrs. Dawes, I mean. I'd forgotten all about that business at the reception the day before, with everything else I had on my mind, but she brought it back to me in a moment. I suppose she was startled to see company at that hour, but in a priest's house she should have been used to that.

I asked for Michael, and she said, as if she was glad to say it, that he had somebody with him.

"And his breakfast getting cold this minute in the kitchen," she said, looking at me with the door still half closed between us, as if she had a mind not to let me in at all.

"Well, I won't keep him from *that*," I said. "But I must see him, so if you don't mind, I'll just come in and wait."

She couldn't say no, so the door was opened and in I went. Father Kaspar was coming down the stairs just as I walked into the hall, and he stopped to say good morning to me, looking surprised to see me and a little subdued. And a good thing, too, I thought, for I'd been hoping Michael had taught him a lesson when he'd tried to interfere about Jack yesterday afternoon at the reception. He's always taken too much on himself, ever since he first set foot in that house, a nasty little man with a mouth like a button and eyes roaming around, seeking whom they may devour. And half the silly women in the parish mad over him, looking for him to lord it over them because they don't get it at home from their milksops of husbands. Well, I wouldn't trust him as far as the end of my little finger, but he's the kind who'll end up a bishop—ambitious and pushing and clever, and always sure to put himself on the right side of everything. While poor Michael will wind up right here in this miserable parish, with a *Monsignor* thrown to him, like a bone to a dog, when he's tottering to the grave.

So he said good morning to me, as if butter wouldn't melt in his mouth, and asked if there was anything he could do for me. I said no, I'd come to see Michael. He said something then about the reception was such a success yesterday, and it was gratifying that so many people had come, and I noticed Mrs. Dawes looking at him as if she was George Washington and he was Benedict Arnold. Then she had to put in her two cents' worth, said yes, but it had left the whole house a wreck, and she didn't know how she'd ever get it straightened out again.

"You know yourself, Mrs. Clohessey," she said to me,

"there's always plenty of help to make a big party, but precious little when it comes to cleaning up."

She was just spoiling for a chance to be disagreeable, you could tell that, and at the same time she kept looking and looking at me, as if she was trying to see right through my skull and find out what had brought me there so early in the morning. All of a sudden she came out with it.

"I hope Mr. John Cournane got home all right yesterday," she said.

I looked her straight in the eye.

"And why shouldn't he have?" I said.

Well, I know all the gossip that's gone on in that parish about Jack, and I know he oughtn't to have come out there yesterday afternoon, but I wasn't going to take *that* from her. It isn't as if I've ever provoked her, the way Una has; I've always been as polite to her as if she weren't starving Michael to death with that dreadful cooking of hers and making enemies for him all over the parish, carrying tales wherever they'll be listened to. That nice old Miss Clemens told me yesterday afternoon there wasn't a doubt in the world she'd done more to put that Mrs. Milligan in as prefect of the Married Ladies' Sodality than any other woman in the parish. Another trouble for poor Michael, the parish slipping out from between his fingers, and the Cardinal after him about the church debt, and then not turning up —the Cardinal, that is—yesterday at the reception: Una was furious about *that*. She thinks he ought to have come to see her if he wouldn't to see Michael, because she considers herself the next thing to the Bishop of Columbiana. But then Una really wore herself out being furious about things yesterday; she had words with Mrs. Milligan, and words with Rosemary, and words with Father Kaspar, and God pity the Cardinal if he *had* turned up, with her in a mood like that.

Anyway, I said to Mrs. Dawes, "Why shouldn't he have?"—and she shot a look at Father Kaspar, who had started to make a motion with his hand as if to warn her or stop her, and hesitated a moment, and then went right on.

"Why, I just meant—I was hoping nothing was wrong," she said, leering at me as if she hoped nothing of the kind. "With that Mr. Cesti turning up here so early," she said, "and now you—"

I didn't wait for her to finish.

"Mr. Cesti?" I said. "Do you mean Mal? Is *he* with Father Cournane now?"

And she said yes, he was, and I said, "Well, then, excuse *me*," and walked up to the study door and knocked and went right in. I didn't care what Mal was talking about to Michael; there were some questions about Amy I felt I had a right to ask that young man.

He was standing over by the window when I walked in, and if I hadn't suspected before that something was wrong, I'd have known it then. He wasn't shaved, and he looked absolutely wild; I've never seen Mal look like that. The minute he set eyes on me, he jumped across the room and asked me, "Have you seen her? Has she come back home?" And when I said no, I'd come to see if Michael knew anything about where she was, he groaned and dropped down in a chair and let his head fall in his hands, the picture of misery.

"My goodness," I said, "it isn't as bad as that, is it?"

I looked over at Michael; all at once, for the first time, I really felt a kind of cold fear coming over me. Because you never know what a woman will do when she is caught between two lives; she may run one way and she may run another, and all you can hope for is that she won't do herself any real harm before she comes to her senses again.

"Where was she last night?" I asked Mal then, straight

out, seeing that neither of them was going to answer me. "Did she really go to see Jack?"

Mal looked up and said oh yes, she'd seen him, and he looked so angry that I was half afraid to ask any more, but that I'd made up my mind to find out. So I kept on pulling it out of the two of them, like a dog worrying an old bone, till finally I could piece some kind of sense together out of what they would tell me. It seemed Jack had made one of his grand resolutions yesterday to turn over a new leaf, and Amy had taken it all in—how he was going to leave that girl and turn into a respectable citizen again. Well, I couldn't blame her, poor thing; she'd believed it because she wanted to, because Jack has always been the greatest thing on earth to her, but you would wonder what she'd learned in her years of going about the world. Because if there's one thing that's harder to do than a camel going through the needle's eye, it's for a man to change his character after he's fifty years old. Or a woman. God help us, the dough is in the oven by that time, and there's no use wishing we'd added more butter or a little less salt.

So if the girl had been wiser it wouldn't have struck her so hard when she saw Jack at his drinking again last night, and the new wife walking in and snapping her fingers and getting him off for herself again. That was what happened, or something like it, and after that—oh, God knows; of course Mal wouldn't talk, but where does a woman turn for comfort when she's had a blow like that? It was plain enough what had happened, only now she'd given him the slip, it seemed, walked out of the room, probably, when he was asleep, and here he was running frantically all over town, trying to find out what had become of her. He'd come to Michael just as I had, because Michael was always the one who knew everything that went on in the family, all the troubles, at any rate, but Michael knew no more than

we did. He looked a little stunned himself at the whole
business, and I wondered if he'd been fool enough to believe, like Amy, that Jack had really meant what he'd said.
It's a grand thing to have two people who love you so much
they can believe you can move mountains, like the saints
in the Bible, but that kind of love is a terrible responsibility
to put on anyone, too.

Well, so there was Jack, back at his old tricks again,
and not likely, I thought, to be found soon again putting
himself in the way of loving daughters and brothers who
were priests, and here were Amy and Mal and Michael
going round and round in their heads like tops that he had
set spinning. It put me in mind of the old days at home,
when he would start up some sort of mischief by putting
the idea into all our heads, and then go off somewhere himself with a book, or to fall asleep in the hammock in the
back yard. So we would be punished and he would get
gingerbread. He was born lucky, till he tried his luck too far.

And I thought if Amy was seeing him now as he really
was, it would be a good thing for her, once she got over the
first surprise. For I had the feeling she'd been going on long
enough believing, the way Jack always has himself, that
somehow everything that was wrong with the world was
going to come right some day—which it won't, no matter
how hard we may try to tell ourselves it will. If there's one
thing I've learned out of all my hard times, it's that it's
better to face up to what you are and what your life has to
be than to try to run away from it, but that is something
Jack will never do, if he lives to be a hundred. I had the
feeling, though, that Amy was doing it right now, and I
can't pretend I wasn't glad of it. For, say what you will, it
is always safer to know the truth, though it is hard for us
sometimes when we first get hold of it. As it was for me,
for example, when I found out about Mr. Duval.

But from that experience I thought I knew something too of how Amy was feeling now, how she would want most of all to be alone for a little, not so much to think about what had happened as to try to gather her self-respect about her again. A woman feels it more than a man when she has been undervalued and set aside, and then when she has done what Amy did, and what I did with Mr. Duval—let her feelings run away with her—she is likely even to under-value herself. I'm sure I used to go about the streets think-ing there wasn't another woman in the town who had made such a fool of herself as I had—and while it was different with Amy, because Mal truly loved her, and would never have run away from her as Mr. Duval had done with me, still she could hardly have been thinking just now that she had done a very wise thing.

So I tried to tell a little of that to Mal.

"You mustn't worry about her," I said. "She'll come home when she's ready; I'm sure she only wants to be by herself for a few hours."

Because the next thing, I thought, was that he and Michael would begin to talk about the police; there's noth-ing else a man can think of when women go off acting in their own flighty way. And Mal said he didn't want her to go home, he wanted her to come to him so he could take her away, and then he looked at Michael and me as if he was daring us to stop him. Poor boy, I'm sure he was feel-ing terrible—and I thought how a love like that can spoil a man, hold him back and keep him on tenterhooks for years, so that he misses doing half the things he is fit for, and having half the pleasures other men have in life. For though Mal never complained, and always had a joke for you when you tried to talk seriously to him about his life, still the jokes were too bitter for him to have been very happy inside.

I sat there now, looking at him and Michael, and I

didn't know which I felt sorrier for. Because Michael is not
the sort of man, priest or not, who enjoys preaching to
people, and yet I could see he felt bound to tell Mal now
that what he was doing was wrong, and that he should let
Amy alone. And then Mal flared up, and I thought there
would be a quarrel, only I happened to hear a kind of noise
outside the door and I said, to quiet them, "If you don't
want this all over the parish in an hour's time, for goodness' sake, speak softer; there's someone there outside the
door."

Of course Michael said it wasn't possible, and he went
over in two of his long steps and flung open the door. And
there was Mrs. Dawes, as big as life, with her ear almost
in the keyhole.

I've never seen Michael so angry before. He told Mrs.
Dawes she was a disgrace to herself and her religion, spying
on the secrets of a priest's study that are almost as sacred
as the secrets of the confessional, and that she could pack
her things and leave that very minute. He fairly faced her
down, for she began by being impudent and claiming she
was only dusting out there in the hall, but before three
minutes had gone by he'd blown all the wind out of her,
and she stood there like an empty paper bag. Still, as she
went off, she threw it back at him, "I have friends in this
parish, Father Cournane, and don't you forget it, and they'll
want to know why I'm being sent away from here for no
good reason and without notice, after all I've done." And I
thought, poor Michael, more trouble for him, and it won't
do him a bit of good in the long run; he'll only end up with
somebody else as bad. Because he is too soft with people,
and always was; he is too good himself to believe the rest
of the world is as wicked as it is.

I believe he was ashamed of himself for firing up like
that, because when he came back into the room he didn't

say a word for a minute or two, but only went over to the desk and put two or three things that were on it in different places. Still, I think it did him good to have his say out and get rid of that woman, who had been a thorn in his side for years with her spyings and intrigues. Mal and I didn't say anything, and after a while he looked over at us and smiled a little, the way I remembered he'd used to when he was a boy, quick and firm, as if he was brightening up inside and he wanted you to know it.

"Well, that's done," he said. "I suppose I shouldn't have lost my temper—"

"You were perfectly right," I said. "Una always said she was a devil for spying and gossiping. I must tell Una; it will set her up for days."

Michael shook his head at me. But I was glad to see he still had his temper, because it made him seem more like my brother again, which he never has since he put on that Roman collar. I remember when he came back from Rome and I saw him for the first time in those clothes; I felt so sad, somehow, I wanted to cry. Because Michael was always one of those boys who wants things run right, like a general; he'd plan things in his head when we were children, battles and excursions and such things, and have them all worked out to the letter, and then we must do exactly as he told us or it would all be spoiled. And of course it always *was* spoiled, because we would never follow him. We were too lazy, or too careless, or just too contrary, and then he would get white, he was so furious, and not say a word, but just throw everything down and walk away.

It wasn't that he was overbearing; he just got more interested in things than the rest of us did. I've often thought he should have been a great general, whom people had to obey, or, better still, a president or governor, and then he might have been able to do things for people that needed to be done, and have had satisfaction in seeing that they went right. And when they went wrong he might have had a comfortable sort of wife at home, who would coax him and cheer him up and say, "Better luck next time, dear."

But how could he satisfy himself when he'd taken on himself the chanciest job in the world, trying to keep people from their sins with nothing but words and exhortations and good example? He's broken his heart over it, that's what has happened, all alone there in that gloomy house with nobody but a bad-tempered housekeeper and a couple of men to come home to. Well, that is fate, I suppose; we all want to do what we can't. Like Una wearing her heart out trying to be a D.A.R., and Mal wanting to settle down with Amy.

But to get back to Mal—of course he wasn't interested in anything but Amy now; he wouldn't have cared if a whole battalion of archangels had just been fired from their jobs. He got up in a minute and said that, since neither Michael nor I was able to help him find Amy, he'd go on looking for her himself. He was bound to go; nothing Michael could say would stop him. Then, since there was no reason for me to stay any longer either, he said he would drive me back to West Haley Street, and we could see if by any chance she had turned up there.

I didn't want him to go near West Haley Street, because I knew what would happen if he and Mrs. Cournane got together now, but what could I do? Finally I made him promise at least he wouldn't go in, if I'd make him a signal from the window whether she was there or not. But I knew if Amy *was* there I couldn't stop him, and he'd go inside no matter what.

So we said good-by to Michael and went out to the hall. We could hear Mrs. Dawes upstairs talking to Father McBride; poor young man, he didn't know what to make of it all, with her going on about Michael and her wrongs. But I looked at Michael and I knew that all that fuss wouldn't do her a bit of good now; if the whole parish was to come begging to him on their knees, it wouldn't change him. He is like all the Cournane men; they will never think the worst of anyone till they have to, and then they are finished with them for all eternity. Pa and that Mrs. Daley, for instance, who almost killed Jack feeding him spoiled fish that time; and we'd tried to tell him and tried to tell him, but no, she was a jewel of a housekeeper till he caught on to that.

And Jack with Rosemary, that was just the same way, anything she'd do and he'd only laugh, turn it aside, even when Una tried interfering in her usual way, trying to bring justice to an unjust world. Well, I'll never know what it was in the end, some little thing, probably, something he couldn't help seeing, that girl was it, Ermina Marlow, and Rosemary trying to take her up at first, maybe something she said, sharp-tongued, the way Rosemary can be. "And immediately the scales fell from his eyes and he saw"—the way it says it in the Bible. He hasn't the least use in the world for Rosemary now—oh, the way he looked at her yesterday, as polite and cool as a stranger, as if they'd never been man and wife, and she ready to suffocate at it, she was so furious.

So we left Michael to his troubles and went out to the car. Mal would hardly say a word for a while after we got in; poor boy, I didn't blame him, though I was chattering on all the while about Michael and that parish of his, trying to take his mind off Amy. It was such a lovely day, too, it was a shame to think of anyone being unhappy in it, the sky so blue even above the city streets, with little white clouds floating around in it. I can't help it, I can't feel really bad on a day like that, not even when I think of all the sad things that have happened to me in my life, Gus dying and René

Duval running off and how hard it is sometimes to keep going on the nasty days and never quite enough money—oh, I don't even like to think about those things on a day like that. It was the kind of morning when everything in the world seems shined up and polished and set in apple-pie order, and you just want to hold your breath and try to keep it that way.

I could tell it made an impression even on Mal, even the way he felt. He calmed down a little after a while and spoke to me like a human being; well, I suppose he had to talk to someone. We talked about Michael a little and then I got him to talking about when he had been over in Europe, oh, some old man with a long beard we passed on the street started him off, Poland and Yugoslavia and Rumania, and all the names of the places I only remembered from geography books when I was in school, Budapest and the Bosporus and Constantinople, where the emperors were, and dukes and kings he had really met himself, as fascinating as a book, and I thought, with all those interesting things and people in the world, isn't it strange that he can only think of Amy? Because there must have been women too, maybe even Turkish ones in trousers and veils, though he said that was all changed now and the Turks look just like anyone else.

But it is so queer to think that wherever we go we can never forget that one little place on earth that we came from, and that it seems to make us what we are, puts us in a kind of prison we are always trying to get out of, and yet always trying to get back into as soon as we feel we're fairly out. That was why Mal had come back here to Amorica last year, and why he had to have Amy, of all the women in the world, and I knew he would never forget her, no, never, not even if she went back to California and Irving Gilman and he was ten thousand miles away. Maybe it is better that way; I don't know. Maybe it's what makes us human, not ever being able to give up what we were and not ever being satisfied with what we are.

So we went on back to West Haley Street. Amy wasn't there, because Josie ran out to the door when we drove up, and I saw she was looking to see if we had brought her. I looked over at Mal.

"What are you going to do now?" I said. "She isn't here."

He just sat there, hunched over the wheel, looking straight ahead. I had a queer idea that if it hadn't been for Amy he would have started the car and driven straight on, clear out of town, just as far as money or credit would take him. After a minute he looked at me and said, "I don't know."

"She'll be all right," I said. "You mustn't worry. Amy's had all sorts of ups and downs, but she's like the rest of us Cournane women; we always manage to land on our feet, like cats. It's only the men in this family who really go to smash. You ought to thank God you're not one of them."

He glanced at me; then he shrugged up his shoulders a little and got out and went around and opened the car door for me. When I got out he stood there looking at me.

"You think she's walked out on me for good," he said. "Is that it, Aunt Dolly?"

I just didn't know what to say. Moral principles are no more to me than beans when I get into a situation like that, and I wanted to tell Mal I thought Amy would come back to him and they would live happily ever after, like the prince and princess in the fairy tales, but I didn't believe a word of it. Because I'd seen how she looked at those children of hers and I'd heard how she talked about Irving Gilman, and it seemed to me that I knew then, just as well as if she'd been standing there beside me saying it to

me, that she'd never go back on them—not for Mal or for
anyone else. For there are all sorts of love in this world, and
nobody, not even the luckiest of us, can have all of them;
there is always a time when we have to choose between
them, and that time, I knew, had come now for Amy.

So I could imagine her worrying her problem out all
by herself, and I felt for her—oh, maybe more even than I
felt for Mal, no matter how unhappy I saw he was—because
a man can always go off and do something interesting and
desperate in a situation like that, like traveling to some
uncivilized country or getting into a war, while a woman
has to sit at home facing the consequences of her decision
day after day. Not that Amy is like Una or Rosemary, to
let something she can't have waste the happiness of what
she *can* have every day for her; she is more like me, willing
to make the best of things—though I take no credit for *that*;
it's the disposition the good Lord gave me. And then she
has some of Pa in her too, the stubborn, enduring, solid-
as-a-rock nature that most people never think of as being
in the Irish, but that crops out every now and again in us
too. When I really thought about it, I thought that that
sort of person makes his own luck in the end—because,
say what you like, Pa had what he wanted out of life, and
Amy would probably get it too, just because she wouldn't
let any dirty little trick fate played on her throw her off her
balance in the long run.

But I couldn't say any of that to Mal, so I just stood
there, and after a minute he said to me, "All right, Aunt
Dolly. I'll let you off the hook."

"Oh, I didn't *mean*—" I said.

"Sure," he said. "I know you didn't." Then he said, in a
queer flat kind of voice, "You don't even have to say it;
she said it for me herself last night. She said we weren't
real—"

"You weren't *real?*"

I didn't know what on earth he was talking about; he was standing there with that old Panama hat he wears pushed back on his head, and if anyone looked solid and real he did, as if you'd have to have a bulldozer to move him out of your way. But then he looked at me and kept on, in that same flat voice, "That no matter how much we wanted it to be real, it wasn't. Not our daily bread and the air we breathed. And I said, 'When has any Cournane ever let that bother him?' Damn it to hell, Aunt Dolly," he said, his face flushing up a little all of a sudden, "you know it as well as I do—there's never been one of you yet that didn't make up a world of his own to live in. So why can't Amy and I make up ours?"

He was upset or he wouldn't have talked to me like that; I knew that. But I knew too what he was talking about now, and that he was right—oh, it was Jack and his young girls, and never facing up to his drinking, and Una with her grand pretensions, and myself—yes, myself with Mr. Duval, even Michael, shutting himself away from the real problems of his life into a sad little world of his own. And Amy was a Cournane too—you couldn't get away from that: she'd proved that once before, years ago, the day she'd run off from her own troubles to marry Irving Gilman.

Still, Amy years ago wasn't the same as Amy now, and somehow I felt Mal knew that too, as he kept on standing there looking at me. I wanted to tell him—it was the only thing I could think of that would be of any help to him now—that Irving Gilman was fifteen or twenty years older than he was, and that in the common course of events he, Mal, ought to be around a good deal longer than Amy's husband—but of course that isn't the sort of thing you can say to anyone. So I didn't say anything at all, and after a minute he just went around and got in the car again, said,

"So long, Aunt Dolly, see you around," and drove right on up the street, fast.

I stood there on the sidewalk, looking after him. After a little Josie came out of the house to me.

"Oh, Dolly," she said, "you didn't find her? And Father Cournane hasn't heard anything either?"

"Not a word," I said. I tried to cheer up a little for her sake. "But she'll turn up," I said. "We mustn't worry."

She came up closer and whispered it to me: "Wasn't that Mal? Where *was* she last night? Did he tell you?"

Well, there is one good thing about collecting bills; you run up against so many kinds of lies in the day's work that when your own time comes you are an expert. I never batted an eye when she asked me that; I lied as splendidly as if I'd been rehearsing what to say for the past half hour.

"She was with Jack," I said. "Then she was upset, and insisted on going home by herself. I suppose she just wants to be alone for a while, but Mal's worried about her— naturally."

I didn't feel one bit bad about it, either; I would have said the same thing before a judge and jury. And it was almost like that with Mrs. Cournane, after I got inside. She was like a hawk, just looking for me to make a slip, but I swore it was all the truth, and then I got her off the subject by telling her about Michael and Mrs. Dawes. Of course she had some old Irishwoman on the string that she wanted the place for the minute I told her, and Josie and I couldn't stop her; she was on the phone in three seconds, trying to tie poor Michael up.

I went on back into the kitchen with Josie. The two children were there at the table, still dawdling over their breakfast in the confusion the house was in, but when Shivaun saw me coming in the door she jumped up and came over and said, "Where's my mother?" The clever little thing knew I'd gone to find her; it's no use trying to keep anything from children like that.

So I tried another lie, God forgive me, and said, "Why, honey, I didn't go to fetch your mother; she'll come by herself when she comes."

She didn't believe a word of it, of course, with Josie there beside me looking as stricken as I felt. The tears came to her eyes and her mouth quivered and then she began to cry. Stephen said, "Shut up, *baby*," to her, but it didn't help a bit. As a matter of fact, he looked upset himself, but like a boy, sullen and a little savage. Poor things, I suppose they felt deserted in that strange house, thousands of miles from their home, without either their mother or their father. It was no use to them that there'd been Cournanes in that house for fifty years; there was nothing of all that life that they knew or remembered.

Josie was trying to hush little Shivaun, but she wouldn't be soothed; she was like all quiet children when they've once let go, crying as if she had a whole salt sea in her eyes. All the while, Stephen sat at the table as if he was too superior to the commotion his sister was making even to look at her, but then all at once he shot at me, "My mother's never coming back—is she?" And I knew he was in it too.

I just looked at Josie, helpless. The child's crying upset me; oh, we live in such a queer old world, where you can't lift your finger for your own pleasure without stirring grief into someone else's cup. I reached over and put my arm around her, and then I heard footsteps outside, and the Captain, who'd been lying on the floor beside the table, got up and went over to the door. Shivaun looked up and stopped crying; a kind of quiet fell over the room.

It was Amy standing there in the doorway. She had on the same white dress she'd worn last night, but she looked strange and remote, as if she'd come from another world. She just stood there, and even the children didn't move—and then it was as if something clicked, and the whole world went back to being normal again.

Amy smiled and came on into the room.

"Hello, you kids," she said to them. "Did you think I was never coming back?"

 *About the Author*

MARY DEASY was born in Cincinnati, Ohio, and attended the Cincinnati College Conservatory of Music.

She is the author of seven novels, of which *The Hour of Spring, The Boy Who Made Good* and *The Corioli Affair* (a Literary Guild selection) are perhaps the best known. Her novels have been published in England, France, Italy, Belgium, Germany, Spain, Norway, Denmark and Sweden.

Miss Deasy has also written several short stories which have appeared in such magazines as *Mademoiselle, Harper's,* the *Yale Review,* the *Virginia Quarterly Review,* the *Atlantic Monthly* and have reappeared in many anthologies including *The Best American Short Stories* volumes and the *O. Henry Memorial Award* volumes.

Miss Deasy now lives in Cincinnati.